CHERISHED ONE

CHERISHED ONE

Melaina Rayne

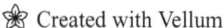

NOTE FROM THE AUTHOR

Cherished One was previously published in 2014, back when I was just a budding new author. After ten plus years of writing and publishing, I decided I would revamp the series. Going on this journey was something I needed to reconnect with the characters. To give them a new voice, new structure, and more depth. I love the end results of each one of the books, and I hope you love them too.

1

Ava waited patiently, watching her boss pace in front of the bank of windows in his office. For the first time in nearly five years of working for him, Jameson showed signs of true stress. And for good reason.

After his father's passing last year, Jameson had stepped up as CEO. He'd been slowly digging the company out of the red. It was an arduous process, but things had been looking up for a long while.

Unfortunately, the last meeting hadn't gone well. Because of this, the future of Ferro Corp hung in the balance.

Last month, an offer had come across his desk from Gray Delcheki, CEO of GrayChek Enterprises. The man was one of the most notorious businessmen in the south. And the most ruthless. He was known for buying up companies, dismantling them, and then selling off the pieces at inflated prices to make a profit.

It worked. He was one of the wealthiest men around,

but his greed ruined lives. Hundreds of lives at a time. And Jameson didn't want that to happen to any of his subsidiaries. He cared too much about the employees and their families to do that. So, he'd turned down the offer.

But due to unforeseen circumstances, Jameson's latest deal had fallen through. A major contract with a big investor. And if he didn't figure something out, he would have to do the one thing he swore he'd never do. Sell off one of his subsidiary companies to stay afloat. That was the last thing he wanted, but he didn't have a lot of options left.

When he finally stopped pacing, Jameson raked his fingers through his dark hair and sighed. "Do I have anything open this week?"

Ava scanned his schedule. "Thursday. Your whole afternoon is available."

"Good. Call Kole. Set something up with Delcheki."

Ava made a note in her planner. *Set up meeting with Delcheki. ASAP.*

Jameson leaned over his desk and typed out something on his computer before looking up at her. "Have you heard anything back from Reggie?"

Ava shook her head. "No, sir."

Jameson blew out a frustrated breath. "Okay. Get with Reggie and find out if he's worked out the details with Ms. England's project. If he has, set up a meeting with him whenever I'm free."

She made the note. *Call Reggie about England project details. Set up meeting if ready.*

Jameson waited until she finished before he continued. "Now then. What do you have for me?"

Ava flipped to her other notes. "Dewain Wray wants you to call him back regarding the Harper account."

Jameson nodded.

"Mr. Eldridge said to tell you, 'Yes.' That you would know what he meant."

Jameson laughed. "Hopeless. Poor guy."

Ava was curious what that meant, but she moved on. "Also, Melissa Brunder called and said she's available for lunch tomorrow."

Jameson shook his head. "I can't do lunch. I have too much to take care of the rest of this week. Call her back and tell her—" He leaned over his desk again and scribbled a note. "Never mind. I'll handle that. What else?"

"That's all for now."

He stared at her for a long moment before adding, "I'm going to say something, not as your boss but as your friend."

Ava hesitated before nodding. "Okay."

Jameson came around his desk and sat on the corner. Keeping eye contact with her, he crossed his arms over his chest. "After this week, I want you to take some time off."

Ava frowned.

"Don't think I haven't noticed how exhausted you've been lately. You look like you're running on fumes, and I don't like it. You need to get some rest."

"But—"

Jameson held up a hand. "I'm not asking. I'm telling you, Ava. You need a break, and you are taking one. I'll have the temp agency send someone in for the next month. You've got to take care of yourself."

"A month? Really," she tried, "that isn't necessary."

Jameson arched a brow at her.

Seeing the look on his face, Ava knew he wouldn't take no for an answer. Ava sighed. "Fine."

"Now, since that's settled, can you run out and get us some lunch?"

Ava nodded. "Greek?"

"Sounds good."

"Do you want me to take her?"

D'mitri lifted his gaze from his niece's sweet face and smiled at Ali. "No, I like holding her."

After a long silence, Ali sat across from him. "Can I ask you something?"

"Sure," he answered, brushing a kiss over the baby's springy midnight curls.

"How are you? Honestly."

Hearing the true concern in her voice, D'mitri met her eyes again. "Tired."

Ali exchanged a glance with Nicolai.

D'mitri knew they both worried about him. He'd been withdrawn and moody since discovering Ali was expecting. Just being near the happy couple pained him because it reminded him of everything he didn't have.

But since Violet's birth, D'mitri hadn't felt quite so hopeless. Something about holding the little angel in his arms gave him a sense of peace. Maybe it was the way she looked up at him with her unusually bright eyes or the way she snuggled in close to him when he held her. It was impossible to be anything but tranquil while holding such a sweet, innocent creature in his arms.

Problem was, the moment he was alone again, the empty feeling came rushing back.

Nicolai sat his glass on the table and searched his brother's face. "Tell me, brother. What is going on with you?"

D'mitri didn't respond. He didn't know what to say, because he didn't know.

"Are you having trouble sleeping again?"

D'mitri reluctantly nodded.

They worried too much about him. But the truth was, over the last few weeks, he'd barely slept. And when he did, he woke disoriented and sweaty. He remembered having intense, vivid dreams. Yet, when he woke, he had no recollection of what he'd dreamed about. Only the overwhelming sense of urgency and an unnerving internal shifting. His jaguar was restless.

As if reading his mind, Nicolai's mouth turned up in a slow smile. "You feel as if you are experiencing your Despertar again."

Not a question. A statement of fact. And D'mitri could only stare at his brother in disbelief. Nicolai was right. That is precisely what it felt like. How had he not made the connection before? D'mitri had spent the last two years feeling sorry for himself, waiting impatiently for his mate. And never once did he consider her coming arrival a possible cause of his growing restlessness.

Nicolai eyed him as he settled back against the couch. "Have the dreams started?"

"I would not know. I rarely remember my dreams. But lately, I feel more on edge. Especially just after I wake."

Nicolai gave him a hopeful smile. "The beginning, perhaps?"

"Perhaps."

Nicolai clapped him on the shoulder. "Soon, brother. You will have her soon."

That should make him feel better. Yet, somehow, it made him even more impatient. D'mitri wanted to know what it felt like to share life with someone. Someone to love with every fiber of his being. A mate who would look at him the way Ali looked at his brother. He was desperate for those things.

He longed for the day he could run with his mate, swim with her in the river, and lay with her in the tall grass, listening to the sounds of the jungle until they fell asleep in each other's arms. He couldn't wait until her mating cycle, so they could spend every possible moment making love under the stars.

But for now, he just wanted to see her face. Who was his mate? Did he know her already? How much longer would it be before they could be together?

2

Ava sat next to her boss, her eyes on the man across from them. Gray Delcheki.

Though Jameson hated the man with a passion, he'd put his personal feelings aside. To keep Ferro Corp from going under completely, he had to make a deal with Mr. Delcheki. Ava still didn't know what exactly Jameson had planned. She just hoped Delcheki went for it.

With his tone even, Jameson began. "Tell me. What is your interest in Healthlink?"

Delcheki laughed. "So much like your father. Always straight to the point."

Ava watched the interaction, knowing Jameson hated being compared to his late father. Fortunately, the only outward sign was the slight clench of his jaw. "I am a busy man. And I don't appreciate having my time wasted."

Delcheki sat back in his chair, studying Jameson with a thoughtful expression. "I bet you are busy. Attempting to get your company out of the hole your father dug beneath it. That's exactly why I wanted to meet with you."

"To discuss my father's inadequacies? Don't bother. I am very much aware of them."

Delcheki shook his head, his mock sympathy not fooling anyone. "It's a shame, what happened. Your father was a good friend to me, so I don't want to see his company go under."

"That won't happen."

Delcheki ignored Jameson's hard tone. "That's why I'm here. I want to make sure it doesn't."

"And why do *you* care what happens to *my* company?"

"I want to return the kindness your father once showed me."

A laugh slipped out before Ava could stop it. She couldn't help it. Jameson Ferro Sr. had never been accused of compassion a single time in his entire life. At least, not that Ava had heard.

Both men shifted their attention to her, both with curious expressions. Jameson raised an eyebrow. Looking back and forth between them, Ava said, "I'm sorry. I didn't mean to interrupt."

"Do tell us, Ms. Brayda," Delcheki propped an elbow on the table as if what she had to say was so intriguing. "What is it you find so funny?"

"Probably the same thing I was thinking," Jameson cut in, saving her from having to answer. Once Delcheki shifted his focus back to her boss, Jameson continued. "I believe you have my father confused with someone else. He was never kind."

Delcheki laughed, surprising Ava. "Kindness wasn't the bigger of his qualities in his later years, no. But he was once a different man. Avoiding details, let me say that he gave me a chance when I was at my lowest. And everything I have today is because of him. I owe him more than I care to ever explain, and since I cannot repay him directly, I would like to do so through you."

Jameson held his stare. "And how would you do that?"

Delcheki took a drink of his water and sat the glass back on the table before saying, "GrayChek Enterprises recently acquired a medical research company, and I am looking to expand. As a medical supply manufacturer and distributor, Healthlink is an ideal asset. It makes things easier for me, to have an inhouse supplier, and taking it off your hands will lift a burden from Ferro Corp.

Jameson shook his head. "As I said before, I'm not looking to sell. Unlike you, I care about my employees and those under each of my subsidiaries. Their livelihoods depend on these jobs, and I refuse to leave hundreds of people jobless because of greed. When I got into the business, I vowed to myself that the individual will always be more important than my big picture. And I will forever stand by that."

Delcheki's expression didn't falter, but Ava could see a brief spark of anger in his eyes. He clearly didn't like being insulted. But who did? Delcheki folded his hands on the table and kept his voice even. "So, if you aren't willing to sell, why are we here?"

"Perhaps, we can come up with some sort of arrangement. Something mutually beneficial. A partnership."

Ava watched Delcheki run a finger over the folded edge of the napkin on the table in front of him. She could almost see the wheels turning in his head. He lifted his dark eyes to meet Jameson's steady gaze. "I'm not interested in a partnership. But just for curiosity's sake, what were you thinking?"

Jameson held his stare. "Instead of buying Healthlink, you agree to order from them whatever equipment and supplies your research facility requires. A win for us both."

Delcheki sat back in his chair. "And the terms?"

"Healthlink provides the supplies your facility needs. And you help your friend's old company by paying ten percent above the usual cost."

"Ten percent?" Delcheki looked deep in thought for a moment, then countered. "How about double cost? If I am to help, I am going to make it worth it."

Jameson held Delcheki's stare. "Why would you offer to pay double?"

Delcheki shrugged. "I cannot repay your father for what he did for me, but at least I can help out his only remaining family."

"And the conditions?"

"None. I pay you double; you provide the supplies I need. That's it."

Jameson snorted. "Mr. Delcheki, I am not new to business. I know there is always a catch. No one, especially a businessman such as yourself, does something like what you've proposed simply out of the kindness of their heart. Despite what you've said, there are always terms or special conditions."

"Someone like me? What does that mean?"

Jameson looked his father's old friend in the eyes. "Someone who buys out other companies and make profits from them for as long as you can before breaking them down to sell to the highest bidder. You don't care about others. You only care about your own profit, so I find it hard to believe you would do something so selfless as to pay double for supplies with no intention other than to simply *help* someone out."

Delcheki had the nerve to look offended. "I'm hurt you would think so little of me."

Another unintentional laugh slipped from Ava, earning her a look of disapproval from both men, but she couldn't help it. She knew Gray Delcheki cared nothing about what others thought of him. Except for women, maybe. That might be why he looked less than thrilled about her reaction.

A faint spark of anger lit his eyes, but he turned back to Jameson. "As I said, there are no terms. No conditions."

The waiter approached with their food and disappeared again once their plates were placed in front of them.

Delcheki drew a breath and offered a half-hearted smile. "Let us speak no more of business. I would rather enjoy this meal and one another's company. We can iron out the details another time."

Enjoying the man's company wasn't possible. Ava didn't like Gray Delcheki at all. Simply being in his presence made her feel like a cat getting its fur stroked in the wrong direction. How could she enjoy her meal with such a man sitting across from her? His gaze settled on her far more often than she felt comfortable with. And the way he blatantly eyed her as if she were a dessert he anxiously waited to devour. She'd never wanted to punch a man in the throat so bad in her life.

Despite the man's creepy aura, Ava managed to enjoy her food and make it through the meal without asking him what the hell he was looking at. She didn't acknowledge his not-so-subtle curiosity with her, and she was beyond glad when it was over.

Jameson paid the check and told Delcheki he would consider the proposal and get back to him. Once they said their goodbyes, Ava happily got the hell out of the restaurant.

She climbed into the passenger seat as Jameson walked around the car. She exhaled a rough breath and lay her head back against the headrest.

Jameson got in and shut the door. He stared out the windshield, deep in thought. Then he turned to her. "Well, what do you think of the offer? Your honest opinion."

Ava sighed. "Well, I think a partnership with Gray-Chek Enterprises would help rebuild Ferro Corp, but I don't like Mr. Delcheki personally."

"That's why I asked your opinion. I trust your judgment. You seem to have a very good bullshit detector, and I have no time for bullshit."

"Well, something about this guy stinks," she mumbled.

With an amused smile, Jameson said, "He was friends with my father."

"And that's definitely not a point in his favor."

"So?" Jameson pushed.

"I didn't get the impression he was lying, but I still don't like him."

Jameson chuckled. "Yeah, I gathered as much."

3

The following Monday, Ava finally went to see her doctor since she had some time off. She told him about everything. The exhaustion. The restlessness. The anxiety. And the new strangely vague dreams that made her feel things she didn't quite understand. The only thing she left out? The bizarre feeling that nothing in her life felt real anymore.

Dr. Engram suggested it might be any number of things. All of which were likely related to a hormone imbalance. He suggested running some standard blood and urine tests to start. But until he got the results, he wanted her to take some time off and catch up on rest. He even offered to prescribe an anxiety medicine, but Ava refused. The last thing she needed was to feel foggier.

After her appointment, she met up with her best friend, Katelyn, at their favorite little mom and pop barbeque place. It was a forty-five-minute drive, but it was worth the trip. Neta's served the best chili cheese dogs in the south. And the chipped beef sandwiches were to die for.

But as hungry as she was, Ava couldn't stop thinking about the doctor's visit. Would the basic tests come back and show something simple? Or would it be some horrible, incurable disease? She'd never been much of a doom and gloom type of person, but the way Dr. Engram looked at her had her thoughts spiraling.

A hand waved in front of Ava's face. "Hello?"

Ava shifted her focus back to Katelyn. "I'm sorry. What?"

She sat her drink down and sighed. "Stop worrying about the test results. Everything is gonna be fine."

"And if it's not?"

Katelyn shrugged. "Then we'll deal with whatever it is together."

Ava gave a faint smile and picked at her onion rings.

"Hey." Katelyn laid a hand on Ava's forearm. "Stop worrying so much. Enjoy your time off. You deserve it."

"Yeah, I guess," Ava let out a long breath and redirected the conversation. "So. What were you saying before?"

Katelyn smiled. "I was saying that I got some good news this morning. You remember my college friend, Maggie?"

"The party girl from Missouri."

Katelyn nodded. "She's getting married."

"Oh, wow."

"I honestly thought she'd never truly settle down. But I guess when you find the right guy, anything is possible. Even if it is Keg Stand Greg."

Ava couldn't help but laugh. Katelyn had told her many stories of those two and the rest of their wild friends.

She supposed even party people had to grow up and be responsible at some point. Right?

Katelyn looked thoughtful for a moment. "You know, I always suspected there was something between them. But man, I never thought either of them would act on it. Guess they finally gave in to the attraction."

"When's the big day?"

Katelyn shrugged. "Not sure yet. But their engagement party is this weekend. I'm taking a few days off work to fly up there. Since you're off too, why don't you come with? I'm paying."

Ava popped a little piece of onion ring into her mouth and contemplated the offer.

"Missouri is gorgeous this time of year. You could get some amazing pictures of the leaves changing. And you'll finally get to meet some of my old friends. Maggie says most of the old gang will be there. Plus, it'll be fun to get away for a few days."

"Yeah, I guess. But with the way I've been feeling lately, it might not be such a good idea."

Katelyn scoffed. "It's a great idea. It'll be good for you. No work. Free food and alcohol. Good company. You know you want to come. And you have nothing better to do than sit around your house, waiting to hear back from your doctor."

"I don't know."

Katelyn leaned in and added, "Don't tell me you're willing to turn down a free trip."

Ava sighed. "Okay, fine. I'll go."

Katelyn squeaked with excitement. "Really?"

"As long as you don't get me shitty drunk."

Katelyn smirked. "No promises."

Great.

"Girl, admit it. The free alcohol was the clincher."

Ava rolled her eyes.

"Admit it."

"No." Ava stuck her tongue out at her friend. Maybe a little. But Ava mostly just wanted to take advantage of her time off and disconnect from her daily life. She needed to let loose. Forget about her troubles. Maybe even get laid.

4

Ava woke before dawn, her heart pounding and her entire body drenched in sweat. All she recalled of the dream were the most intense green eyes she'd ever seen. Iridescent and glowing in the darkness. She didn't feel afraid though. She felt alive and her senses more stimulated than they'd ever been in her life.

Unable to go back to sleep, Ava dragged herself out of bed and took a much-needed shower. When she finally emerged, she snuggled on her couch with the newspaper and drank her morning coffee while waiting for the stores to open.

She had to find a dress for the engagement party. According to Katelyn, Maggie didn't throw ordinary parties. She went all out, and Ava was glad to be able to dress up for once.

The first shop Ava stopped in had nothing she liked. The next two had a couple of dresses that looked good on the hanger, but Ava didn't like the way they fit. They didn't flatter her figure at all.

At the fourth shop, Ava finally found the perfect dress. It was a low-cut, shin-length gown that the owner of the little boutique recommended. Ava wasn't sure about the cobalt blue, but once she had it on, she loved it. Not only was the color perfect, but the fabric hugged her petite, curvy frame like it was made just for her.

Ava stepped out of the dressing room to get a better look at herself in the full-length mirror.

The woman who'd helped her stood a short distance away, refolding shirts on the display table near the center aisle. The moment Ava stepped in front of the mirror, the woman looked up and beamed. "I was right. That color is amazing on you."

Ava blushed as she smoothed her hands over the soft fabric. "Thank you. I never would have picked this out for myself, but I love it."

The woman's smile widened even further. "I'm so glad."

Once Ava got changed back into her regular clothes, the woman packaged the dress in a lavender-colored box, folded neatly in tissue paper printed with the boutique's logo.

Ava left the little shop with a pep in her step. She couldn't wait to wear the dress. It wasn't often she got a chance to dress up. Sure, she'd been to a handful of events through Ferro Corp, but never anything so fancy that wasn't work-related.

Katelyn was right. She needed to take advantage of her time off. To let loose and live her life to the fullest. And if she was lucky, she'd meet someone at the party that would take her gorgeous new dress off her by the end of the night.

After taking the package to her car, Ava walked down the block to her favorite bookstore. She figured it wouldn't hurt to grab a book or two for the trip. Even if she didn't have time to read during the four-day weekend, she'd at least have something to keep her occupied once she got home.

Ava wandered over to the stationery section. She didn't need any more notebooks or journals. She had a drawer full of them at home, but she couldn't resist looking to see if they had anything new.

When she didn't see any that she had to have, Ava wandered over to the romance section. She skimmed the new releases, picking one up and reading the back cover.

It was about a grumpy loner mountain man and a curvy city girl with a sunny disposition. She gets caught in a blizzard while taking photos for her blog. He rescues her and takes her back to his cabin, where they get snowed in together.

Forced proximity. Opposites attract. Ava loved those type of books.

She scanned the shelves, looking for one more book, but none of them piqued her interest. Not until she reached the last section. And in the center of the last shelf, something caught her eye. A face on one of the books. Half of it, that of a beautiful black jaguar. The other half, a man that stole her breath.

Ava stood in the middle of the bookstore, captivated by the image on the cover. Not only because both man and beast had the most striking sage-green eyes she had ever seen, but also because she recognized those eyes from her dreams. She didn't know how it was possible, but she knew one thing. No matter what the book was about, it was coming home with her, and she'd be reading it before day's end.

Ava spent the next few hours getting ready for the trip. She washed her last load of laundry, watered all her plants, and unloaded the dishwasher. The house didn't need to be spotless, but she didn't want to come home from the trip to chores that needed to be done.

Once she had everything in order and packed for the trip, she settled on her bed with a bag of white cheddar popcorn and the book she'd been waiting half the day to read.

Leaned back against the headboard, Ava rested the book on her lap and read until she fell asleep.

This time, she dreamed of a vibrant jungle teeming with life. She closed her eyes and enjoyed nature's music as she sank into the tall, soft grass. When she opened herself to the world around her, Ava sensed someone watching her. She slowly opened her eyes and looked around before realizing where the feeling came from.

Just in the fringe, she saw those eyes again, peering out from the darkness beyond the small clearing where she sat. She tried to see the face that went with those beautiful, hypnotizing eyes, but it stayed just out of the dim light.

D'MITRI DRAGGED himself to bed and fell asleep before his head fully settled on the pillow. For the first time in a long time, he dreamt. He stood in the jungle with shadows surrounding him. And from out of the dark, a soft glow penetrated the night. Eyes like none he'd ever seen. Luminescent orbs that drew him in and held him captive. Deep,

20

golden amber with a starburst of electric green. They were a Jagara's eyes. Her eyes. And they were stunning.

He woke the next morning, a mix of emotions overwhelming him. He felt incredible relief and joy knowing the dream was only the first taste. A sign that his mate's Awakening had begun. But no matter how happy he felt knowing that their time approached, he had no idea how long it would take.

He still didn't know who she was or even what she looked like. So, he tried his best to go back to sleep, in the hopes of seeing her face or some clue to where she lived. But his excitement kept him awake.

That day was the longest of his life. He tried to busy himself in his shop, but no amount of sanding and carving could keep his mind from wandering back to his mate and those wild, beautiful eyes.

The next day, D'mitri sat on the couch across from Grandi as he fed Violet a bottle of milk. The youngling was nearly four months old, and Ali hadn't been away from her since giving birth. According to Grandi, Ali hadn't taken her jaguar form since well before the little one was born. But Nicolai had finally convinced her to leave Violet with Grandi and go for a much-needed run.

Grandi sighed. "I am glad she has finally let the youngling breathe. She needed a break. She was growing too clingy."

D'mitri smiled. "Ali or little Violet?"

Grandi smirked. "Yes."

D'mitri chuckled softly.

Grandi looked at his granddaughter. "Ali more so than the little one. She was in much need of a run. She has been under much stress lately."

"She worries too much for everyone," D'mitri agreed.

Grandi looked up at him then. "She worries for you, D'mitri."

He sighed. "I know. As does everyone else. But there will be no need for worry soon enough."

Grandi arched a brow. "And why is that?"

"I have dreamed of my mate."

Grandi's eyes widened, but before he could respond, Ali burst into the room with Nicolai close behind her. Though breathless from their run, Ali beamed when she saw him. "D'mitri! What brings you here this morning?"

He rose to greet her. "News, sweet sister."

She eyed him with curiosity when she registered his cheerful mood.

Nicolai chimed in. "What sort of news?"

D'mitri smiled, clasping his brother's shoulder. "Dreams of a beautiful female with eyes like none I have ever seen."

5

Ava knew Katelyn's friend must have some serious money if she'd sent a private jet and her personal driver to pick them up. Still, she was impressed when they pulled up to the massive iron gates and waited for them to open. Ava had never seen anything like it in person. Only in movies and on TV.

The three-story mansion beyond the gates stole her breath. With the oranges and pinks of the setting sun reflecting off the windows, the view was spectacular.

An older woman greeted them at the front door and then led them down the wide hall to an enormous room. The sunset shone through the floor-to-ceiling windows, casting a red-orange glow across the pale walls, and highlighting the built-in bookshelves.

"Oh, wow," Ava whispered to herself.

"Katie!"

Ava turned to see a leggy brunette coming in through the massive French doors with a wide smile on her face.

Katelyn's eyes lit up as she hugged the other woman. "I wouldn't miss the party of the year."

When Katelyn stepped back, Maggie surprised Ava by giving her a quick hug. "I'm glad you decided to come."

"Me too. And I have to say, your house is beautiful."

"Thank you," she beamed. "My mother fell in love with it instantly, and my father, not being able to deny her anything, bought it for her as a wedding gift."

"That's sweet."

"Yeah, well, to tell the truth, he spoiled us both." She was quiet for a beat before asking, "So, are you two hungry?"

Katelyn laughed. "Starved."

"Good," Maggie said, motioning for them to follow her. "Because I made sure there would be enough for both of you and some for Greg when he gets home later."

They crossed the hall and went through the double doors and into a gorgeous dining room with dark, heavy-looking oak furniture.

"I was about to ask you where he was."

Maggie looked back at Katelyn and rolled her eyes. "His boss had him drive up to Weston to pick up his nephew. Apparently, the little punk got into some trouble, and his parents want him to come down here and stay with his uncle. Problem is, they have a vacation that's been planned for months that they can't cancel. And his uncle doesn't get back into town until next week. So, he asked Greg to keep an eye on the boy until then."

"That sounds like fun," Katelyn said sarcastically.

"I know, right? There's nothing like babysitting a trouble-making teenager when you're supposed to be on vacation."

Katelyn laughed as the three of them sat together at one end of a long table. "That shouldn't be too hard for Greg. They should get along just fine. He's just a big teenager himself."

"You don't have to tell me," Maggie snorted. "But at least he won't be the only one. The entire gang will be here."

Katelyn smirked. "This should be fun."

"Interesting as usual," Maggie grinned. She turned to Ava. "I don't know how much Katie has told you, but the old gang can be a little wild. Every time we all get together, there's some sort of excitement. Last time, Gareth and Kurt got into a fight."

Katelyn snorted. "I still don't know what happened. Neither of them would tell anybody what started it. We were all hanging out on the patio after most of the other guests had gone home. One second, they were sitting there talking while us girls danced and goofed off. And the next, Gareth clocked Kurt, knocking him out of his chair."

"Totally killed my buzz," Maggie added.

"Tell me about it. I just wish I knew what triggered it."

"There's no telling. They were both wasted, and you know how Kurt likes to talk shit."

"Yeah, but Gareth? He's usually the mellow one. Something had to set him off."

Maggie nodded. "Who knows? Maybe it was just the Jack. It has the same effect on Debbie."

Katelyn burst out laughing. "I forgot about that. Shit. That was a rough night. We practically had to carry her out of the club, but she was livid once we got her in the car. It took Gareth sitting on her to keep her in the seat."

Ava laughed.

"Yeah, you laugh," Maggie said seriously, "But you weren't there, and you don't know Debbie. She's this tiny little redhead with the sweetest, easygoing attitude, but that night she was the devil. She fought like a madwoman, cussing out Gareth, and threatening to cut off his balls if he didn't get off her."

"Thank God she wore herself out and passed out."

Katelyn snorted again. "Yeah, after almost an hour. I thought we weren't ever gonna go home that night."

Maggie frowned. "How did we get home?"

Katelyn stared at her for a long moment before she cracked up. "I honestly have no idea."

Ava spent the rest of the evening listening to Maggie and Katelyn tell story after story about their friends. And she had never laughed so hard in her life.

By the time she finally crashed for the night, Ava was a little tipsy and completely exhausted. Traveling always tired her out, and this time was no different.

———

D'MITRI COULDN'T GET the dream out of his head. He kept seeing it over and over. Her curvy little body, slinking slowly through the tall grass as he lounged near the water's edge.

Her wavy hair, darkened by the water, hung just below her shoulder blades. But D'mitri hadn't been able to look away from the way her hips swayed as she made her way to the tree line. The look she threw him over her shoulder stole his breath. That seductive little glance in his direction just before she slipped out of sight is what did him in.

D'mitri replayed the dream over and over in his head, enjoying the catlike way she moved and how the color of her skin glowed, even under the thick canopy of the trees.

Waiting for her would be pure torture. He felt like he'd lose his mind before the time came and he could hold her in his arms and kiss her lovely lips.

———

Ava lay in the bath, her eyes on the ceiling but her thoughts on the vivid dream she'd woken from twenty minutes ago. The rich scents and vibrant colors like nothing she'd ever experienced. And the man in the dream was the most striking she'd ever seen.

His beautiful, masculine features. His mouthwatering body with the hard muscles and smooth, golden skin. The way the light played over his midnight hair was beautiful, and she wanted to feel it between her fingers.

But it was the eyes that did her in. Eyes that she recognized from her other dream, and his breathtaking face from the cover of the book that she'd bought just before coming to Maggie's.

Strange how the brain worked sometimes. Taking things you see, think, or do during your waking hours. Plucking select ones from your memories and then merging them together to create dreams.

Problem was, dreams usually began to fade once she woke, but those of the gorgeous stranger seemed to burrow into her mind like they belonged there. Like *he* belonged there.

Ava finished her bath and got ready for the day. Once

she dressed in a pair of comfy jeans and a long-sleeved T-shirt, she dried her hair and tugged it into a loose ponytail.

She joined the others downstairs. Katelyn and Maggie sat at one end of the huge table, chattering quietly. And next to Maggie sat a gorgeous, well-built man with dirty-blond hair that stuck up in short, messy spikes.

He was the first to notice when she walked into the room. He stood to greet her with a wide, welcoming smile. "Hey. You must be Ava."

She nodded. "And you must be Greg."

After a quick handshake, Ava settled at the table, across from Katelyn.

"How'd you sleep?" Maggie asked her.

Ava shrugged. "Not too bad, I guess."

"Oh, that doesn't sound good. It's not my bed, I hope."

"No," Ava assured her. "I've just had trouble sleeping lately. Strange dreams."

"Ah. My friend had that problem a couple of years ago," she said with an odd tone. Then she gave an encouraging smile. "It didn't last long though."

Perhaps picking up on the strange vibe, Greg looked back and forth between them before he changed the subject. "When are they getting here?"

"Should be some time before lunch."

Greg grinned. "I can't wait to see Violet. I bet she's getting so big."

"Who is Violet?" Ava asked before taking a bite of a croissant.

"Ali and Nicolai's baby," Maggie answered. "She's almost four months old. She's the most adorable thing you've ever seen."

"You aren't biased either, are you?" Greg asked, laughing.

Maggie poked him in the ribs and glared at him. "What, I can't think my goddaughter is beautiful?"

"If you like," he teased. "She's okay for a baby, I guess."

"Uh huh. I'm telling Ali you said that, and she won't let you hold Violet at all while they're here."

"Whatever." Greg rolled his eyes. "She loves me. Nobody can resist my charm."

Maggie scoffed.

"What?" Greg smirked. "It got you into my bed, didn't it?"

Maggie snorted. "Technically, it was my bed."

"Still worked."

"Uh-huh. Don't make me hold out on you until the wedding, smartass."

Greg threw his head back and laughed loud enough for it to echo off the high ceiling. "I bet my favorite pajamas you can't hold out for one night, nympho!"

"Watch me, baby."

"Oh, I will. And you are so gonna lose." Greg's voice then dropped into a husky purr. "You can't resist me when I do that thing."

A flush bloomed on Maggie's cheeks, but Ava knew it wasn't from embarrassment when Maggie breathed, "That would be cheating."

"Cheating? There would have to be rules for me to be cheating." He smirked as he took Maggie's hand and kissed her knuckles.

Maggie's eyes went hazy for a moment. Ava looked

across the table at Katelyn, who seemed equally entranced. Ava felt a little embarrassed watching them behave that way, so she focused on fixing herself a plate instead.

She suspected with how Maggie looked at him, Greg might be right about her giving in before the night was over. They might be lucky to make it through breakfast.

6

Ava sat on the end of the bed, only half paying attention to the conversation as Katelyn and Maggie stood next to a set of double doors that opened into a huge walk-in closet.

"Hey, girlies."

Maggie looked toward the bedroom doorway and squeaked, "Hey!"

Ava turned to see who the gentle, raspy, feminine voice belonged to. Maggie met the beautiful woman in the middle of the room and hugged her so tight Ava thought the poor woman might stop breathing.

When Maggie finally released her, the woman smiled at Katelyn. They exchanged pleasant greetings and Katelyn motioned toward the bed. "Ali, this is Ava, my friend from Louisiana."

When Ali turned to say hello, something in her amber eyes shifted, and her smile faltered a heartbeat before she greeted her. "Nice to meet you."

Feeling a peculiar familiarity, Ava searched the

woman's face. "Have we met before? You seem familiar to me."

"No. I don't think so." She offered her a faint smile, but Ava saw the flicker of unease in her eyes.

Katelyn must have noticed the underlying awkwardness as well because she drew Ali's attention again. She tugged Maggie's hand forward and all but shoved it in Ali's face. "Have you seen this ring?"

Ali took Maggie's hand and inspected the sparkling diamond on the intricate platinum band. "Wow. It's even more gorgeous in person."

Maggie beamed. "I still can't believe this is happening."

Ali scoffed. "I can't believe it took Greg this long to propose."

Katelyn spoke up. "I'm still processing the whole thing."

Maggie rolled her eyes. "I know. I know. Keg Stand Greg is settling down. Who'da thunk?"

They all laughed. Then Maggie asked, "Where's Violet? Is Greg hogging her already?"

Ali smiled and nodded. "Giving Nico a break. He gives me shit about holding her too much, but he holds her more than I do. If it wasn't for me telling him no, she'd sleep in our bed with us."

Maggie nodded. "I can see that. He's such a softy when it comes to her. That man is wrapped around both of those tiny pinkies of hers."

Katelyn chimed in. "I just hate to think of when she gets old enough to date. He's gonna be a beast."

Maggie and Ali exchanged a look and burst out laughing.

"Come on," Maggie said with a smile. "Let's get back down there. I wanna see my girl."

Ava followed the others back down the stairs, and into the den where the men sat chatting. When they both looked up, Ava nearly tripped over her own feet.

She vaguely heard Maggie gushing over the baby and the baby's happy babble echoing as if from a distance, but Ava's focus was on the man who rose from the chair next to Greg. It was him. The man from her dreams.

Katelyn's hand waved in front of Ava's face, but Ava barely noticed it.

"Hello?" Katelyn stepped in front of her, blocking her view.

Seeing the odd expression on her friend's face, Ava cleared her throat. "Yeah?"

Katelyn frowned. "Are you okay?"

"Yeah. I just…" Ava swallowed.

"What?"

Ava looked around Katelyn and forced a breath before asking quietly, "Is he a cover model for romance novels?"

"No." Maggie's friend said from beside her. "But he is on the cover of my latest book."

Ava looked over at Ali, and she could see so much pride in the woman's golden eyes as she watched the man approach. This guy was Ali's husband. Ali. Katelyn told her that Maggie's friend was an author. Feeling like a complete idiot, Ava breathed, "You're Alessandra Montez."

Ali nodded.

"I'm reading your book. He…" she glanced at the guy again as he said a quick hello to Katelyn. "Oh, wow."

"That's my man." Ali smiled proudly.

He turned to Ava then. "Hello, I am Nicolai," he said with a gorgeous smile and a not-so-subtle Portuguese accent as he took her hand, touching his forehead to the back of it before he straightened.

When he released her hand, she cleared her throat. "I'm Ava."

His piercing green eyes held her gaze and seemed to see deep inside her. She felt like he knew she'd dreamed of him. Which was ridiculous. There was no way he could know that.

"So," Maggie broke through the awkward tension. "Does anybody want food or drinks?"

Ali laughed. "Don't you think it's a bit early for drinks, Mags?"

She shook her head. "It's wine o'clock somewhere."

"You are such a lush," Katelyn chimed in.

Maggie rolled her eyes. "Fine. We'll wait. Killjoys."

They settled at the table. Some of them ate lunch while others just sat and talked. Although her aunt spoke Portuguese, Nicolai's accent captivated Ava. Okay, maybe it wasn't the accent. Or, at least, that wasn't the only thing. His voice, those eyes, the way he smiled—everything about him was familiar to her. Yet not.

Ava looked down at her plate and pushed the food around with her fork, trying to concentrate on anything but him. She felt an obsession over the guy growing already, and she'd just met him.

"It sounds so perfect," Ali said, drawing Ava's attention. When she looked up, Ali was smiling across the table at Maggie.

"It won't be nearly as beautiful as your wedding though. That was the most…" Maggie shook her head.

"I've never seen anything like it. I wish we could have a ceremony like that."

Unable to help herself, Ava asked. "What was it like?"

Ali looked at Nicolai with a beaming smile and squeezed his big hand before she turned to Ava. "It was the traditional tribal marriage ceremony of our people. It took place in the middle of the jungle on the ancient tribal grounds. There was a huge stone platform in the center, and everyone stood around it. On either side was a hut for each of us to get ready, and when the elder called us out, he presented each one of us to the crowd."

Nicolai spoke low, but his smooth voice was clear. "I knew you were the one for me. There was no doubt. But when I stepped out and the crowd parted, my breath left me. The reality that you were mine was nearly too much for me to take." He brushed his fingers over Ali's cheek and smiled. "You were the most beautiful creature I had ever seen, like an angel who came down from heaven just for me."

There was a quiet moment, and something passed between the two of them. Ava was mesmerized by the way they seemed to speak to each other without saying a word.

A gagging sound brought everyone's attention to Maggie. She had her finger in her throat, faking disgust. Nicolai grabbed a napkin from the table and hurled it at her. "I feel the same way watching you two drool all over each other."

"Anyways," Ali said, frowning at Nicolai.

He gave her a small grin before continuing. "The elder bound us together with the ceremonial words and then said a prayer over us before presenting us as one. The best part of the day—other than the kiss—came at the end of the ceremony."

Ali held her hand out, palm up, and Ava leaned in to inspect the line of symbols tattooed on Ali's forearm. They were very similar to the ones her aunt Lilah had.

Ali smiled proudly. "It's Nicolai's name in the old language. He has mine on his arm too."

Nicolai turned his arm over so she could see his tattoo as well.

"They're beautiful," Ava said, turning her focus back to Ali. "As a bride, what do you wear in a tribal marriage ceremony?"

Ali started explaining but stopped when Nicolai shifted his weight and took out his wallet. He slipped a picture from the folds and pushed it across the table to Ava.

She ignored the shirtless Nicolai in the picture. Just the sight of him brought her dream back into the front of her mind, and that was the last thing she needed at the moment…or ever. Ava then forced herself instead to look at Ali in the photo, who wore a long, sheer skirt. A criss-cross of white fabric covered her chest, and her golden hair was pulled back from her face and adorned with a large orange flower.

"Wow!" Ava looked across the table at Ali. "That is gorgeous. You looked like an island princess or something."

"That's what I told her," Maggie beamed.

"What's it like being in the jungle?" Katelyn asked.

Ali and Nicolai exchanged an odd look before Ali answered. "It's a million times more beautiful than any picture I have ever seen. The colors and scents are unbelievable. The sounds are so soothing, and to be honest, I miss it horribly when I'm gone."

"I've always wanted to go to South America, but I've never had a chance."

Ali nodded. "Oh, it's worth it. If you're anything like me, you will absolutely love it. You won't want to leave once you get there and take your first good breath of jungle air."

Ava agreed. "It is beautiful there."

Katelyn shot a surprised look at her. "You've been?"

Ava nodded. "When I was fifteen. I didn't get to enjoy it too much though. I was there for my uncle's funeral."

"How did I not know that?"

Ava shrugged.

Greg must have read the tension rolling off Katelyn. He quickly drew her attention "I was a little nervous when we went. But they're right. It was amazing there. Maggie wants to go back for our honeymoon and spend some time out in more of the remote places."

Ava's brows shot up. "Really?" She looked at Maggie. "No offense, but you don't seem like the 'roughing it' type."

Greg laughed. "She wasn't before we went."

After scowling at Greg, Maggie smiled at Ava. "I guess it's just one of those places you can't help but love."

7

The party was everything Katelyn said it would be. Gorgeous people, delicious food, and enough alcohol to drown an army.

At dinner, conversation flowed all around her as everyone ate, but Ava didn't hear much of anything. And though the food looked good, she barely touched her plate. With Ali and Nicolai sitting across from her, she didn't have much of an appetite.

Ali was beautiful and she seemed like a sweet woman, but Ava couldn't stop looking at Nicolai. She felt terrible for staring at another woman's husband, but every time she looked away, something always dragged her focus back to him.

To make matters worse, she didn't see the man in the nice clothes. All she could see when she looked across the massive mahogany table was Nicolai in all his naked glory, his body stretched out in the grass next to a shimmering pool in the middle of the jungle.

He and Ali seemed to, for the most part, be in their

own little world, feeding each other pieces of food and then leaning in close to kiss or whisper something that made the other smile.

When Nicolai reached for a small piece of meat on his plate, his eyes lifted for a mere heartbeat. Still, the intensity in the depths of those eyes stole Ava's breath and held her gaze captive for that fleeting moment. Then he offered her a polite smile before turning his focus back to his wife.

How embarrassing. Had he felt her staring, or did he blow it off as them by chance looking up at the same time and making awkward eye contact? He didn't seem awkward about it. Or even bothered by her looking at him. So, maybe he didn't notice how long she'd been staring.

A hard nudge under the table drew her attention to Katelyn. Her friend leaned in and hissed, "What is wrong with you?"

Ava's heart sank. Apparently, someone had noticed. Dammit.

Katelyn glanced at the happy couple before lowering her voice even more. "You've been eye-fucking a married man for the last thirty-five minutes with his wife sitting right there."

Ava's face flushed with embarrassment, and she glanced around the room. Thankfully, no one paid her any attention.

With the drone of conversation buzzing around them, Katelyn leaned in closer. "When dinner is over, we're getting you some drinks and then I'm introducing you to some of my guy friends. The single ones."

Ava snorted.

"I'm serious. You clearly need the distraction." Katelyn tossed another quick glance across the table, but

Ava didn't bother looking. She knew exactly what her friend meant. And she was right. Ava desperately needed something—or someone—to take her mind off Nicolai.

Over the next thirty minutes, people slowly trickled out of the dining room and made their way to the massive library across the hall. Ava felt a bit of relief when the couple across from her followed.

Katelyn pushed her chair back and stood. "Come on. I'll introduce you to some people."

Ava reluctantly got to her feet and smoothed her dress.

Her friend snorted. "Don't look so excited."

Ava rolled her eyes. "Fine. Let's get this over with."

Katelyn linked arms with her, and they walked together into the other room. Having her friend at her side made it easier, but Ava didn't know if she was ready to socialize.

Katelyn dragged her up to the first group of partygoers and introduced her to them all. The next hour was a blur. Usually, she had a hard time remembering names, but between recognizing some of them from Katelyn's social media and connecting some of the names with stories she'd been told over the years, Ava was able to keep up just fine.

Three glasses of champagne later, Ava felt buzzed, so she wandered over and asked the bartender for a bottle of water.

Over to her right, a group of friends stood in a semi-circle at the end of the bar. What she overheard wasn't the guy-talk she expected when she first spotted them. Instead, she discovered how hopelessly in love with Maggie Greg really was. All he could talk about was how much he looked forward to being her husband and having a handful of kids together. And the genuine happiness radiating from their friends made Ava smile.

"Hi."

Ava looked to her left to see who'd spoken. A muscular guy stood an arm's length from her with a warm smile on his handsome face. She recognized him from at the dinner table, but they hadn't been introduced yet. "Hi."

He angled his big body more toward her and offered his hand, "I'm Joseph."

She reluctantly slipped her hand into his. "Ava."

He smiled. "Beautiful name."

She forced an awkward "thank you" because she didn't know what else to say.

The guy made her a little nervous, honestly. Not because she got bad vibes from him, but because of his height. He towered over her. Which wasn't hard. Topping out at only five-foot-three, most people were taller than her.

He nodded over his shoulder. "You want to dance?"

Ava glanced toward the center of the room where a handful of people had paired up. In the mix was Nicolai and Ali. She'd managed to avoid them for the last hour and a half. She wasn't about to go anywhere near them now. Turning back to face the bar again, she muttered, "No. I'm good, thanks."

"How about just some company, then?"

She didn't feel much like being social. She'd rather go to bed, but being alone with her thoughts wasn't the best idea. Instead, she took a deep breath and turned to face Joseph. "I'm warning you. I might not be the best company."

He grinned. "Somehow, I doubt that."

Behind him, at the other end of the bar, Ava caught sight of Katelyn smiling in their direction. Ava couldn't tell if her friend had sent Joseph her way or if she was just excited that Ava was finally talking to someone. Either way, she should probably be a little nicer and really talk to the guy. She needed the distraction, that's for sure. But she didn't know if she could muster enough enthusiasm to not come off as unfriendly.

"Look, I'm just kind of trying to relax."

Though he nodded in understanding, Ava could see the disappointment in his deep blue eyes.

As if she didn't feel bad enough already, Ava glanced toward Katelyn again. Her best friend gave her a hard frown and mouthed, "What are you doing?"

Ava knew she wouldn't hear the end of it if she didn't at least feign a little interest. Lucky for her, the guy didn't give up so easily. He leaned into the bar, propping himself on his elbows. "I was about to get another drink. Do you want one?"

To satisfy Katelyn, she looked up at Mr. Redhead and gave him the best smile she could muster. "Sure."

When the drinks were in front of them, Joseph asked, "So, how long have you known Maggie and Greg?"

"Almost two days."

He arched a brow. "Really?"

"Yeah. Katelyn dragged me up here from Louisiana. How about you? How long have you known them?"

He looked deep in thought for a few seconds before he said, "I've known Maggie about seventeen years."

"Oh wow. So, you basically grew up together."

"Yeah. My family moved here when I was nine. Our parents met through one of the Jennings' charity events.

They became good friends after that, so me and Maggie spent quite a bit of time together. Hell, we even ended up going to the same college. That's where we both met Greg." Joseph turned to face the rest of the room. "Most of the people here are friends from college."

Ava turned and scanned the room. She couldn't imagine having so many friends. There had to be at least thirty people there. And more trickling in since dinner was over.

She leaned back against the bar next to Joseph and sighed. She felt herself finally starting to relax…until she saw Ali and Nicolai. They were no longer on the dance-floor. Instead, they stood near the bank of windows away from the rest of the crowd.

While Joseph kept talking, her attention was on the couple who looked as if they were oblivious to everyone else in the room.

Ali lounged against the bookshelf, and Nicolai leaned into her, running his nose along the edge of her jaw. When his lips brushed over her ear, Ali closed her eyes and smiled. Ava watched, envying her as Nicolai's big hand slid over Ali's hip and he pressed himself into her tall, slender frame.

Ava could barely breathe from the intensity those two radiated, and she wanted that. She wanted…

"They're hot, right?"

As if she hadn't felt like a complete voyeur before, Joseph knew exactly what she'd been looking at, and she could feel her face turning red.

"Don't be embarrassed. It's hard not to notice those two."

Notice them? She wished it was that simple. If you

noticed someone, it was a mental acknowledgment of their existence in the world. But then you moved on to something else. Ava couldn't move on. Her gaze just kept returning to Nicolai.

Ava turned her back to the room and asked the bartender for something a little stronger than champagne.

"Bourbon?"

"Sounds good."

He sat a double shot in front of her, and after a quick thank you, Ava slung it back in one go. Big mistake. She covered her mouth with a shaking hand and fought hard not to cough. The smoky, harsh flavor made her eyes water.

"You okay?" Joseph asked with a chuckle.

Ava nodded but had to blow out a breath to compose herself. The burn that traveled down her throat and into her stomach reminded her why she wasn't a bourbon drinker. She preferred something lighter and easier on the senses. Sure, champagne would get her the buzz she was after, but Ava wanted to be wasted to the point of forgetting about Nicolai completely. For a little while, at least.

"Another?" the bartender asked.

When Ava indicated the glass, he poured a second, and she tossed that one back as well. She shivered as she looked up at Joseph through watering eyes.

He grinned. "You all right?"

"Yes," she coughed. "One more."

He arched a brow in surprise. "You sure?"

"Absolutely."

Ava didn't miss the look Joseph exchanged with the bartender, but the guy poured another anyway. Both men watched with a wary expression as she fired back the third and final shot.

With her palm on the center of her chest, Ava let out a rough breath to try and calm the burn.

Joseph handed her his beer. "Here, this will cool things down a bit."

She took the bottle without hesitation and drew a long pull of the dark, hoppy brew. The flavor was awful, but the relief it provided her throat and gut was instant. She handed the bottle back to him. "Thanks."

"You want to talk about it?"

The genuine concern in Joseph's voice surprised her, but Ava couldn't look at him. He seemed nice enough, but the guy was a stranger. He didn't need to be playing therapist to whatever messed up crap was going on with her. She honestly just wanted to get the night over with, go home to Louisiana, and try to forget she'd ever met Nicolai.

Instead, the vivid vision of him forced itself back into the forefront of her mind. The dream of him lounging naked in the thick grass by the river's edge. His bronze skin. His long, midnight hair. And those intense green eyes never leaving hers as she prowled toward him.

Ava squeezed her eyes shut and forced herself to take a deep, calming breath. She had to stop this. She really was obsessing over him, and it was wrong. He had a wife. And a baby.

"Hey. You okay?"

No. She wasn't okay. She felt like she was losing her mind.

A warm, gentle hand brushed her arm. "Come on. Let's get you some fresh air."

Ava lifted her eyes to meet his. Air was probably a good idea, but searching his handsome face, she couldn't help thinking maybe Katelyn was right. Maybe a good roll in the sheets with a stranger was exactly what she needed. "I have a better idea."

Ava knew she should feel guilty about using the guy as a distraction, but she didn't allow herself to dwell on the thought. Besides, judging by the shift in Joseph's expression, she didn't think he'd object to being used in the way she had in mind. And that solidified her decision to get the hell out of there.

Ava took Joseph's hand, and without another word, she led him upstairs. The room she stayed in was spacious, but when she closed the door, cutting the two of them off from the rest of the world, it felt almost claustrophobic. Joseph was a big guy, but it wasn't his physical size that made the vast room feel almost suffocating.

Joseph sat his drink on the corner of the dresser and then turned to face her. As the silence stretched between them, she didn't know how to get things started. Sure, she'd been brave enough to drag him to her room, but she didn't know how to initiate the next step.

Joseph must have seen the indecision in her eyes because he leaned back against the dresser and assured her. "Look. We don't have to do this."

She leaned back against the door because she needed the support. "No. I want to. I just…"

When her words trailed off, Joseph approached her with slow, precise steps.

As he stepped in close, Ava rested her head against the door and looked up at him. "I've never done this before," she blurted without thinking.

Joseph frowned slightly but brought his hand up to cup her chin. "You're a virgin?" he asked softly, awe apparent in his voice.

Ava laughed, some of the tension leaving her. "No, that's not what I meant. It's just that I've never slept with someone I just met. Usually, there is dating first. In fact, I have a strict five-date rule."

Joseph blinked. "Oh."

"But tonight is far from my usual." Ava admitted. "It sounds harsh to say it this way, but I honestly just need the escape."

He grinned, his eyes softening as he stepped even closer. "I'm okay with that."

Good. At least she didn't have to feel guilty about using him.

Joseph leaned down, hesitating for a heartbeat before his mouth brushed against hers. At first contact, butterflies took flight in Ava's stomach. It had been a long time since she'd last been kissed. She'd almost forgotten what it felt like.

When a ragged little breath escaped her slightly parted lips, Joseph's tongue got involved. He slowly licked at her mouth, inviting her to open further to him. And she did.

The guy could kiss. The teasing strokes of his tongue combined with the alternating soft, then firm play of his skilled lips took her away from her thoughts of others. Ava enjoyed the diversion. Unfortunately, that didn't last.

Even though Ava found him physically attractive, but beyond that initial jolt, she just wasn't feeling the spark she'd hoped to feel. Maybe that was part of having a one-night stand. Sure, they shared the physical, but she could see just how much mental and emotional bonding created true intimacy.

Needing more, Ava let her hands roam over Joseph's toned chest and up to grip his nape. Ava ignored the uneasy feeling building in her belly and deepened the kiss.

The low groan that escaped Joseph's throat told her how much he enjoyed what was happening. As did the way his rough hands traveled down her side and gripped her hips.

Ava's breath left her in a rush when she felt the evidence of his excitement press against her stomach. Joseph took her reaction as arousal, but Ava ignored the strange feeling building in her gut. Determined to push through the uneasiness, she fumbled with the buttons of his shirt.

Joseph shifted, helping her as she pushed the material off his shoulders. And when his arms were free, he brought his hands up to cup her face as he continued kissing her, breathing into her as her heart rate increased.

Joseph broke away from her mouth, trailing kisses along her jaw and whispered into her ear, "You smell incredible." He groaned when she moved against him, and he whispered into the hollow just below her ear, "You feel amazing too."

Ava wrapped her arms around his waist and held on, gripping his bare back as he traced his tongue over her throat. Sliding his thumbs beneath the straps of her dress, he tugged gently, nibbling at her collarbone as he pushed the material from her shoulders.

Ava exhaled another ragged breath when the dress hit the floor at her feet. She clutched Joseph's shoulders, trying to stay calm, but when he tucked an arm around her waist and pulled her fully against him, she was on the verge of something intense.

Shaking a little, Ava tried not to focus too much on the fact that she stood before a virtual stranger in nothing but a pair of heels and a thong. With her bare breasts pressed firmly against Joseph's hard torso, she buried her fingers in his hair. The second she closed her eyes, a troubling picture flashed in her mind. The man from her dreams was pressed against her, her fingers in his hair and her head thrown back in pure ecstasy as he plunged into her trembling body.

Opening her eyes to reality, Ava tried to force Nicolai from her mind and focus on what she had right in front of her. But the moment she caught sight of Joseph's reddish-brown hair, an overwhelming wrongness came over her. Betrayal. She felt it deep inside. She didn't understand it, but she tasted it on her tongue and felt it crawling over her skin.

Joseph's free hand slid over the curve of her bare ass and his open mouth brushed over the top of her breast.

When Ava began to squirm, he lifted his head. The moment they made eye contact, Ava felt the panic rise.

"Let go of me," she rasped.

Joseph frowned. "What?"

Ava pushed at him, her breaths quickening. "Please."

Joseph released her and took a step back. "What's wrong? What just happened?"

Breathing too heavy, Ava quavered, "I can't."

Worry filled his bright eyes. "Did I do something wrong?"

Burying her hands in her hair, Ava shook her head. "I just can't do this."

"Ava," Joseph said softly.

But all she could think about was how she'd lost her mind. She was about to sleep with a perfect stranger because she wanted to forget about another. She couldn't understand the heavy dread and the undeniable feeling that she was betraying someone. And not just herself. But, who? Was it Nicolai? His wife? Someone else?

"Ava," Joseph said a little louder. When she finally looked up, he assured her in a calm, gentle voice. "It's okay. We don't have to do this."

All too aware of just how little she wore, Ava covered her bare chest as her vision blurred with unshed tears.

Joseph grabbed his shirt from the floor and wrapped it around her. "Please don't cry."

As the tears spilled over her lashes, Ava tugged his shirt closer. "I'm sorry. I don't know what's wrong with me."

"It's all right. Just breathe."

Ava took a shuddering breath. And when her stomach churned, she knew the alcohol was about to make a second appearance. Forcing another breath, she tried to ease the feeling building inside, but it kept growing no matter how many breaths she took. Her throat worked as she forced air in and out of her lungs.

She closed her eyes, attempting to get a grip on her churning stomach, but she could hold it back no more. Not wanting to puke all over Joseph, she lunged for the bathroom. She barely made it to the toilet before the retching took over.

When she felt Joseph's fingers gather her hair, she tried to push him away, but he insisted. "Let me help you."

"No," she mumbled, fighting the churning in her stomach. She really didn't want him to watch her puke her guts up.

Still, he stayed, crouching behind her, his gentle hand on her back as she lost the contents of her stomach. "That's it," he soothed. "Just let it go. You'll feel better."

When she finally finished, Ava lifted her heavy arm and flushed the toilet, so she didn't get sick again from the smell of the alcohol. Laying her head against her arm, Ava forced herself to breathe while Joseph stroked her cheek and neck.

They sat in silence for a long time, Ava dozing, and Joseph never leaving her side. At some point, he lifted her from the floor and her vision swam. She tried to protest, but he whispered, "Shh, I've got you."

Exhausted and unable to keep her head up, Ava let her cheek rest against Joseph's hard shoulder as he carried her.

Once he settled her in the bed, Joseph stretched out on top of the covers beside her. Ava felt a bit relieved that she didn't have to be by herself, but she felt bad for Joseph. He was stuck babysitting the drunk girl when he could be downstairs with his friends.

Ava rolled onto her side, trying to ease the sick feeling in her stomach. "I'm sorry."

Joseph hesitated, his eyes meeting hers. "For what?"

"For everything. But mostly, for getting sick."

He brushed her hair from her face. "No apologies necessary. Just get some sleep. And I'll be right here if you need anything."

Ava hoped so, because she felt like shit, and she didn't want to be alone.

8

Ava finally dragged herself out of bed around noon. After showering, she made her way downstairs to see who all was up and moving around. She hoped to find some food, because she was starving.

Happy chatter greeted her when she stepped into the dining room. Maggie and Greg sat at one end of the table talking with Ali and Nicolai, along with a few other familiar faces from the night before. Joseph and Katelyn sat toward the other end, seemingly deep in their own conversation, until Joseph looked up and motioned for Ava to sit beside him.

When she joined them, Joseph offered her a warm smile. "How are you feeling?"

She shrugged. "Okay, I guess." She hesitated, glancing at Katelyn before she asked him, "How about you?"

"I'm good." He grabbed an empty glass from the center of the table and poured her some orange juice. "Here, drink this. You look like you need it."

Ava gave a weak smile. "Thank you."

"You want some food?"

When she shook her head, he turned back to Katelyn, jumping right back into their conversation. "So, I told him my dad worked for the company back when I was a kid, and I always wanted to follow in his footsteps. I loved listening to the old man talk about his job and the work-ings of an oil rig. As far back as I can remember I've wanted to throw a chain. He asked my dad's name, and when I told him, he laughed. Turns out he and my dad worked together back in the day."

Katelyn smiled. "That's cool."

"Yeah," he laughed. "I thought so too, until I found out the truth about all the stories the old man told me growing up. The ones about all the crazy roughnecks he worked with. Damn near every one of those stories was a lie. Not because they didn't happen. But because he was the crazy roughneck at the center of them."

Katelyn snorted. "That shouldn't have been a surprise. Remember what he did the time that kid, Frankie, stole your brother's baseball glove?"

Joseph nearly choked, and Ava watched his face as he laughed. "Oh shit. I forgot about that."

Curiosity got the better of Ava. "What did he do?"

Joseph sat back in his chair and grinned. "The crazy son of a bitch dragged me and Jimmy down to the kid's house and knocked on the door. When the mom answered, Dad spoke politely and asked for Frankie. When the kid came to the door, he stood there trying to look all innocent until my dad lifted the baseball bat and slapped it against his palm as he asked if Frankie wanted to catch some balls."

"Oh, my gosh. What did the boy's mom do?"

"She didn't get what was going on, but Frankie understood perfectly. He ran into the house and came back with Jimmy's glove. He threw it at my dad and hauled ass upstairs so fast he stumbled twice before he reached the landing."

Ava laughed. "That poor kid."

"He never even rode his bike past our house again." Joseph chuckled. "I bet the little shit never stole another thing in his life after that."

"I bet," Ava said before taking another drink of her orange juice.

"The best part was afterward, when the mom shut the door. Dad looked at me and my brother and said, 'That's how you get shit done.' I'll never forget the smile on his face as he handed the glove back to Jimmy." Joseph sat back in his chair and said in a barely audible voice, "I miss that man."

Feeling like she was intruding on the moment, Ava shifted her focus to the others seated at the table. Greg gave her a warm smile and then turned his attention back to Maggie's conversation with Ali. Ava wasn't really paying attention to what they were saying. She just watched their demeanor. The two of them were close, just like Ava and Katelyn.

Lately though, Ava felt like she was drifting away from everyone and everything. She wasn't feeling like herself at all, or even acting like herself. Last night was the perfect example. On a normal day, she would never consider hooking up with someone she'd just met. What was wrong with her?

Sure, she could blame it on the chaos that sometimes came with being personal assistant to a CEO. But truth was, now that she had so much free time, there was no denying it was so much more than that.

What little sleep she did get was disrupted by unsettling dreams. She didn't always remember them once she woke. But the ones she did recall were strange, to say the least. Still, they were nothing compared to the vivid dreams she'd had lately. And after meeting Ali and Nicolai, she wished she could forget those as well.

Greg and Maggie sat listening to Ali talk about some sort of martial arts training. She talked with animated movements, but Ava had a hard time following the story.

Nicolai sat close to Ali, with his arm draped over the back of her chair, but he wasn't listening to the conversation either. His knowing eyes were focused wholly on Ava, and the way he stared at her made her squirm in her seat.

Ava turned her focus back to Joseph and Katelyn. But no matter how much she tried to listen to their conversation, she felt like she couldn't breathe. She could still feel Nicolai's intense eyes on her, so she pushed away from the table and went outside to get some fresh air.

Ava stepped out onto the massive patio, and the second the cool October air surrounded her, she felt some of her tension ease.

9

When D'mitri left his home, he'd set out to clear his mind with a hard run, just as he had every day since his Awakening. It usually worked, but this morning was different. He felt different. When he woke from the vivid dream of his beautiful mate, he'd thought it was time, but then it hit him. He had no clue who she was or where to find her. And when he tested their mate bond, he received no reply. Now he felt as if he might lose his mind. He wanted her. He needed her with him, and he grew more impatient for her by the second.

D'mitri ran until his legs ached, and he could go no farther. He collapsed mere feet from the river, barely mustering enough strength to draw his next breath. His body was exhausted, but his mind was still in total chaos. He forced his burning lungs to draw another breath. Running wasn't working anymore. It was too close to time for her to come to him, but his woman, his mate, was still out of his reach, which drove him mad. He blinked away tears of frustration and rolled onto his back. Staring up at the sliver of sky showing through the canopy of leaves above him, he forced another breath.

D'mitri lay there for a long time, trying unsuccessfully to think of anything other than his woman. After a while he forced himself to swim for a few minutes to loosen his aching muscles. When he was done, he climbed out of the water and dressed before heading back toward his home.

He took his time, and when he finally arrived back home, he drew a bath and lay there for some time, hoping to soothe his mind as much as his body. When he finally dragged himself out of the bath, he made his way down to the dining room to fix himself a drink. He thought maybe he could drink enough to just pass out and dream of his woman again. This time, maybe he could learn her name. He would be beyond thrilled to know where she lived so that he could go to her.

D'mitri nearly jumped out of his skin when a hand landed lightly on his shoulder. Surprised, he turned to see his father.

"I am sorry, son. I did not mean to startle you." Burian frowned. "I called your name several times, but you did not answer."

D'mitri took a deep breath and released it slowly. "I apologize, pai."

"Are you well?" his father asked, worry clearly in his rough voice.

D'mitri nodded. "Only thinking."

Burian searched D'mitri's face carefully before asking, "Would you like to join me for another drink?"

D'mitri looked down at his empty glass and nodded. "I will have one more before I go to bed."

Burian took D'mitri's glass and poured him another. When he handed it back, D'mitri thanked him and turned toward the big window that faced the jungle. He couldn't stop his thoughts from drifting back to his mate.

He wanted to scream in frustration. Nothing he could do would speed the progression of his mate's Awakening. Nature must take its course, but D'mitri's patience ran thinner by the moment.

"Son, please sit. You make an old man nervous with all the pacing." When he didn't stop, Burian slapped a hand on the table. "D'mitri!"

He wheeled around and looked at his father. Burian rarely raised his voice. But when he did, everyone took notice.

"Sit with me, my son." Burian pushed the chair away from the table with his foot and waited for D'mitri to sit. Burian leaned forward, resting his elbows on the table. "What troubles you this night?"

He stared at his father for a long moment before he said, "I dream of her, pai. I have seen her beautiful face, yet she is out of my reach."

"Be patient, son. You have waited this long."

D'mitri shook his head. "I have no patience. I want her with me now."

"I understand. When your mae came to my dreams, I thought I would lose my mind with the need to be with her." Burian leaned back in his chair. "See, back then, her tribe resided beyond the west river, as far south as Prateya. But I did not care. I threw out tradition and ran, not stopping until I reached her village."

D'mitri stared at his father in disbelief. "You ran all the way to Prateya?"

Burian grinned. "Of course. She was mine, and nothing would have stopped me from going to claim her."

"You never told me that."

Burian looked down at his glass for a long time before he lifted his clear eyes. "I suffered much like you have, so I understand what you have been through as of late. But trust that the time fast approaches. You will be with her soon, and she will be well worth the wait, my son. Just as your mae was worth every second of every torturous mile I ran."

———

BY THAT EVENING, most of the other guests had gone home. But along with Katelyn and Ava, Joseph, Nicolai, and Ali were still there. They all sat in the den, chatting while some sipped their drinks.

Not Ava. She drank water. She'd had enough alcohol at the engagement party to last her an entire year. Sure, she'd made a new friend in the process, but the embarrassment and guilt? That, she could have done without.

Ava sat on the cozy chaise lounge, her shoulder leaning against one curving end with her feet tucked beneath her. Joseph sat on the opposite end, listening to the casual chatter. Ava wasn't paying attention to the conversation because, surprise, her attention focused elsewhere.

She'd had crushes before, of course, but never in her life had she felt such a strong pull toward someone. If she wasn't careful, it would become an obsession. She told herself to stop thinking about him and pay attention to the conversation, but her thoughts kept circling back to him. Him and those dreams.

Ava

Her eyes jumped to Nicolai. He was staring at her again.

Can you hear me?

Ava's breath left her in a rush. She'd heard him alright. It was like he spoke directly into her mind. At first, his voice sounded distant with a slight echo. Like someone talking to her from the end of a long tunnel.

Ava. It came again. This time a little clearer. More insistent. *Tell me you can hear me.*

She didn't want to answer. Didn't want to acknowledge his voice. Because if she did, she would have to admit that she was losing her mind. No sane person heard voices. Especially not the voice of a man she had no business even thinking about. Or worse, dreaming about.

Please. Talk to me, Ava. I need to hear your sweet voice.

That was it. She couldn't just sit there and act like everything was fine. She shot up from her place on the lounger and mentally shouted at him. *Stop it! Stop talking to me!*

Katelyn asked if she was all right, but Ava ignored her friend and hurried from the room. She pushed her way through the double doors leading out onto the patio. She paced from one end to the other, drawing in the crisp afternoon air. She couldn't take this. Not only was she hearing his voice in her head, but her body felt odd. Her skin felt tingly and hot. She shook uncontrollably, and she knew she had to get a grip. Because she was losing it.

"Hey."

Ava turned abruptly, startled by the sound of Joseph's gentle voice.

"Sorry. I didn't mean to scare you."

Ava blew out a ragged breath. "You're good. I was just in my head. I didn't even hear you come out."

"You okay?"

"Yeah. I just needed some air."

Joseph studied her for a moment. "Panic attack?"

Ava thought about denying it. But she recalled the feeling that overtook her that night in her room, when guilt had overpowered her senses and left her so unnerved. It was the same overwhelming anxiety she felt when she heard Nicolai's voice in her mind. She wasn't sure it was a full-fledged panic attack, though. "Possibly. I don't know. I've never had one before."

"My mother used to have them. And my sister has bad ones. Mom always needed space. Jess needs comfort, someone to rub her back and distract her with conversation." Joseph searched her face. "What do you need?"

Ava shrugged and turned to look out across the huge yard. "A new brain would be great."

Joseph chuckled softly. "I can't help you with that. But I've heard I give good hugs."

Ava gave him a shaky laugh. "I don't doubt that."

"Come on." Joseph opened his arms to her.

Ava didn't even hesitate. She stepped into his embrace and let him draw her close. She'd try just about anything to calm her racing thoughts.

"Relax," Joseph whispered. "I've got you. Just breathe."

Ava took a deep breath and leaned into him, resting her forehead against his chest. His wide palm made slow, gentle circles up and down her spine. The soothing, repetitive movements slowly melted away every ounce of tension in her body.

Joseph whispered against her hair. "There. That's better."

Ava finally lifted her head again and offered him a grateful smile. "Thank you."

"I'm glad I could help."

Behind Joseph, the patio door opened, and they both turned to see who'd joined them. Ava wasn't surprised to see Katelyn standing there.

Her friend pulled the door closed behind her, eyeing them both. "Everything okay?"

Ava nodded. "I just needed some fresh air."

Katelyn glanced back and forth between them. Ava could see the skeptical look on her face. And even though she didn't say anything more about it, Ava knew she would ask about it later.

"Well, I just wanted to let you two know Nicolai and Ali are heading out soon, and they want to say goodbye before they leave."

Though Ava didn't care to see Nicolai again, she couldn't be rude. Besides, she liked Ali. Even though she was a bit odd, she'd been nothing but nice to Ava the whole weekend.

Two and a half hours later, Ava and Katelyn stood in front of the airport saying their goodbyes to Joseph.

He put his number into her phone and made her promise they would keep in touch. With a wide smile, he hugged her and Katelyn to him with an arm around each of them and kissed them both on the cheek. "Safe travels, ladies."

She and Katelyn replied in unison. "You too."

Joseph chuckled as he turned to head back around to the driver's side of his truck. Once he climbed in, he gave them one last wave before he drove off.

The second he was out of sight, Katelyn bumped Ava's elbow. "So?"

Ava frowned. "So, what?"

Katelyn waggled her eyebrows. "You gonna give me all the dirty details or what?"

"Nope. Nothing to tell."

"Oh, come on. Clearly you two made a connection."

Ava shook her head. "Just friends. There's nothing else growing out of this weekend, that's for sure."

Katelyn scoffed. "Please."

Laughing at her friend's skeptical expression, Ava assured her. "Just friends. Trust me."

Katelyn's voice dropped a few octaves, mimicking Joseph's accent. "I'm glad I met you. I hope this isn't the last time we see each other. Keep in touch." She made an exaggerated kissing noise.

Ava snorted. "Yep. Sounds just like him."

Katelyn took Ava's phone off the top of her bag. She tapped the screen and scrolled. "Uh huh." She turned the screen toward Ava. "See. Smiley face next to his name. He 'likes you' likes you."

Ava looked. Sure enough. Joseph had put a smiley face at the end of his name. Joseph :) Patrick. She didn't have a picture of him to add to his contact profile, so at the top of the screen, a grey bubble with his initials took up space where his picture would've been. And Ava's heart sank.

Katelyn's smile faded. "What is it?" She turned the phone around and inspected the screen. "What's wrong?"

"JP," she whispered, her eyes wide as she stared up at her friend.

Confused, Katelyn asked, "What?"

Ava knew that name. Katelyn had talked about the guy many times. She'd had the hugest crush on him but that's as far as things had gone. Or so she thought. Feeling frustrated with her friend, Ava smacked Katelyn's arm.

She looked at Ava like she'd lost her mind. "What the hell was that for?"

She snatched the phone from Katelyn's hand and pointed at the little bubble on the screen. "JP. Joseph is JP."

Katelyn's expression faltered. "What?"

"The JP you were obsessed with your whole freshman year of college."

"Yeah. So."

"Do you still have a thing for him?"

Katelyn didn't answer. She just shifted her weight uncomfortably.

"Woman!" Ava scrubbed a hand down her face. "Why the hell didn't you say something? I never would have taken him upstairs if I'd known who he was."

Katelyn shrugged. "Doesn't matter. He's never shown any interest in me. Never shown interest in anyone other than you. That's why I sent him to go talk to you the other night."

Ava shook her head. "I knew it. I knew something didn't feel right."

Katelyn frowned. "What do you mean?"

Ava sighed. "We didn't go through with it. I didn't sleep with Joseph."

The relief in Katelyn's eyes was palpable. And Ava had never been so glad she'd listened to her instincts.

10

D'mitri felt helpless. For the last thirty-eight hours and nineteen minutes, his mate refused to speak to him. He could feel the presence of the mate bond. It grew stronger by the minute, but she'd somehow managed to throw up a barrier between them.

"I know you just got home, but I am on the verge of panic. What do I do, brother? Without her letting me in, I cannot find her and go to her."

Nicolai seemed to be equally perplexed by his predicament. "You are certain she is no one we know? No one from the remaining tribes?"

D'mitri gave his brother a frustrated scowl.

"Tell me. What does she look like?"

D'mitri closed his eyes and described every detail. From her thick, dark hair and unique eyes to her plush, pouty lips and luscious curves.

Nicolai didn't say a word, and when D'mitri opened his eyes again, he saw they were no longer alone. Ali had returned from putting Violet to bed. She stood in the doorway with the oddest expression on her face. She and Nicolai stared at each other, clearly communicating through their own mate bond. Something they did often. But this was different.

D'mitri's entire body tensed. "What is wrong?"

Nicolai turned back to him and sat forward in his chair, resting his elbows on his knees. "Tell me, brother. Do you know her name?"

With his heart in his throat, D'mitri answered. "Ava."

Nicolai's gaze shot back to his mate, and Ali let out an excited screech. "I knew it!"

Her reaction confused D'mitri even more.

"I knew she was one of us. I should have said something."

Nicolai disagreed. "You did the right thing by staying quiet. If she has shut him out, odds are she may not even know she is Jagara."

"I bet that's the reason she was acting so weird and why she kept staring at you so much. She probably thinks she's dreaming about you."

Nicolai nodded.

"Wait." D'mitri cut in, his heart pounding. "What are you saying? You know my mate?"

Nicolai chuckled. "We have spent the last few days with her."

D'mitri stared at his brother in disbelief.

Nicolai crossed to his side and clasped his shoulders. "She is a little thing, but she has fire in her eyes."

D'mitri knew that. He could see it in their shared dreams. But he didn't care about that now. All he could think about was having her with him in the waking world.

With desperation clear in his suddenly hoarse voice, D'mitri demanded, "Tell me where she is."

Ali and Nicolai exchanged another glance before Ali grabbed the phone. The silence seemed to stretch on forever and his heart pounded against his ribs.

"Hey, Maggie. You won't believe what I just found out. Ava is one of us!" Ali nodded as if her friend could see her. "I know. She's D'mitri's mate. He dreamed of her while we were gone."

D'mitri heard Maggie's shocked response from across the room, but he couldn't hear precisely what she said.

"Yeah. That's the main reason I called. I wanted to ask where she lives so he can go to her."

There was a pause.

"Oh."

Another long pause.

"Yeah. Okay. Bye." Ali disconnected the call and turned to D'mitri with a sigh. "Maggie is calling Katie to get Ava's address. She'll call back as soon as she can get ahold of her. But it may take a bit. They had a five-and-a-half-hour flight back home and they might not have landed yet."

The next forty-seven minutes were the longest of D'mitri's life. The seconds ticked by like hours, and he was half-crazed by the time Ali's phone finally rang. D'mitri paced back and forth, fighting the urge to take the phone from her and ask Maggie himself.

When Ali pulled out a pen and wrote on the notepad Nicolai handed her, D'mitri hovered, reading as she jotted down what Maggie said.

Louisiana. His mate was in Louisiana.

AVA AMBLED down the narrow path that curved through a dark, damp forest. It was beautiful, but her senses were working overtime. Something out there made her uneasy. It was a feeling more than anything, like her body was hyperaware of her surroundings, but her mind hadn't fully processed every detail yet.

One thing stood out to her, though. A scent that hung in the air. A scent that didn't belong. Deep. Earthy. Masculine. And though she saw no one, she knew she wasn't alone. Someone or something followed her. Watching her from the shadows. She could feel the eyes on her.

Then she heard a familiar voice whisper. "Ava."

She wheeled around but saw no one.

"Run," the voice commanded.

Though uncertain where his voice came from, Ava instinctively obeyed. With her heart in her throat, she raced down the path as fast as she could go, afraid of what else might be out there.

Something trailed her. She could hear it running alongside her. She didn't see it at first. But then, she spotted the pale figure streaking through the trees nearly fifty feet off the path. A man. And though she ran impossibly fast, he easily matched her pace.

Ava tried to outrun him, but he overtook her, circling around to cut off her path of escape. She skidded to a stop and faced the most frightening man she'd ever seen.

He was tall with odd, angular features. His skin pale, as if he'd never seen a drop of sunlight in his entire life. And his waist-length hair was almost the same shade of his pallid skin. He looked like death warmed over, and his cold, black eyes held no emotion. Just raw, animal hunger. Not like the sexually charged moments in her favorite romance novels. But more like a blood-starved vampire with ill intentions.

Something about the man felt familiar. Ava knew she'd never seen him before, but she felt an eerie sense of déjà vu. She felt an undeniable draw to the frightening male, and though everything in her said she should be running, her body refused to listen.

The moment she took a step toward him, a wicked, satisfied smile spread across his face. And despite her fear, Ava couldn't stop herself from going to him.

"Yes," he coaxed her. "Come to me. Take my hand."

Though her survival instinct told her to get as far away from him as possible, Ava had no control of her own body. No matter how much she wanted to run away, she kept moving toward him.

Then, suddenly, everything changed. Her vision grew sharper, the colors around her more vivid despite the surrounding darkness. Every joint in her body ached. And even her gums throbbed as if they had a heartbeat of their own. She didn't know any other way to explain it, but it felt as if something inside her clawed its way to the surface. Like a long-dormant part of her was finally waking.

She was on the verge of tears when the man's expression faltered, and his attention shifted to something behind her. The frustrated, almost distraught look on his strange face made her reluctant to turn and see what had captured his attention.

But with his invisible hold on her weakened, Ava

slowly looked over her shoulder, and her next breath froze in her lungs.

Not twenty feet away, on the path behind her, stood an enormous black jaguar, its beautiful, fearsome face twisted in a silent snarl.

Sure, the animal could tear her to shreds. But, somehow, the man felt much more menacing. Especially when he bared his teeth and hissed at the jaguar. "I will have her."

His words sent chills dancing up Ava's spine. And when he suddenly lunged toward her, all she could do was squeeze her eyes shut and brace herself for impact.

Funny. Never once had she thought about how she might react in a dangerous situation, but standing still and closing her eyes was not what she would have imagined. Apparently, her fight or flight response was broken.

A massive body hit her, taking her to the ground, but the impact came from the opposite direction she expected. Ava didn't move a muscle, but she let out a scream when two rough hands gripped her arms.

"Ava."

Her eyes snapped open, and there in the darkness of her bedroom, a broad-shouldered man knelt over her. She couldn't see his face. The heavy curtain of his dark hair shielded his features. But she'd know that mouthwatering, masculine scent anywhere. She'd dreamed of him enough over the last week.

Ava's heart pounded, her breath coming in ragged little draws. She couldn't figure out if she was still asleep or if the man truly was in her home, hovering over her like a wraith in the night.

As if sensing her unease, he released her arms and he sat back.

Ava scrambled back against the headboard, grateful for the distance between them, even if it was mere feet.

From his new position near the foot of the bed, the contours of his face caught the pale light filtering through the blinds. Ava blinked. She was right. It was him. He looked different. Much like he always appeared in her dreams. His midnight hair wild around his shoulders and his pale green eyes so bright they almost seemed to glow in the dark room.

Ava let out a relieved breath and relaxed against the headboard. He wasn't really in her room, sitting on her bed. It was another dream.

Sure, she'd wanted to stop dreaming about him because of the guilt she felt whenever she did. But she would gladly welcome more dreams of him, so long as she didn't have to see that terrifying pale-haired guy again. He scared the shit out of her. Honestly, he looked like something out of a horror flick. And Ava had never been a fan of scary movies.

11

Ava woke in the morning with a strange achy feeling radiating through her entire body. It felt much like when she spent too much time in bed. Or that one time she had the flu when she was nineteen. Man, she hoped she wasn't getting sick.

Ava rolled over and stretched, groaning as she arched her back. It felt incredible, but she needed to get up. Sure, she was on vacation, but Ava couldn't lay around all day and be lazy. It just wasn't in her nature.

She sat up, immediately frozen in place when she felt the chill of the early morning air on her bare skin. Reluctantly looking down at herself, Ava breathed, "What the hell?"

She tossed the covers back and confirmed her suspicions. She didn't have a stitch of clothes on. When had that happened? And why? Had she gotten overheated in her sleep and stripped her clothes off to cool down? Possibly.

With an aggravated sigh, Ava flung herself back

against her pillows and covered her eyes. If it wasn't one thing, it was another. She hated feeling so out of whack. And if the doctor couldn't figure out what the hell was wrong with her, she wished whatever was making her body go haywire would go away already. She just wanted to feel normal again. Or at the very least, be able to enjoy her time off.

After a much-needed shower, Ava made herself a big cup of coffee and curled up on the couch to watch TV. But after mindlessly scrolling through her watch list for fifteen minutes, she shut off the TV and tossed the remote on the cushion beside her with a heavy sigh. Nothing looked appealing.

In all honesty, she should call her Aunt Lilah. They hadn't talked in a while.

The phone rang twice before Lilah's cheerful voice answered. "Good morning, love. How are you?"

Ava instantly felt the tension easing from her shoulders. "I'm good. How've you been?"

"Doing well. Been spending a lot of time in the garden this week, enjoying this lovely weather."

Ava cringed internally. "If I'm honest, my flower garden is a little neglected. I haven't weeded in a couple weeks."

Lilah tsked. "Working too hard again?"

Ava rolled her eyes. "Yes, but don't worry. Jameson made me take a few weeks off. I have plenty of time to catch up on my gardening. And anything else I need to do around the house."

"Good." Lilah chuckled. "But don't spend your whole vacation staying busy. Enjoy the time off. Sleep in. Be lazy.

Easier said than done. Ava was accustomed to waking up at five in the morning. Going non-stop for ten to twelve hours. Then crashing on the couch with whatever prepackaged meal she pulled from the freezer and watching mindless TV until time for bed.

"Remember, love. Everything is about balance. You don't have to lounge around the entire time. But allow yourself time to rest and relax."

Ava sighed. "I know. I'll try."

"Now, are you going to tell me what troubles you?"

For a moment, Ava considered telling her everything was fine. But Lilah knew her too well. And though Ava didn't want to burden her aunt with all the weirdness, she needed to talk to someone about it.

"Are you not feeling well?"

Ava drew a deep breath and admitted, "I've had some pretty strange dreams lately and it's been stressing me out."

"You want to tell me about it?"

Ava drew her feet onto the couch and tucked them beneath her. "It's kind of embarrassing, honestly."

"Oh now. I'm sure it's not that bad."

Ava dropped her head back against the cushion and stared up at the ceiling. She didn't know why she felt so nervous. She'd always been able to talk to Lilah about anything. But once she started talking, it all just spilled out of her. "I've been dreaming about being in the jungle. And there's this man. He's probably the most beautiful man I have ever seen. He has a feral aura that scares me and excites me at the same time. And in one of the dreams, he changed."

"What do you mean?"

Ava swallowed the lump growing in her throat. "He turned into a massive black jaguar."

A long silence hung in the air before Lilah asked something Ava didn't expect. "Do you remember the stories your uncle and I told you and Darien when you were young?"

She had a vivid recollection of huddling close to her cousin with a heavy quilt wrapped around their shoulders, and Lilah and Kale sitting across from them. She remembered how she felt in those moments, but for the life of her, she couldn't recall a single detail of the actual stories themselves. "Not any specifics."

"They were stories that my father told when I was a child. Old tribe lore about jaguar shapeshifters."

"Really?" Interesting.

"Maybe something triggered your memory of those stories."

"Yeah, maybe." Ava suspected Ali's book had a little to do with that.

Lilah asked, "Did I ever tell you that my Kale and I dreamed of each other before we were together?"

Shocked, Ava breathed, "No."

"We did. I knew him before, of course, because his tribe lands were close to mine. I saw him quite frequently when we were children, but as we got older and things grew unsafe, some of our tribes dispersed and went to live in the busy cities, far from the heart of the jungle."

Ava's brows shot up. "You never told me that. I didn't realize when you spoke about your tribe that you meant it that way. I didn't know you lived in an actual tribe when you were a girl."

"Oh, yes. Our lands were deep in the jungle. And my tribe was one of the last to flee to the more modern villages. I miss that simpler way of life sometimes. Especially since my Kale passed."

Ava could understand that. She would love to live a simpler lifestyle. Something much less fast-paced than the big city and her demanding job. That would be amazing. "Do you ever think about going back?"

"I've sometimes wondered if I should because of Darien. But I don't think I could leave you. I would miss you too much."

Ava knew the feeling. "I would miss you too, but I'm a grown woman. I'll be fine if you decide you want to go back. Besides, it would give me an excuse to visit the tribe lands."

Lilah sighed. "I don't know. I have a life here. I couldn't just up and move. What about the house? My garden? My friends?"

Ava smiled to herself. "Tia, your friends aren't going anywhere. Kerri and Tilda would miss you, but they would be happy for you. Besides, I could take care of the house and the garden."

"I guess."

Hearing the reluctance in her voice, Ava said, "What if we just take a trip there? I do have a few weeks off. We could go visit some of your old friends. And I would love to see Grandpa Bazyli again. Who knows. Maybe we'll even see Darien while we're there."

Lilah was silent for a few moments before she asked, "How soon can you be ready?"

D'MITRI ARRIVED in Louisiana just before noon. He wanted more than anything to go straight to his mate. But he wasn't sure how to approach her. By what Nicolai and Ali said, he couldn't be sure if Ava even knew what she was. And if that was the case, showing up at her front door might be a bit startling.

But what else would he do? Wait for her to leave the house and pretend to have a chance meeting? He didn't have the patience for that. Instead, he took a taxi to the address on the crumpled piece of paper in his pocket.

The driver pulled up to the curb in front of a white wood frame house. Cedar shutters framed the windows, and the door was painted the same vibrant shade of green as his favorite swimming hole. Though the yard appeared slightly neglected, it was beautiful. It reminded D'mitri of his mother's flower garden. Organized chaos, she used to call it.

D'mitri wasn't sure how his mate would react to seeing him standing on her front porch in broad daylight. He had no idea how their first official meeting would go, but he didn't want to delay it any longer. He walked straight up to Ava's front door and knocked.

His heart hammered as he waited for her to answer the door. And when she didn't, he knocked again.

From the neighbor's yard, a gentle voice called, "She's not home."

D'mitri spotted a blonde woman kneeling next to a long flowerbed that lined the short white fence separating the two yards.

She sat back on her heels and watched D'mitri as he approached.

"Do you know where she is?"

The woman gave him a onceover. "Who wants to know?"

D'mitri didn't know how to answer that. He didn't want to give her his name. But what did he say? He couldn't tell the woman the truth. He couldn't tell a human woman that he was Ava's mate. He wasn't technically her friend, either. Not yet anyway. But that was the safest answer. "A friend of Ava's. I have traveled a long way to see her."

The woman pushed to her feet and brushed at the bits of grass clinging to her knees. "You didn't tell her you were coming?"

"It was meant to be a surprise. Do you know when she will return?"

D'mitri could see the caution in the woman's eyes. She shifted her weight. "I don't. But she asked me to keep an eye on the house and water her plants."

"For how long?"

The woman didn't need to speak her mistrust. He could read it in her wary eyes.

"I understand. You do not know me. But I have limited time. I came all this way to see her. If you could help me out, I would greatly appreciate it."

The young woman placed her hands on her hips as her dark eyes slid over him once more. She must have decided him trustworthy enough because she sighed. "I'm not sure how long exactly. Maybe a week or so."

"You are certain you do not know where she has gone?"

She shook her head. "All I know is that she went with

her aunt. They mentioned something about going home, but other than that, I have no idea. I always thought she grew up here in town."

D'mitri's heart skipped a beat. Could she have gone to the homelands? Did she know her origins after all? And who was her aunt?

He thanked the woman for her time and walked back toward the street, dialing his brother's number as he went.

***

BY SOME MIRACLE, Ava managed to get a same-day flight, and Lilah made arrangements for them to stay with the Juani family. Even though Ines and her husband would be out of town for the next week, they were more than happy to open their home to Ava and Lilah.

Ines and Lilah were childhood friends and the Juani family had visited nearly every summer when Ava was young. Still, she felt uneasy about being in their home while they were away. Fortunately, their youngest son, DeMario would be housesitting until they returned from their trip.

After the thirteen-and-a-half-hour flight to São Paulo, they had another two hours on a tiny plane, and arrived at almost two-thirty in the morning to an airport in the middle of nowhere. Ava was exhausted, but the excitement of being in the jungle again had her wired. She couldn't see much because of the late hour, but the sounds and scents overwhelmed her as she stepped off the plane.

Ava knew DeMario planned to pick them up, and she was excited to see her old friend. The last time she'd seen him, he'd been a lanky fifteen-year-old boy. He had always been tall, but Ava wasn't fully prepared for the six-foot-four linebacker of a man strolling with confidence across the tarmac. She was so shocked by his appearance she nearly dropped her bag.

Sure, she had seen the transformation in pictures over the last eight years. But seeing him in person was a whole different story. Gone was the shaggy-haired boy she'd had a crush on most of her life. And in his place stood a mountain of a man with a faint shadow of a beard on his chiseled jaw.

Ava watched as he and Lilah greeted each other. And when he turned to her, DeMario offered her a warm smile, his dark mahogany eyes sparkling with excitement. "Good to see you again, Ava."

She returned the sentiment. "It's been a long time."

He'd always been the sweetest, most down to earth guy. That much, at least, hadn't changed. Too bad she couldn't find someone like him back home. Someone she could actually be with, instead of obsessing over a man that belonged to someone else.

Ava had always liked DeMario. Hell, he'd been her first crush. And her first kiss. If they didn't live in different countries, they might have given it a real shot. But Ava's home was in Louisiana, and she knew he would never leave the jungle behind. Not for her or any other woman. She knew how important his family was to him.

DeMario took their bags. "Come. Let us go. We have a long drive ahead of us."

Ava and Lilah followed DeMario to his truck and strapped in for the bumpy three-hour drive to Keintara. As uncomfortable as it was, Ava couldn't help but enjoy just being in the jungle again.

They reached their destination just after sunrise, and DeMario showed them to their rooms. Ava didn't even bother getting cleaned up from the trip. She crashed the second she crawled into the enormous bed.

va woke feeling more rested than she had in a very long time. She rolled over and looked at the old clock on the wall. Quarter to five. Damn. She'd slept almost eleven hours. She needed to get up and get moving. Just because she was on vacation didn't mean she wanted to sleep the day away.

By the time Ava got up, bathed, and got dressed, a mouthwatering aroma had drifted up to her from the kitchen. Her stomach let out a loud growl in response.

Ordinarily, she couldn't even think about eating for a least four or five hours after waking. This time, though, she felt starved. Sure, she'd snacked on granola bars and the bag of pre-shelled pistachios that Lilah had stashed in her purse. But Ava was ready for something more substantial. Whatever hearty meal was being prepared downstairs, it made her mouth water.

She made her way downstairs, and in the kitchen, DeMario stood in front of the stove preparing dinner. And on the stool next to him sat an adorable little girl with dark auburn ringlets that hung just past her shoulders. She chattered happily, swinging her feet as DeMario stirred the food in the pot.

Across the kitchen, sitting at the table with her aunt Lilah, was a man that Ava recognized. Zavier. DeMario's older brother. He hadn't changed much in the last eight years, but he didn't have the same spark in his eyes that he once did.

Still, he rose to greet her before he turned to the duo in front of the stove. "Breya."

The little girl looked over at him. "Sim, papa?"

"Be polite and come say hello to Ava. In English, please."

The little girl hopped down from the stool, her midnight-blue eyes sparkled when she turned to Ava and smiled. "Hello, Miss Ava."

Though surprised by how polite and grownup the little girl sounded, Ava returned her greeting. "Hi. It's nice to meet you, Breya."

The little girl beamed up at her. "Uncle D said you and Mrs. Lilah live in North America, and life is very different there."

"It is," Ava agreed.

"What do you think of the jungle?"

"I love it," she answered honestly. "I wish I could live here. It's so much better than where I live."

Breya smiled. "What do you think of my uncle?"

Ava glanced at DeMario before she answered. "He's very nice."

"He is handsome, no?"

Ava blushed when she saw the smile that touched DeMario's lips before he turned his head. She felt the heat rising in her cheeks, but she answered. "Um... yes."

"He has no mate yet. Maybe you could be his. He thinks you are very pretty. He said so to my papa."

Ava didn't know how to respond to that little bit of information.

Lucky for her, Zavier cut in. "That is enough, Breya. You are embarrassing her."

Wide midnight eyes met Ava's again. She apologized in her sweet, heavily accented voice. Then scurried back over to her uncle's side and climbed onto the stool again.

Ava joined Zavier and Lilah at the table, and the three of them chatted while DeMario finished cooking.

Conversation continued over dinner, DeMario joining in, and Ava enjoyed every second. Aside from the occasional weekend at her aunt's, she didn't often get the chance to socialize over a good, homecooked meal.

Out of nowhere, Breya smiled up at Ava. "I cannot wait until I dream of my mate. I want to have one like my papa. He is strong and loves my mama still, even though she has left us."

Everyone grew quiet, and that one innocent comment sucked all the air from the room. The loud clatter of Zavier's fork dropping onto his plate echoed in the otherwise silent kitchen. He didn't move or even lift his head. He just sat there, staring at his plate.

Ava looked around at the others and waited for someone to speak. She didn't dare say anything. She didn't know the details about what happened, but she'd heard through Lilah that Zavier's wife had gone missing while out for a run. And that had been more than two years ago, if Ava remembered correctly.

When Zavier finally pushed his chair away from the table and stalked from the room, DeMario whispered something to Breya that Ava didn't quite hear.

Breya glanced at both Ava and Lilah, a sad expression on her young face before she slipped out of her chair and followed Zavier outside.

Tears stung Ava's eyes. She couldn't imagine what the little one felt in that moment, knowing she'd upset her father.

Ava, Lilah, and DeMario finished the rest of their food in silence. And when they were done, Lilah offered to clean up.

DeMario spoke up. "Thank you, but I will take care of things. You are my guest."

Lilah scoffed. "You cooked. I will clean up. You two go sit on the porch and catch up."

When DeMario looked like he was about to protest, Lilah gave him a stern look. He laughed under his breath. "Yes, ma'am."

They sat out back for hours, reminiscing and talking about how much everything had changed since they'd last seen each other. DeMario had bounced around from one job to another, trying to figure out exactly what he wanted to do with his life. His latest endeavor was working for Marius, Zavier's brother-in-law.

"How's that going?"

DeMario leaned back in his chair. "If I'm honest, I don't know how I feel yet. As much as I love the water, the ocean is a different beast altogether. I will give it a fair shot, but I can't see commercial fishing being something that my heart is in. Not in the long run. I just don't have the heart to tell my parents that yet."

Ava frowned. "Why?"

DeMario shrugged. "They are supportive, but I feel like my father is getting impatient with me. He hasn't said much about it, but I see it in his eyes each time I move on to something new."

Ava reached over and laid a hand on his forearm. "Your dad loves you, and I'm sure he understands that you're just trying to find your way."

DeMario looked skeptical.

"You'll figure it all out eventually. And you have time. You're still young."

DeMario arched an eyebrow. "You do recall that you and I are the same age, do you not?"

Ava laughed. "Yes. I am aware. But we all figure life out at our own pace. I just got lucky and found a job fresh out of high school."

"And you still like what you do?"

"Yeah. I tend to get restless when I have downtime. So, working for Jameson keeps my mind busy. I don't have a whole lot of time to just sit and let my thoughts wander."

DeMario took another sip from his glass, looking thoughtful. "Must be nice."

"Jameson is a good boss. And a good friend. I wouldn't even be here right now if he hadn't made me take a month off."

DeMario nodded, searching her face. "I am glad you came. I hope you enjoy your time here and you find everything you need."

Ava just smiled at him. "Thank you."

She wasn't sure how else to respond. Was she reading too much into it, or had there been a hint of hopeful undertone to his words? And what was he hoping for? That she'd changed her mind after all these years and wanted to have some sort of long-distance relationship with him? That she would decide to move to South America?

Ava turned back to stare out at the gentle rain. Was that something she wanted? Sure, DeMario was a gorgeous, sweet man. They'd always had chemistry. But if Ava was honest with herself, a relationship was the last thing she needed. She was confused enough. She didn't need to add a romantic relationship to the mix. And she didn't want to hurt her friend if things didn't work out between them.

Ava let out a long breath and stared out into the darkness. Funny how without the burden of the city lights, you could see much clearer and farther. And with nightfall, the sounds of the rainforest had grown louder.

It was like a symphony. The low hissing whispers of countless raindrops in the trees. The animals chattering and chirping. The insects buzzing. All of it soothed her. And though she grew up in Louisiana, being in the jungle —in the homelands—felt like coming home.

They sat in comfortable silence for a long time, sipping their drinks and enjoying each other's company.

When Ava yawned, DeMario smiled. "Tired?"

Ava shrugged. "Maybe a little."

Truth was, despite all the sleep she'd had that day, she felt like she could sleep another twelve hours. Maybe it was jetlag or the fact that she hadn't had a good vacation in years. Either way, she felt bad for going to bed so early. DeMario didn't seem to want the night to end.

"If you and Ms. Lilah have no plans for tomorrow, I would like to take you somewhere. I have only been there a few times since I was a kid, but I think you would like it."

"Yeah?"

"It is called Sun Point. The highest ridge in Jagara territory. There is a massive cliff that overlooks miles and miles of jungle. Treetops for as far as the eye can see. It is beautiful."

Ava smiled. "That sounds amazing. I'd love to see that."

"It is a bit of a hike, but well worth it."

"I'm okay with that."

"Good." The way DeMario's eyes lit up made her pulse flutter.

"Well." Ava stood and stretched. "I should go get some rest."

DeMario stood as well.

"Thanks for the drink and the conversation."

"Of course." He smiled down at her. "Pleasant dreams, Ava."

"Thanks. You, too."

Ava gave him a quick hug and made her way upstairs. Though she wanted nothing more than to crawl in the tempting bedding, she forced herself to go through her nightly routine. She brushed her teeth. Washed and moisturized her face. Changed into her pajamas.

By the time she climbed into bed fifteen minutes later, she felt wide awake again. She tossed and turned for over an hour, her thoughts refusing to quiet.

Flopping onto her back, Ava stared at the ceiling. All she could think about was the father/daughter duo and the shitty situation life had thrown at them. Ava felt so sad for them. They'd both lost the most important person in their life. Zavier, his wife. And little Breya, her mother.

Ava couldn't imagine what that was like. She didn't

even recall her own mother and father. She was only an infant when they died. And everything she knew about them was second-hand memories and a shoebox full of old pictures.

She hadn't been without by any means. Though technically, Lilah and Kale were her aunt and uncle, they had essentially been her parents. They'd taken her in when Darien was only a year old. The four of them were a close-knit family unit. And after Kale had taken Darien back to the homelands, Lilah and Ava had grown even closer. Especially after Kale passed away a few months later.

In a way, Ava understood what it was like to lose a loved one. But she couldn't fathom how lost little Breya must feel without her mother.

And seeing the pain in Zavier's eyes when Breya spoke of her mother so casually, broke Ava's heart. She didn't know how he managed to stay so strong after losing his wife. Mate. Breya had said mate.

But why that word? Something about it triggered an unusual sense of familiarity in Ava's tired mind. She'd heard it used in the same context before. Not only in Ali's book, but somewhere else she couldn't quite put her finger on. Was it something one of the others said? Something Lilah said?

Unable to let it go, Ava dragged herself out of bed and went to Lilah's room. The light was still on. She could see the soft glow under the door.

She knocked gently, and after a moment, Lilah opened the heavy panel. "Can't sleep?"

Ava shook her head. "I know it's late, but can I talk to you about something?"

"Of course, love. Come on in." When Ava didn't speak right away, Lilah frowned. "Is everything okay?"

She didn't know where to start. Didn't know what to say without sounding a touch crazy.

"Maybe I'm reading too much into things. Or maybe I'm just tired and overthinking. I feel like everything and everyone around me isn't what I thought."

Something in Lilah's eyes shifted. A hint of worry, maybe?

"My life feels like it's finally coming together but falling apart at the same time. Things are just too coincidental. I mean, I just…" Ava shook her head. "Breya said some things that kind of struck me as odd but strangely familiar. Maybe I am reading too much into it because of everything else, but I don't know."

Lilah sat on the small sofa in the corner. "Just say what you want to say, love."

Ava flopped down beside her and sighed. "This whole mate thing and dreaming about the jungle. Dreaming about this man. I don't know what to think. Is it a coincidence or am I just losing my mind?"

Lilah drew a deep breath and slowly released it. "I had a feeling this was coming."

Ava frowned. "What do you mean?"

"We are overdue for a conversation, love. I just don't know where to start."

Ava didn't know how to respond. It vaguely sounded like a precursor to "the talk" and she was pretty sure they'd had that discussion multiple times throughout her childhood and teen years. Each time had consisted of the most current age-appropriate content. But judging by the nervous look on her aunt's face, the coming talk was not about sex.

Lilah turned sideways on the sofa, fully facing Ava. "As I told you before, your uncle and I dreamed of one another before we got together. This is something that happens with our people. They are called mate dreams, and it is how we find each other."

She stared wide-eyed at her aunt.

"That is also why you've always dreamed of the jungle. It is a part of you, just as it is a part of us all. When our Awakening begins, our nature draws us, not only to our mates, but also back to the homelands."

Ava opened her mouth to speak, but what the hell did she even say to that? It was a common thing among their people? What was it, exactly? Some cosmic spiritual connection?

Lilah reached over and took Ava's hand. A soft smile on her face. "Now that your mate dreams have begun, it won't be long until he is with you. I am so happy for you. You will have your mate soon, and I can't wait for you to experience that kind of closeness."

That's when her brain finally caught up and everything clicked into place. Ava's heart dropped into her stomach. If what Lilah said was true, that meant Nicolai was her mate. Panic rose in Ava's belly, and she whispered. "It can't be."

Lilah gave her hand an encouraging squeeze. "I know it sounds incredible, but like I said, it is the nature of our people."

Lilah didn't understand. It wasn't so much that Ava didn't believe everything she'd just said. Somehow, she believed every outrageous word. But one simple factor had her nearly hyperventilating. It wasn't that she'd dreamed of Nicolai. It wasn't even that she'd heard his voice in her head. It was what hearing it meant. If what Lilah said was true, Ava never wanted to hear that deep, sensual voice again.

Lilah moved closer and tucked her arm around Ava's shoulders. "I know how all this sounds but try not to worry. He is your fated mate. You two are perfect for each other. You'll see."

"Not possible," Ava choked out. "He can't be mine."

Lilah frowned. "Why would you say that?"

"Because I've met him, and he's with someone else."

Lilah shook her head. "No. You are mistaken."

"I'm not. He's married and they have a baby." The sympathetic look on Lilah's face made Ava want to cry, but she managed to hold the tears at bay. "He's not my mate, Tia."

"Nature would never give you someone that wasn't right for you. The man you dream of is the only one for you. Your one true mate. You will love him, and he will cherish you."

Ava shot to her feet and paced away from Lilah. "Just stop. I can't. I can't do this." She closed her eyes, wanting to scream at her aunt. She didn't understand. Nicolai couldn't be her mate.

"Okay," Lilah tried to soothe her. "Why don't we just talk about your dream. Tell me about this man."

Ava scrubbed her hands down her face. "Honestly, I just want to go to bed."

Because the more Lilah talked, the more confused and stressed she felt. She just needed to get away. Get out of that suffocating room.

"I'm tired, Tia."

"Alright, love. We can talk more tomorrow."

Ava left without another word, leaving her aunt sitting on the sofa. She slipped into her own room and made her way out onto the balcony for some fresh air. Leaning against the railing, she took a deep breath and shoved her thoughts away.

The scents that floated in the thick, fragrant air soothed her. She liked the rich moisture that seemed to cling to her like a needy lover. It made her long for someone to share the night with. Someone that wasn't the man on her mind. He belonged to another woman. A woman Ava liked.

Tears blurred her vision. Why couldn't she stop thinking about them or what Lilah said?

Exhausted, Ava went back inside and crawled into the soft bedding, hoping it would drag her into a deep sleep with no dreams. But that didn't happen. Her aunt's words lingered. *You will love him, and he will cherish you.*

Cherish? Why had that one word stood out among all that Lilah had said?

13

T he last two days were pure hell. D'mitri had missed his mate by mere hours. And it took him another fourteen before he could get a flight back home. How Nicolai had found out where she was, he didn't know, but he was grateful. Especially when he reached the Juani family home.

His mate's scent drifted on the slight breeze, drawing him to the room upstairs. He leapt quietly onto the balcony and listened for movement inside.

"D'mitri Montez," a deep voice said from the shadows. "What has you prowling around my family's home at this time?"

D'mitri recognized that voice. It was the youngest Juani brother, DeMario. "My mate brings me."

DeMario stepped from the dark corner. "Am I to be the protective brother and warn you to treat my sister well, or are you here for the lovely Ava?"

"Ava."

"Lucky bastard."

D'mitri narrowed his eyes. He'd heard the hint of jealousy in DeMario's tone, but he couldn't be sure if it was directly connected to a desire for his own mate in general or a desire for Ava specifically.

Before he could question him, DeMario nodded toward the open door closest to D'mitri. "Go to your woman. We shall speak more in the morning."

When DeMario disappeared through the door at the far end of the balcony, D'mitri turned back to Ava's room. He listened for movement inside. And when he heard nothing but the sound of her soft breathing, he slipped inside.

His mate lay stretched atop the bedding, with nothing on but pale pink cotton panties and a thin white T-shirt that clung to her like a second skin. The decent part of him wanted to turn around and go back out the way he came in. But even if it was the respectful thing to do, the desperate feral need to be near his mate wouldn't let him. He couldn't walk away now that he'd finally found her.

Careful not to disturb her, D'mitri eased into the bedding beside Ava and lay facing her. The sheer awe he felt overwhelmed him. The mate dreams had not done her justice. His mate was even more beautiful in real life. Her silky chestnut hair, flawless bronze skin, and the rosy lushness of her lips called to him.

She looked so peaceful, but he couldn't help himself. He had to test their mate bond and see if she'd finally let her guard down again. And when he closed his eyes and touched her mind, he found her wide open.

In her dream, everything looked different. In their mate dreams, he saw through his own eyes. This time, he saw everything through hers.

Ava lay on a thick bed of leaves and grass, staring up at the clear night sky. The stars shone bright, and the colors around her were brilliant and vivid. The heavy, damp air filled with a multitude of scents, both pleasing and not. But Ava felt content in the moment. No worries. No frustrations. Just her and the beauty of nature surrounding her.

D'mitri didn't want to burst his mate's contented bubble, but he couldn't wait any longer. He needed to fully connect with her. So, as gently as he could, D'mitri whispered her name.

Ava let out a long breath before responding. *I wondered when you would be back.*

D'mitri smiled to himself. *You locked me out after the last time we spoke, but I can understand why.*

She scoffed. *Right.*

You have been dreaming about me and do not want to be because of who I am. You are angry and confused. And you do not understand what is happening to you.

Ava sighed. *You are half right. I had a conversation with my aunt tonight that opened my eyes to something I never could have imagined. I'm still trying to process it.*

Do you want to talk about it?

Ava sighed and let her head roll toward him. After a heartbeat, she reached out, her fingers brushing over his stubbled cheek. "You always look so different in dreams."

D'mitri's body came alive. His mate touched him for the first time and every nerve ending in his body woke with a vengeance. But he pushed aside his physical response and forced himself to explain to her. "That is because I am not who you think I am."

Ava searched his face. "What do you mean?"

97

He placed his hand over hers and watched her pupils flare wider. "My name is D'mitri."

Ava blinked.

"You dreamed of me. You have been speaking to me through our mate bond. Not Nicolai."

She shot upright in the bed. "What?"

He sat up beside her and offered in a gentler tone. "Nicolai is my brother."

He didn't have to listen in on her thoughts to know they were in disarray. He could see the chaos in her eyes.

"I understand if this has confused you. How could you have known?"

After staring through the open door into the night, Ava turned to look at him again. "This isn't a dream, is it? You're really here."

"And I traveled a long way and back again to be here with you."

Ava scrubbed both hands down her face. She took a deep breath. "I've been lying here alone, thinking about what my tia told me. I was okay with the idea of it all, but what bothered me was, if all this was real, it was unfair."

"Because you thought you dreamed of Nicolai?"

Ava nodded. "I'm so relieved that you're not him."

The unshed tears in his mate's eyes made D'mitri want to drag her into his arms. But he held back.

"I know I see the subtle differences between you two, but I honestly don't think I'll fully believe it until I see the two of you together."

"Then let us go to him when the sun rises."

Ava nodded. "Okay."

They sat for a long time, staring at each other. D'mitri

wanted to express the relief and delight he felt now that she was with him. But he didn't want to come on too strong since all this was new to her.

"Something I don't get is how all this started because of me reading a book. Ali's book."

D'mitri frowned. "What do you mean?"

"I picked up her book by chance and after reading it, these crazy dreams started. Honestly, I wouldn't even be here right now if it hadn't been for those dreams and my aunt Lilah."

D'mitri didn't know how to respond.

"Actually, now that I think about it, the dreams started before. I picked up the book because of the face on the cover. Your face." Ava gave herself a shake. "Well, Nicolai's face, I guess."

"Your nature brought you here. And just in time. I can feel the change coming. I can smell it on you."

Ava's brows crinkled. "What do you mean?"

The confusion in her soft voice made D'mitri hesitate. "Your Awakening. Your jaguar is surfacing."

Ava's eyes grew wide. "What?"

Nudging at the mate bond, D'mitri listened in on her thoughts to get a hint on what was going on in her head. He felt a little guilty for just blurting it out when he realized she didn't know what he was talking about. But she quickly made the connections between what her aunt had told her earlier in the night and Ali's book.

Ava shook her head in denial, her words coming out as nothing more than a whisper. "It's not real. It can't be."

"I am sorry. I did not realize your aunt had not told you."

Ava stared at him, her eyes wide with disbelief.

"It must be a lot to take in."

She snorted. "You think?"

He could feel her panic begin to build. Her breaths coming in short, panting draws. She was in shock as she played over everything. The stories. The conversations with Nicolai and Ali. The strange kinship she'd felt toward them both.

She squeezed her eyes shut. "This can't be real."

"It is."

Still shaking her head, she met his stare again. This time D'mitri saw tears shimmering in her eyes. The overwhelming need to comfort his mate overrode his decision to give her a little space. He couldn't help himself. He reached out and drew her close.

Ava tensed at first. But when he murmured reassurances to her, she relaxed into him and rested her head against his shoulder.

D'mitri stroked her hair, hoping to soothe her further. And it worked. Eventually, she brought her arms around his middle and melted in his arms, slowly drifting into a much-needed sleep.

D'mitri was torn. He was overjoyed to be with his mate. Holding her in his arms filled an empty space in his heart that had been hollow for far too long. But he felt a sadness and an uncharacteristic anger that made him worry he might not be able to control himself when he spoke to Ava's aunt. He couldn't understand why the woman would, or could, keep something so significant from Ava.

D'mitri sat with her cradled in his arms, snuggled against his chest. She looked so peaceful, but he knew when she woke again, her mind would be anything but.

She would likely be hurt or angry with her aunt for not telling her everything. And D'mitri wanted to be there for her, but he wasn't sure if that was the best idea. She might not want him around for something so emotional, but he wasn't sure if he could be away from her so soon after finding her.

14

D'mitri sat across the table from Lilah and stared at her as she took a sip of her tea. He waited patiently for her to gather her thoughts after he had explained who he was and how confused Ava was over her dreams.

"So," Lilah finally answered, "I must tell her everything now that you are here."

"She knows. That is why I have come to you. How could you not tell her?" he asked calmly, although he was raging inside.

Evidently, some of his anger showed, because she frowned. "You do not understand. I wanted to keep her safe."

"Safe?" D'mitri snapped, his frustration overcoming his control. "With her mate is where she is safe!"

Lilah blanched at his tone. "Not if that brought her back here."

"You brought her here," D'mitri said angrily.

"Because I knew she was coming into her Awakening.

I wanted her to be here when she went through her first emerging." Lilah shook her head and added softly, "In a way, I hoped her grandmother's blood would dominate and she wouldn't go through this."

"Go through this?" D'mitri growled. "You wished for her not to have her mate! Are you so heartless that you would deprive her of her fated happiness?"

Lilah shook her head. "It wasn't like that. That's not what I meant. I always knew she would be like us. There were just too many little things about her that proved she would be. That's why I told her the stories. I wanted her to be familiar with it all even if it was only in the stories. I did plan to tell her everything, and I tried so many times, but there was always some reason for me not to."

D'mitri slammed the side of his fist into the table. "Do you know how frightened she is, how hurt she is that you did not tell her?"

Lilah's pained expression was clear when she lifted her eyes to meet his angry gaze again. "Yes, I can imagine. But I tried last night, and she just shut me out. I tried. I really did, but when she gets her mind set, there is no telling her anything."

"You blame her?" D'mitri asked in disbelief.

Lilah shook her head. "No. It is my fault. I should have told her from the time she could understand the words, but I didn't."

D'mitri could understand her wanting to protect Ava, but this woman was supposed to be.…

"Good morning," DeMario said, striding into the kitchen. He looked back and forth between D'mitri and Lilah. "How is everyone?"

Glad to be distracted from the conversation with Lilah,

D'mitri stood and clasped hands with DeMario. "I am well. And you?"

"Life is good." He smiled, but a hint of sadness crept into his eyes. "Slow for us Jagara without a mate, but good." As he turned to get a cup of tea, DeMario asked over his shoulder, "How are your brother and his new family?"

"They are very well. How is your brother?"

"He has been better. But he has also been much worse."

"Still no news of Mina?" D'mitri asked.

DeMario shook his head sadly and turned to stir a little honey into his tea. When he turned to lean back against the counter, his expression instantly shifted, and he smiled. "Good morning."

"Good morning," a sleep-roughened voice answered from the doorway.

D'mitri followed DeMario's gaze. Ava stood just inside the kitchen. Her dark chestnut hair in disarray, the wild locks framing her gorgeous, heart-shaped face. Her sleepy eyes focused on him, and D'mitri could see the relief in her expression. She was glad to see him.

Then he watched Ava's focus shift toward her aunt, and for a moment, he felt every ounce of hurt and resentment his mate felt toward the woman. He wished he could bear the weight of the betrayal she felt. But it was hers to work through, and he had enough anger of his own directed at the woman. Still, he could support his mate and be there for whatever she needed.

"Tea?" DeMario offered Ava.

She took a cup from him with a small, grateful smile. Then turned and leaned against the counter beside him.

D'mitri stood quietly, knowing her distant expression had nothing to do with him. The tension from last night's events hovered between the two females, but as angry as D'mitri was with Lilah, he hoped the coming conversation wouldn't cause any permanent animosity between the two females.

"Did you sleep well?" DeMario finally asked, breaking the silence.

Ava swallowed the sip of tea before she answered. "Yes. Once I recovered from last night's information dump."

DeMario glanced at Lilah, who seemed to be studying an imaginary smudge on the table. Then he tossed a curious look toward D'mitri.

D'mitri watched Ava. She stared into her teacup, avoiding eye contact with her aunt at all costs. He could feel everything she felt. The hurt. The anger. The betrayal. All the chaotic emotions from the night before came flooding back.

Surprising everyone, Lilah spoke up. "Boys, would you mind giving me and Ava some time alone?"

D'mitri saw Ava tense. She didn't protest, but her eyes met his over the rim of her cup.

Do you want me to stay?

Ava gave him a faint shake of her head. *I don't know if I'm ready for this conversation, but there's no point putting it off.*

I am only a thought away if you need me.

He didn't miss the slight tug at the corner of her lips. *I appreciate that. But I think I'm okay.*

D'mitri turned to DeMario, "Come. Let us give them a little space."

DeMario cleared his throat. "Of course."

WHEN THE MEN had left the room, Ava turned and looked out the window. She had no idea what to say to Lilah. Yes, her aunt had been there for her all her life, treated her as if she were her own daughter. She treated Ava no differently than she had her birth son, Darien. But she'd lied. Kept the truth of Ava's true heritage a secret.

Ava drew in a breath and released it slowly. "I don't understand why you would keep something like this from me."

"I wanted to tell you," Lilah answered softly. "I tried many, many times, but there was always some reason not to."

Ava set her cup on the counter and closed her eyes. "You should have told me anyway."

Ava heard a chair push away from the table, and when Lilah laid a gentle hand on her back, she said, with regret heavy in her voice, "I know, love, and I'm sorry I didn't."

Unable to stand her touch, Ava wheeled around, knocking Lilah's hand away. "You lied to me!"

"You're all I have left, and I didn't want to lose you too. I only wanted to keep you safe," Lilah explained with a pained tone.

"Safe from what?" Ava snapped at Lilah. "From having this connection with him? From knowing about my amazing heritage?"

Lilah shook her head. "It wasn't like that."

Ava said in disbelief. "I was kept in the dark all my life. I don't even know who I am."

And then it hit her. If her aunt had kept all this from her, what else had she not been truthful about?

"What else did you lie about, Tia?" Ava asked angrily. "Are you even related to me?"

Lilah looked at her as if she'd lost her mind. "Of course I am."

"What about my parents? Did they even die in an accident?"

The expression on her aunt's face was all the confirmation Ava needed.

"What really happened to them?"

Tears shimmered in Lilah's eyes. "Ava—"

"Don't!" Ava ordered. "Just tell me the truth."

Lilah was quiet for a long moment before she said, almost reluctantly, "Technically, your father's death was an accident. Or so your mother said."

Ava frowned, her anger faltering. So her mother said? What the hell did that mean?

After taking a steadying breath, Lilah continued. "Your mother was taken by a Naymati—one of our people's enemies. When your father went after her, he and the Naymati fought. During the struggle, your father fell from a high ledge. Seeing her mate fall to the cavern floor…" Lilah cleared her throat before continuing. "Nara lost control of her jaguar and attacked the Naymati. When he was down, Nara went to your father, but he was too injured to move. Your mother couldn't carry him, so Zorion made her leave him and go for help. By the time she returned with the others, the Naymati was gone, and your father had succumbed to his wounds."

Ava stared at her aunt, shocked by what she was hearing. She really would've preferred a normal accident because the story sounded unreal. Ava was afraid to hear anymore, but she had to know. "How did my mother die?"

"I don't know, love."

Ava frowned. "What do you mean you don't know?"

With a pained expression, Lilah said, "One day I was watching you for Nara, and she simply never returned. And before you get a crazy idea in your head, your mother loved you. She would never have willingly left you behind. Something happened to keep her from returning."

Ava stared at her aunt, unsure of how to react. "How, Tia? How could you not tell me this? How could you keep something like that from me all my life?"

"I didn't know how to tell you. You had so many other problems, and I didn't want to add to them with something like that?"

"With the truth?" Ava shouted. "You should have told me!"

"I didn't want—"

"Screw what you wanted or didn't want. This is about me. My life. My parents." Ava drew a shaky breath and rasped, "I can't do this right now. I need some air." Without another word, she moved around Lilah and headed for the door.

As she left the room, Lilah called after her, but Ava ignored her. She had to get away. She couldn't talk about it anymore. Not right now. She just wanted to be alone. Honestly, she wanted to go to D'mitri and let him wrap his comforting arms around her, but he was busy talking with his friend. Instead, she pushed her way out the back door and drew in a breath of the thick jungle air as soon as her feet hit the ground.

Closing her eyes for a moment, she breathed in the

wild scents that hung in the air, and when she caught the hint of something she liked, she let her nose carry her feet in that direction. She followed the scent down a well-worn path through the yard to the edge of the jungle, hesitating only a second before continuing down the path.

Ava walked slowly, enjoying the feel of the thick, damp air on her skin and hair. She might normally be uncomfortable, but for some reason the air soothed her. Ava loved the peacefulness of this place. Though it wasn't quiet, it seemed to quickly draw the stress and tension from her.

She looked up at the thick canopy above her and smiled. She loved it here. She didn't want to leave. She could stay there forever and be completely happy never having to go back to the city again.

D'MITRI'S conversation with DeMario was very short. When his old friend saw how distracted D'mitri was, he promised they would catch up at a later, more convenient time. D'mitri slipped from the house, knowing he had to give his mate and her aunt more time to talk. He kept his mind closed off from hers, giving them the privacy they needed.

He found a spot far out of sight of the house. Where the sounds of forest life surrounded him and blocked out the stresses of the morning.

He was so absorbed in the bustling life around him that he didn't hear Ava approach. He didn't know she was near until she stepped around the tree and brushed her palm over the leaves of the large fern next to him. He sat quietly watching as she stroked every plant within her reach as she inched along the thin path.

When she stopped to investigate the trees above her, D'mitri smiled. She seemed so content in the wild. Away from other people. Away from her aunt. He didn't want to disturb the peace radiating from her, but he felt the need to touch her mind. *Ava.*

Her shoulders stiffened for a second before the corner of her mouth curved into a slight smile. *Yes?*

Are you feeling better?

Much.

Good. I am glad.

Ava reached out and touched the closest tree, smiling as she ran a gentle hand over the bark.

Would you like some company? D'mitri asked, feeling hopeful.

Ava's smile widened. *That would be nice. I'm out in—*

I know where you are.

She frowned. *How?*

D'mitri smiled. *Because I see you.*

Ava looked around, and when their eyes locked, she slowly approached. "What are you doing hiding out here?"

"Not hiding. Enjoying the sounds of the jungle." D'mitri closed his eyes. "It calms me."

"I know the feeling."

After an awkward silence, D'mitri beckoned her to him. "Come. I want to show you something."

Ava closed the distance between them, and when she slipped her hand into his, he guided her to sit beside him. "Do you like monkeys?"

She nodded. "I love them. Why?"

Tearing his focus from her beautiful eyes, D'mitri looked up, and Ava followed his gaze.

Sitting on a limb not twenty feet above them was a lively little squirrel monkey.

Ava's face lit up and she made a cooing little sound in the back of her throat. "He's adorable."

The little monkey hopped down to the limb below his original perch to get a better look at the two of them. Ava sat motionless, careful not to scare him away, and D'mitri made a soft clicking sound.

The little monkey looked at him and Ava watched in awe as it descended to the limb only five feet over their heads. D'mitri repeated the clicking noise until the monkey hopped onto the ground a few feet away. He chattered softly while looking at Ava, then glanced at D'mitri before inching closer to her.

Ava couldn't believe this was her life. She sat cross-legged in the middle of a South American jungle next to this beautiful, wild man, with a cute little squirrel monkey slowly making its way toward them as if knowing they posed no threat.

Though she remained focused on the little monkey, she was acutely aware of D'mitri's proximity as he eased closer to her. She could feel the heat of his body and the calm energy radiating from him. With exquisite gentleness, he took her hand and slipped something into her palm.

Berries, he whispered into her mind.

The gray and gold monkey watched D'mitri's every

move, curiosity flaring in its little face when it saw the berries.

Slowly extend your hand to him.

Ava did as D'mitri said, and he made the soft clicking sound.

The monkey eyed them both as it inched forward. And after a slight hesitation, stretched out its tiny hand, taking one of the berries from her palm. The amusement and sheer joy Ava felt threatened to bubble out of her in the form of a laugh, but she didn't want to scare the little guy away.

Instead, she sat perfectly still and watched in awe as his tiny hand took all the berries, one by one. When he was done, he chattered his thanks and hopped back into the tree with the others.

Once the happy little guy disappeared back into the branches above them, Ava beamed at D'mitri. "That was amazing. Thank you for that."

"You are most welcome."

D'mitri's genuine, pleased smile made Ava's heart flutter. She didn't fully understand the whole mate thing, but she could feel the bond growing stronger by the second. It had nothing to do with the undeniable physical attraction she felt for him. It was more about her curiosity.

Ava leaned her head against the tree trunk and studied D'mitri's handsome features. Sure, he looked eerily similar to Nicolai, but she could see so much more than their near-identical features. It was in their eyes. In their overall auras.

D'mitri appeared to be a bit more rugged than his brother. Yet, the wildness in his sea-green eyes held an underlying softness she hadn't seen in Nicolai's. Something much more intimate.

Ava jumped when D'mitri's palm cupped her cheek, her breath catching in her throat. Her entire body reacted to his gentle touch. Her internal temperature rose. Her heart thumped harder. And her breath froze in her lungs when his thumb lightly grazed her bottom lip.

Ava could have melted on the spot the way his intense eyes lingered on her mouth. D'mitri was about to kiss her, and although she had no doubt it would be nice, Ava wasn't sure she was ready for that yet.

To her relief, D'mitri's hand fell away, and he eased back, giving her a little room to breathe. The last thing she needed was to rush into the whole mate bond thing. They had time. And she wanted to get to know him first.

15

"I love your accent."

D'mitri's pale eyes narrowed. "What accent?"

Ava smiled. "You have a very thick Portuguese accent. Your English is obviously recently learned. Only within the last few years, I'm guessing."

"How do you know that?"

She laughed softly. "Am I right?"

He nodded. "Nicolai and Kaela taught me."

She loved the way his accent caressed the words, especially names. Hers in particular. He pronounced this one Ky-Ella. Almost jealous of the way the woman's named rolled from his tongue, Ava asked, "Who is Kaela?"

"She is like a sister to me. She came to live with us when she was very young, and now she helps take care of my father."

Ava heard the hint of sadness in his voice. She asked softly, "What's wrong with your father?"

"We must watch him closely, because he sometimes loses himself."

She frowned. "What do you mean?"

"He forgets things. Important things. And he can be very confused at times. Mostly he is himself, but there are days when he is completely lost."

"That's sad," Ava said before she realized the words had slipped out.

"It is. But at least we still have him."

"I can't even imagine what that would be like. Not knowing who you are must be very scary." When D'mitri nodded in agreement, she asked, "How does your mother handle it when he gets like that?"

Something flashed in D'mitri's eyes, and he looked away from her. Ava almost regretted asking as she saw the look on his face. He exhaled a shaky breath before saying quietly, "She passed many years ago, before Father became sick. I am glad she never had to see him that way. It would have broken her heart."

After an awkward silence, Ava whispered, "I'm sorry. I didn't realize—"

"It is all right. You did not know."

She stared at his profile, watching him for a few moments. "Is it all right if I ask what happened to her?"

D'mitri turned to her, his expression serious. "I am your mate, Ava. Never be afraid to ask me anything."

The utter honesty in his tone made her feel a little less intrusive.

"To answer your question, when Nicolai and I were young, our mother passed while birthing our sister. Neither of them survived."

Tears burned behind her eyes, but she didn't have time to fully process the stirring emotions.

D'mitri suddenly stood and offered her his hand.

"Come. Let us not sit and be sad over the past. Walk with me."

Ava took his offered hand and let him help her off the ground. She expected him to let go. Instead, D'mitri laced his fingers with hers and led her deeper into the jungle. The intimacy of that simple connection made Ava's heart flutter.

"Where are we going?"

"There is a place I want to show you. But first, we can stop by Ali and Nicolai's. It is on the way."

Although nervous about seeing Nicolai again, Ava knew she needed to see the brothers standing side-by-side to fully believe there was two of them. "Okay."

They walked a good thirty-five minutes before the vegetation thinned and the sound of water perked her interest.

"Are we close?"

D'mitri pointed ahead of them. "Just around that next bend."

Just beyond a grouping of massive ferns, the trail curved to the right. Another hundred yards, a two-story house begin to come into view, and the gentle sound of water grew louder.

"Oh wow," Ava breathed when they reached the source of the sound.

A river ran along the back edge of a vast lawn, and an old fallen tree served as a bridge across. Ava stopped in the middle to admire the view. The water looked inviting, and she'd love to go for a swim. Somehow, she knew the water would be the perfect temperature.

"I can't imagine having a river in my yard. I'd be in it so much I'd grow fins."

D'mitri chuckled. "I will take you swimming later if you want."

Ava beamed up at him. "Really?"

"Absolutely. I have the perfect place. But for now"—he nodded toward the house—"we go see my brother and his mate."

Just as they hopped down off the natural bridge, Ali pushed open the back door. As soon as she saw them, a wide smile broke across her face. "You're here!"

She rushed down the steps and met them halfway across the yard. Ava didn't expect a hug, but the leggy blonde wrapped her arms around Ava's shoulders and squeezed like they were old friends and hadn't seen each other in ages.

Ali released her and smiled. "I knew you were one of us. I could feel it in my bones, but Nico wouldn't let me say anything. But after learning that you weren't raised Jagara, I'm glad I kept my mouth shut."

Ali turned to hug D'mitri as well.

"You, sweet brother, really do have a beautiful mate."

Ava didn't think Ali's whispered words were meant for her ears, but somehow, she'd managed to hear them. And they made her feel a little awkward.

"Ava." A familiar voice came from behind her. She turned just as Nicolai approached. He offered her a hand and a genuine smile. "It is good to see you again."

To her surprise, seeing him in the flesh again filled her with a kind of relief she hadn't expected. And after spending the night and half the day with D'mitri, seeing Nicolai made their subtle differences glaringly obvious. "Good to see you too."

Nicolai's hand briefly touched her shoulder as he

stepped around her and clasped D'mitri's nape. He brought their foreheads together. "I told you she would be worth the wait."

When the brothers released one another, Ali smiled. "Is everyone hungry? Grandi fixed an ass-load of javali stew, and I made cheese bread."

"That sounds amazing," Ava admitted.

"Good. Because I'm starved and I didn't want to be rude and pig out in front of you guys."

D'mitri took Ava's hand and followed Ali inside with Nicolai bringing up the rear. At the far end of the long galley kitchen, an older man stood with his back to them, stirring the food in a massive pot on the stove.

"We have company for dinner," Ali announced cheerfully.

The man turned, a wide smile on his handsome, weathered face. "D'mitri. I heard the news."

"I am sure you did." D'mitri laughed, cutting his eyes at Ali and Nicolai, before turning to Ava. "Grandi, I would like you to meet Ava. My mate."

Grandi shifted his focus, and the second his strange, golden eyes met hers, his smile faded. He hesitated a moment before taking her outstretched hand. With an awed expression, he whispered, "You are Ahava Parmali."

Those were the last words she expected from the man. And judging by the look the brothers exchanged, they recognized the name as well.

Ava swallowed, her heart in her throat. "How do you know that name?"

She wasn't sure who she was asking. Grandi, D'mitri, or Nicolai. But Grandi smiled down at her. "You are the Cherished One."

The Cherished One? Words suddenly flooded Ava's mind. Words she hadn't heard in a long time.

Behold, the sole youngling of our beloved Zorion. Let us always remember his spirit and his love for Nara every time we lay our eyes upon his precious daughter. Today it is with great honor and great respect to her departed father that I bestow her with the name she shall be blessed with for the rest of her days. May her whole life be lit with the love of our people and anyone she decides to allow into her heart. With love, I call her Ahava, the Cherished One.

Lilah had told Ava the story many times. The day her grandfather, Bazyli, presented her to the tribes. Her naming ceremony. And as many times as her aunt had told her the story, Ava had never fully understood. To her, it was always just another story. But recalling those words as an adult hit her with an unexpected flood of emotions.

As if she wasn't already overwhelmed, Grandi stared down at her, a soft smile on his weathered face. "But for your eyes, you look exactly like your mother."

Ava felt tears burning behind her eyes, but by some miracle, she managed to keep them contained. "You knew my mother?"

"I knew Nara well. She and my mate were the best of friends. Inseparable."

Oh wow. She didn't know how to react to that bit of information.

Grandi looked back and forth between Ava and Ali. "Your mothers would be so happy to see you two standing here together. Despite all the hardships and obstacles that took you both on such different paths in life, you still ended up here. Family."

Ava looked over at Ali. The odd kinship Ava had first felt toward her the moment she walked into Maggie's bedroom seemed to make so much sense now.

With tears in her eyes, Ali closed the short distance between them and pulled her into a tight hug.

AVA SAT on the back steps chatting with Ali while the brothers stood by the river, staring out across the water.

Violet was fussy, and Ali stood, bouncing the unhappy baby girl on her hip. "I don't know what's wrong with her. She's never like this."

"You want me to hold her? Give you a little break?"

Ali let out a relieved sigh. "Thank you. My arms are killing me. She's getting so heavy."

Violet went quiet, her wide eyes on Ava's face when Ali handed her over.

Ava smiled. "Hi."

Violet grinned, her watery eyes crinkling at the corners.

"What are you fussing about, huh?"

Violet snuggled close, resting her chubby little cheek against Ava, and let out a shaky little sigh. She didn't make another sound. Just stared up at Ava.

Ali settled on the step beside them. "Looks like somebody favors her auntie."

Gently rocking side to side, Ava stared down at Violet's sweet little face. She supposed she was the little one's aunt. Or she would be.

I like the way you look at my niece. Ava's gaze jumped to D'mitri's, and he smiled the moment their eyes met. *I long for the day I see you holding our child in your arms.*

Though she knew it was way too soon to think such things, Ava found herself smiling. Sure, they had just met, and they had a long way to go in getting to know each other. But the idea of having a family of her own, of having *his* children, made Ava's heart fill with an unexpected warmth.

The satisfaction in his expression made her feel like she couldn't breathe. A little overwhelmed, Ava pushed the thought in his direction. *Stop looking at me and pay attention to your brother.*

D'mitri just smiled and shifted his focus back to Nicolai.

"Your connection seems strong already," Ali observed.

Ava nodded. "It's so weird though. You'd think I'd be freaking out over all this, but it's strangely comforting."

Ali smirked. "Yeah, you would think that, but all this is natural to us. I mean, I was a little freaked at first, but I thought I was going crazy. I already had other major issues, but when my dreams got weirder and I started hearing Nico's voice in my head, I was lost. I didn't know what to do."

That bit of information surprised Ava. "Really?"

"Yeah. If you'd met me before, you'd swear I was a different person." Ali's expression grew thoughtful. "I used to have horrible panic attacks. And it got to the point where I couldn't even leave my apartment for fear of it happening in public."

"You're right," Ava admitted. "Seeing how carefree you seem now, I never would have guessed that about you."

"Yeah, well, I had to work at that. It took something traumatic happening to break me out of it. I still struggle from time to time, but having Nicolai makes it much easier to deal with. Because of the mate bond, he sometimes catches my mental triggers before I do and helps head things off before I spiral."

The thought of having that kind of deep connection with D'mitri was a mixed bag. Being so open to someone that they had firsthand insight into her needs and desires sounded incredible. But letting him see all the dark recesses of her mind? Terrifying.

"Can I ask you something?"

Ava glanced over at Ali. "Sure."

"When we first met, did you know you were Jagara?"

Ava thought about it for a moment before she answered. "I knew my family were from Jagara tribes, but I didn't understand fully what that meant. I knew I was born here, but I had no clue about the telepathy and the shapeshifting."

Ali nodded. "We suspected as much."

"It's so surreal. I grew up on the stories, but that's all they were to me. Just stories. And, honestly, until I started reading your book, I'd forgotten all about them."

Ali looked thoughtful for a moment, a flicker of sadness in her amber eyes. "You're lucky you had that much. I didn't know anything. I came into this completely blind."

Ava didn't feel lucky. Her aunt had kept the truth of her heritage a secret her entire life.

"But I want you to know that you aren't alone in all this. If you ever have any questions or just need to talk, I'm always here. Okay?"

Ava swallowed the lump that suddenly formed in her throat and nodded. "Thank you."

The brothers made their way back over to them and D'mitri crouched in front of Ava. "You look so natural with a little one cradled to you like that."

Before she even had a chance to respond, Ali reached out her foot and shoved against D'mitri's knee, sending him backward onto his ass. "Don't scare her off with baby talk this soon! What's wrong with you?"

Everyone laughed, but D'mitri looked up at Ava again. *I am not scaring you, am I?*

No. The instant relief on his face made Ava smile. "Are you ready to take me for that swim?"

After handing Violet over to Nicolai and giving Ali another hug, Ava took D'mitri's hand and waved to the happy little family as he all but dragged her toward the river. Laughing, Ava let him lead her over the natural bridge and into the jungle once again.

They were barely out of sight of the house when D'mitri brought her hand to his mouth and kissed her knuckles. Heat flooded her as he smiled down at her. "Run with me."

"Run?"

He nodded. "I want to run. Come. You will enjoy it. Trust me."

Though skeptical, Ava couldn't resist the little sparkle of excitement in his sea-green eyes. "Alright. Lead the way."

Laughing to herself at the enthusiasm he radiated, Ava watched as he broke away from her and ran off down the trail. She loved the way he moved, his movements fluid and smooth despite his bulk. And damn, he was fast.

"Come, Ava! Run!" he called over his shoulder.

When she finally shook herself out of the trance, she followed him.

"Try to keep up!"

Hearing the taunt in his voice and in her mind, Ava pushed herself, running as hard as she could. She followed him, slowly seeming to catch up with him. He suddenly veered off the trail and headed off from the way they'd come—down a path she hadn't even seen.

It was narrow, and the tree limbs hung low over her head. The ferns and low-lying plants slapped at her legs as she continued, and when D'mitri slowed to tug his shirt over his head, Ava was distracted enough that she slowed her pace to enjoy the view.

His shoulders were thick with muscles. She loved the way they moved under his dark skin as he ran. She couldn't help but notice the firm, thick muscles of his legs and ass as well. She couldn't wait to see the rest of him bare before her eyes.

He ran a little farther before slipping out of his pants so quickly that she wasn't sure she even knew how he'd done it. One second, he was running in his well-fitted jeans, and the next he was completely nude.

This time Ava didn't just slow. She nearly stumbled.

She could hear his laughter in her mind, but when he shimmered out of sight and an enormous, black jaguar took his place, Ava tripped over her own feet and fell. She skidded to a stop. Breathing hard, she lifted her head to see the giant cat coming toward her.

She knew her eyes were huge with shock, but she couldn't stop staring. As it moved closer, Ava pushed herself up and scooted backward until her back hit something solid.

Do not be afraid.

When Ava realized she had her hands up in defense, she took a deep, unsteady breath in and forced herself to drop her hands. "I'm sorry. That was a little unexpected."

D'mitri shifted back to his human form and crouched in front of her. Ava forced her eyes to meet his, but her peripheral vision had always been excellent. She didn't have to be looking directly at his package to know what he was working with.

D'mitri took her hands, gingerly turning them over to inspect them.

Ava was shocked to see the abrasions on her palms.

"Please forgive me. I did not mean for you to be hurt. I am so happy to have you here with me, I did not think of what your reaction might be when you saw my other form."

With the amount of adrenaline racing through her system, she couldn't even feel it. "It's all right. They don't hurt."

He stared at her as if he didn't believe her.

"I'm just in a little shock. I wasn't expecting you to change like that," she admitted. "But I have to get used to this sooner or later, right?"

He nodded.

"So," she said, "let me see it. Show me again."

"Are you sure?"

Ava drew in a calming breath and nodded. "Yes."

He watched her warily as he moved back a few feet and shifted back into his jaguar form.

Though she was somewhat prepared, her breath caught

in her throat with such a big creature so close to her. She had to remind herself that it was only D'mitri and not some random wild animal in front of her.

She stared at his eyes. They were so much like D'mitri's, but there was an iridescent sheen making the richness of the color stand out. Ava liked the way they sparkled, and the contrast of his pupils added to their intensity. Human or jaguar, he was equally as beautiful.

When he inched closer on his belly and stretched his head toward her, he said, *Touch me, Ava.*

She slowly lifted her hand, and when he dropped his big, black head onto her lap, Ava closed her eyes for a second before lightly brushing her fingers over the surprisingly soft hair on the side of his face.

More, he growled softly into her mind.

Her hand stroked over his wide head and down over his muscular shoulders. When a loud purring started, vibrating against her leg, Ava laughed. *You're like a big housecat.*

That should offend me, but coming from you, it is anything but an insult.

His intense eyes drifted closed. Ava continued to stroke the side of his face and down his thick neck. "I didn't mean to hurt your feelings by being freaked out."

Do not worry. If anything, it was my fault by not warning you.

"But I feel horrible," she argued.

Then make it up to me by finishing the run we started and come swimming with me.

As he rose from her lap and turned to move back down the path, Ava watched in awe at the beauty of this magnificent beast.

I am your *beast, my sweet.*

A smile broke across her face, and she followed him as he trotted down the path. As she ran to catch up, D'mitri picked up his speed. She followed him for a while longer, enjoying the run, and he allowed her to keep up. When he slowed, Ava followed suit.

And as they cleared a small rise, Ava's breath nearly left her.

16

"Oh my gosh!" Ava said breathlessly. "It's so beautiful here."

It is my favorite place to be.

"I see why," Ava said in awe as she moved to the edge of the falls and looked down at the churning water nearly thirty feet below. "This may be *my* new favorite place."

D'mitri paced away and trotted back the way they came. Ava was about to ask where he was going when he turned and sprinted straight toward her. She almost panicked, thinking he was going to knock her over the edge, but then he veered at the last second and leapt hard, launching himself nearly halfway across the river. He landed with a great splash, and when he surfaced, he was no longer the beautiful, frightening jaguar.

D'mitri threw his hands into the air. "Join me, Ava!"

She shook her head, unable to stop herself from smiling at his exuberance. "I'm not jumping! You're crazy!"

His smile widened. *Come. You wanted to swim.*

Not like that. I can't jump.

Yes, you can. Do not think. Just jump. She was still debating it when he added, with an adorable smirk, *Unless you are afraid.*

Don't taunt me! It's not necessary. She kicked off her shoes and looked nervously over the edge.

Stop delaying and jump.

Okay, I'm coming. Give me a minute. Ava took a deep breath before she drew her T-shirt over her head and tossed it aside.

D'mitri smiled wider. She made a face at him as she undid her jeans and slipped them from her legs. She knew her thin cotton bra and low-rise panties, both of which were white, didn't leave much to the imagination. But she could at least pretend they allowed her a little modesty. D'mitri looked up at her with a hopeful expression, and maybe a little lust.

Ava shook her head. "I'm not getting naked with you, you wild man."

"Just jump!" he yelled, humor lighting his gorgeous face.

Pacing away from the edge, Ava took a deep breath and let her fear go. She didn't allow herself a chance to think. She just ran those fifteen feet and leapt. The air rushed at her for mere seconds before the river wrapped around her like a warm cocoon.

She kicked for the surface and came up laughing. D'mitri greeted her with a smile. "That was beautiful."

"That was fun!" Ava beamed.

"I am glad you enjoyed it."

"Enjoyed it? That was almost orgasmic."

The second the words left her mouth, Ava regretted

them. Heat rushed beneath her skin, and she could feel her face turn red.

"Do not do that." He swam closer, and Ava avoided eye contact as he brushed her hair back from her face. "Never be ashamed of your thoughts or your feelings. Especially not with me."

Ava didn't know why she felt embarrassed. But with D'mitri so close and the intensity radiating from him, she felt overwhelmed.

With a gentle touch beneath her chin, he whispered, "Look at me."

She reluctantly lifted her eyes.

D'mitri gave her a soft smile. "You can be so bold at times. Yet, other times, you seem so meek. Makes me wonder what you would be like if I kissed you."

Breathless. That's what she'd be like. That's what she already felt like as he moved even closer. His intense sea-green eyes focused on her mouth, flickering with a hint of that beautiful iridescent sheen from before.

Ava could only stare up at him as his thumb slid over her parted lips.

She saw the moment he decided. D'mitri's hands cradled her face. Then he leaned in and simply brushed his mouth over hers. The moment Ava's lips parted to take in a ragged breath, he smiled against her mouth.

She'd been thinking about it ever since she woke that morning, wondering what it would be like. Now that she knew it was pure heaven, she had to have more. On a rough exhale, Ava gripped his forearms and drew herself closer. The moment she pressed her lips to his, D'mitri made the most animalistic sound in the back of his throat. It sent a wave of heat straight to her core.

D'mitri shifted their bodies closer, pressing against her, reminding Ava of just how naked he was. His arousal was impossible to ignore, pinned between them the way it was.

It should bother her because she had never been the kind of girl to just sleep with someone she'd just met— Joseph was proof of that—but this was different. D'mitri was different. It felt right to be against him like this, and she didn't want to stop.

They were deep in the jungles of South America, alone but for the animals, and she was going to indulge in this beautiful man.

D'mitri's tongue teased at her mouth. His breath smelled and tasted incredible. Like an unknown spicy fruit that she could quickly become addicted to.

He gently sucked Ava's bottom lip, drawing a low groan from her, and she moved even closer to him.

"See," D'mitri whispered against her mouth. "So meek, yet so bold."

Ava wrapped her arms around his neck and pulled his mouth harder to hers. A deep growl rumbled in his chest, and he claimed her mouth with a fierce kiss. He slid one hand into her hair, fingers gripping her scalp and holding her mouth to his as he devoured her. His other hand rested on her bare back, fingers spread wide, touching as much skin as he was able.

Ava loved every second, matching his fierceness with her own and still wanting more. Drawing her legs around his hips, Ava pulled him even closer, but when D'mitri's firm hand slid down her spine and beneath the band of her panties, her heart thudded hard.

He kept kissing her, letting his hand drift farther down, gripping her firm cheek as he pressed her against the hard length straining between them. A mere scrap of material separated them, and it would be so easy for him to push it aside and sink into her overheated core.

Ava had never wanted anything so much in her life. But what was she thinking? It was too soon.

The moment she had the thought, D'mitri stopped. Resting his head against hers, he drew deep, ragged breaths. He kept his legs kicking, keeping them both afloat while he just held her close, allowing them both time to recover from the intensity.

When D'mitri lifted his head and looked at her, he smiled. "There was nothing meek about that."

She shook her head, still unable to speak. D'mitri forced another calming breath. Allowing a little distance between them, he tilted his head back and closed his eyes.

Ava took the opportunity to breathe. She pulled away from him and swam around, allowing her body to calm.

After a while, D'mitri asked if she was ready to head back.

Ava shook her head. "I don't want to go back just yet. I would like to see your home though. Can we do that?"

D'mitri smiled. "I would like that."

Ava was glad. She looked forward to seeing his home and meeting his father. And Kaela.

D'mitri climbed out of the river, Ava took the opportunity to admire his glorious form. He was gorgeous. His big frame towered over her, his muscles flexing as he leaned down to take her hand.

D'mitri cleared his throat. When their eyes met, Ava felt a blush redden her neck and cheeks. He'd caught her looking at his body, but he didn't seem to mind. He just held out his hand.

Ava let D'mitri pull her onto the bank. He hesitated, his eyes drifting down. With a nervous smile, she tucked one arm over her chest to hide how her nipples puckered under his appreciative gaze. She motioned for him to lead the way back up the thin trail to the top of the falls.

After Ava was dressed again, D'mitri took her hand and led her back the way they'd come. She was grateful when he found his jeans and tugged them back on. He was gorgeous to look at, but the thoughts that came to mind as she watched him moving fluidly through the jungle were distracting when they were trying to get somewhere.

By the time they reached D'mitri's home, Ava was exhausted and starving. All she wanted to do was eat something and crawl up in a bed somewhere. Instead, she drew on the little strength she had left and forced herself to follow him inside.

They entered the house through the back door, stepping into a spacious eat-in kitchen. D'mitri snagged a banana from the counter and offered it to her. Then he pulled a pitcher of juice from the fridge and poured her a glass. That first sip was heaven. The sweet, rich flavor burst to life on her tongue. It tasted like mango, pineapple, and another fruit that she couldn't quite place.

As D'mitri peered into the fridge, looking for something else to eat, Ava heard a woman's cheerful voice from across the room. "I thought I heard you come in."

The woman was gorgeous, with deep-bronze skin and raven hair. She strode into the kitchen, her dark, chestnut eyes smiling at D'mitri. When she saw Ava leaning against the table near the back windows, the woman hesitated before asking cheerfully, "Who is this?"

A wide smile broke across D'mitri's face. He moved to

stand close to Ava. "Kaela," he said happily, his fingers threading through Ava's hair, "This is Ava. My mate."

The woman's dark eyes flared. "Truly?" When D'mitri nodded, she laughed out loud and hugged him, standing on her toes to kiss his cheek. "I am so happy for you!"

She then turned to Ava, kissing her cheek before saying, "You are such a blessing!"

"What are you going on about, girl?" a deep voice boomed from beyond the kitchen entrance.

Ava stood a little straighter, taking a step closer to D'mitri.

A sturdy-looking man with wide shoulders came striding into the room. She might have thought him to be D'mitri's older brother, if not for the white streaks at his temples that stood in sharp contrast to his blue-black hair.

The man hesitated when he saw Ava standing next to D'mitri, knowledge blooming in his bright eyes.

Ava expected him to say something like what Kaela had. Instead, he rasped, "You are Ahava, the Cherished One."

"And my mate, pai," D'mitri said, beaming with pride.

His father moved in closer. "I always wondered what happened to you. Where have you been all this time?" he asked, his eyes searching her face.

When Ava didn't know how to respond, D'mitri spoke up for her. "She was with Lilah."

His dark brows came together. "Lilah? Delilah Parmali, Zorion's sister?"

Ava nodded. "She goes by Brayda now."

"She was mated to Kale, then?" he asked, and when Ava nodded, he smiled. "Such surprises!" He looked at

D'mitri and beamed. "The Cherished One, my boy! She is yours!"

D'mitri nodded, a huge smile on his handsome face as his father wrapped his arms around them both.

"My sons have found their destiny. Joy fills this old man's heart." He pressed his forehead to D'mitri's and gripped the back of his neck as he whispered, "I could pass to the next world and go with a smile on my face knowing you suffer loneliness no longer."

THEY EVENTUALLY MADE their way into the dining room with their plates. They chatted over dinner, and Ava listened to stories of the twins' childhood. She was quite amused, but D'mitri gave his father a look of disapproval several times before the night was over.

Ava talked a little about her childhood, how close she'd been with Kale and Lilah, and their son, Darien. She told them about the problems they'd had with Darien in his teen years. And how Kale had brought him back to the jungle to help with those issues. She went on to tell them about Kale's passing. D'mitri could see that the news saddened Burian. He sat quietly for a while, seemingly reflecting on the news.

Eventually, they moved to the sitting room to relax. D'mitri settled on the couch, tugging Ava down beside him. Burian sat across from them, smiling and talking with them excitedly about Ali and Nicolai. He again said how happy he was that both of his sons had found their women.

Ava rested her head on D'mitri's shoulder while they sat listening to his father talk proudly about his own mate,

D'mitri's mother, Dalah. He remembered her vividly but sometimes forgot that she was no longer with them. Today wasn't one of those days. D'mitri listened in awe of the love that his father still had for her. Burian missed her terribly and wished that she were here to see her sons with their mates.

When D'mitri heard Ava exhale a long, slow breath, he brushed her hair back from her face and smiled. She was sound asleep, her lips slightly parted.

"Take her to bed, son," Burian said in a low voice.

D'mitri said goodnight to his father and carried Ava up to his room. He lay her on the bed, but when he drew his arms from beneath her, she stirred a little and reached for him without opening her eyes. "D'mitri, don't leave."

"Shh," he whispered. "Rest, meu doce. I am here."

She relaxed a little at the sound of his voice, but she still slid her hand over the bedding trying to find him. D'mitri quickly pulled his shirt over his head, tossing it aside before he climbed into bed next to her. She instantly relaxed the moment he slipped his arm around her and drew her close.

D'mitri lay with his mate tucked against his side, her head on his shoulder. He closed his eyes to absorb the way her body fit so perfectly with his. For the first time in a long time, he truly felt content. And he drifted off to sleep with a smile on his face.

17

D'mitri woke to the most intoxicating scent. Ava. His mate. She smelled like sweet jasmine and warm summer rain. He could lay there for hours with her curvy little body pressed against him and soak up the satisfaction of knowing his mate was finally with him.

He didn't want to open his eyes, for fear that it was all a dream. But when he felt a soft hand glide slowly over his bare chest. He had to look.

Those exotic golden eyes with the burst of green at their centers greeted him. Ava gave him a sleepy smile. "Good morning."

D'mitri brought his free hand up and pushed the heavy fall of dark hair from her cheek. "It is when I wake to your beautiful face."

Ava turned her face into his chest and laughed softly.

"What is funny?"

Ava lifted her head again, a small smile still on her

lips. "I have sleep in my eyes. My hair is a mess." She covered her mouth, and added from behind her hand, "Not to mention I probably have the worst case of morning breath ever."

D'mitri shook his head. "Your breath is sweet like nectar."

"You lie."

He shook his head.

Her starburst eyes searched his before she asked, "Can I use your toothbrush? I left mine at DeMario's." When D'mitri nodded, she placed a quick kiss at the center of his chest before she slid out of bed.

Once she disappeared into the bathroom, D'mitri closed his eyes and savored the mouthwatering scent she'd left behind. Ava was so close to her Awakening, even the smell of her breath drew him in.

D'mitri knew others would catch her scent, but only his body would react so strongly to her. Only he would feel blood rush to his groin with such ferocity.

He rubbed his aching length in an attempt at some relief, but it made things worse instead. Only one thing would satisfy the insatiable need for his mate. Ava herself. Nothing short of sinking into her perfect body would ever slake his undeniable hunger for her. But no matter how much he wanted that, he knew it was too soon.

D'mitri let out a shaky breath and scrubbed both hands down his face. He knew he was in trouble. After yesterday's kiss, he hadn't been able to think about much else. The way she tasted. The way she felt against him. The smell of their blended scents.

Ava called out from the bathroom, her words garbled, "I can't believe I fell asleep on you last night."

D'mitri cleared his throat and replied. "You were very tired. It was a long day for you."

She made a sound of agreement.

"You had much to take in. As did I."

D'mitri heard her spit, and she said, "My tia is probably worried about me. I should call her and let her know I'm okay."

"Not necessary. She knows you are with me."

The water shut off, and seconds later, Ava stepped into the doorway. "That's why she'd worry. I mean, look at you. She'd know that any woman would fall all over you. And into your bed, apparently."

"I assure you. No woman has ever been in this bed."

Ava arched an eyebrow at him. "Really?"

"Yes. And you did not fall into my bed. I laid you in it gently."

Ava smirked. "You know what I meant, smartass."

"I do. I also know that your aunt will be okay. She knows you need your space. But she knows you are safe with me."

Ava smiled and crawled back into bed beside him. D'mitri tucked an arm around her and pulled her close again. She relaxed into him and rested her head on his shoulder with a contented sigh. "I really shouldn't be this comfortable with you already."

D'mitri brushed a few strands of hair from her cheek and tucked them behind her ear. "You are at ease with me because you were born for me. Just as I was born for you."

Ava closed her eyes, but D'mitri could hear her thoughts. She was happy. Taking a deep breath, she reveled in the utter peace she felt just in lying with him.

D'mitri felt and heard the change in her when his

fingertips caressed the curve of her throat. Her breath escaped her as a gentle exhale, and Ava searched his face from beneath heavy lashes.

"I still can't believe you're real," she whispered.

"I am," D'mitri replied softly.

Ava dragged herself closer until he thought she might kiss him, but her mouth hovered a scant inch from his. She said, with a gentle rasp, "Prove it."

D'mitri brought both hands to her dark hair and searched her eyes. He didn't know how to prove his existence to her, but he would show her the fire burning in him, a fire that burned only for her.

D'mitri brought his mouth to hers and captured the sigh that escaped her lips. He kissed her slow and easy, letting his hands slide down her spine. With a firm grip on her hips, he dragged Ava on top of his raging body. She made a hungry sound in the back of her throat.

His hands roamed, smoothing over the soft expanse of skin at the base of her spine before following the suppleness beneath her shirt and up her back.

Ava arched under his hand, her spine following his touch. The low, inhuman sounds she made told him just how close her jaguar was to surfacing. And when his thrumming growl rose in answer, Ava lifted her head again. Surprise flickered in her eyes, quickly giving way to arousal.

The fire that ignited in her eyes called to his jaguar, but D'mitri forced him down. That first time was about connecting. And releasing any awkward energy still lingering between them. There would be time enough for more another time. For now, he needed to savor the feel of his mate's perfect curves and the heat of her mouthwatering body pressed against him.

D'mitri held her stare, those gold and green eyes intense as Ava sat up, straddling his hips. In one swift motion, she pulled her shirt over her head and tossed it aside. When she reached to unhook the front clasp of her bra, D'mitri gripped her hips and watched as she revealed herself to him.

Sure, he'd seen right through her thin water-soaked bra during their swim yesterday, but the unhindered view was pure heaven. The sight of her puckered, rosy nipples made his mouth water, but they would have to wait. Because the moment Ava dropped back down, and her bare, hot skin met his, D'mitri knew he didn't have the patience to take his time and savor every inch of her perfect body.

With a growl rumbling in his throat, he pulled her mouth back to his, and he claimed her with a ferociousness that even surprised him. But he couldn't stop. He rolled her beneath him and pressed her into the bedding, his weight holding her much smaller body in place as he rocked against her restless hips.

Unable to bear the offending material between them, D'mitri rose above Ava and stripped her pants from her shapely legs. He didn't stop to fully admire the view, because her scent drove him mad. He wanted to fall face-first between those thick thighs and feast for hours, but his body had other plans. He needed to be inside her.

D'mitri kicked his pants off and dropped onto the bed, his body covering hers again.

The pure delight on Ava's beautiful heart-shaped face only spurred him on. D'mitri kissed her. Deep, drugging kisses that drew the most satisfying little sounds from her. He enjoyed the feel of her full mouth under his and her satin skin caressing his as they moved together. He was in heaven already, and he had yet to sink into her slick heat.

Please, Ava pleaded through their mate bond.

D'mitri couldn't resist her. He lifted his head and looked into her hungry eyes as he aligned their bodies and sank into her tight grasp. The soft little gasp that escaped her nearly did him in. It took every bit of his self-control not to pound into her and find his release.

D'mitri held himself still, watching her eyes glaze, and Ava didn't move. Her mind was utter chaos. Pure, blissful chaos. She was so lost to sensation that he had to remind her, *Breathe, love.*

She let out a shuddering breath and drew another before D'mitri retracted his hips and sank into her again, inch by slow inch.

D'mitri drew a ragged breath and released it slowly. "You feel unbelievable."

He wanted to fully appreciate the moment, to savor the feel of her gripping heat surrounding him. But his little mate had other plans. Ava arched her back and rolled her hips. "Keep going. Or roll over and let me."

D'mitri stared down at her, surprised by her aggressive tone.

"Move, dammit!" she ordered from between gritted teeth.

Knowing that her desperation for release matched his own, D'mitri gave her what she wanted, what they both needed. He let go of his control and drove into her with sure, even strokes.

Ava's hips rose to meet his every thrust, and she clutched at him, her fingernails digging into his back. Those sharp little points amplified every other sensation washing over him. And though he barely clung to his sanity, D'mitri didn't want to stop until she was shuddering and breathless.

And just when he thought he would lose his mind from the sheer pleasure, they both flew over the edge and into a mind-numbing release.

AS THEIR BREATHS and their heartbeats returned to normal, Ava lay in D'mitri's arms with her head tucked beneath his chin.

He slipped his fingers into her hair and whispered, "I am sorry for not savoring the moment."

Ava pulled away enough to see his face. "Do you see me complaining?"

D'mitri shook his head.

"Then shut up and enjoy *this* moment."

When D'mitri smiled, Ava snuggled close again. He slid his free hand down her bare back. And after a long silence, he asked her, "What do you want to do today?"

Propping herself up on an elbow, Ava searched his expression. "I love it when you speak Portuguese. The way your words roll off your tongue makes me…" She smiled but didn't finish her thought.

"Makes you what?" D'mitri asked as he tucked her hair behind her ear.

Ava shook her head. "I really like it. If you never spoke English again, I wouldn't complain."

"Good," D'mitri laughed quietly. "I very much like when you abandon English as well."

She gave him a funny look. "When did that happen?"

D'mitri flashed a beaming smile. "When you were screaming for me not to stop."

She felt her cheeks grow warm again. She laughed. "Did I really?"

"Yes," D'mitri chuckled. "Now, will you answer my question?"

She looked at him, confused. For the life of her, she couldn't remember what he'd asked.

"What would you like to do today?" he reminded her.

Ava laughed and covered her face, a little embarrassed that he could make her forget things so easily. Unable to stop grinning, she said, "Swimming again would be nice."

D'mitri agreed. "Yes, and I would be more than happy to take you."

"Can we have breakfast first? I'm starving." Ava was thoughtful for a moment before she asked, "Will your father be eating with us?"

D'mitri eyed her carefully. "Why do you ask?"

Ava shrugged one slender shoulder. "I was just wondering. It would be nice to spend more time with him before we head out."

D'mitri closed his eyes and rolled onto his back, reluctantly leaving the warmth of her body.

"You okay?" Ava asked, her gentle fingers tracing over his furrowed brow.

D'mitri nodded, taking her hand before kissing her fingertips. "I am only glad you like him."

Frowning, she asked, "How could I not? He's sweet and funny. Not to mention he looks so much like you.

Well, technically, you look like him, but you know what I mean." Sliding a single finger along the edge of his jaw, Ava added, "Besides, how could I not like someone who helped create you?"

Smiling, D'mitri dragged her to him and placed a gentle kiss to her lips. "You are a sweet angel." When Ava laughed, he added, "Come. Let us wash up before we join my father and Kaela for our meal."

D'MITRI SAT AT THE TABLE, watching his father and Ava interact. He could see the bond quickly growing between them, and it made him happy to see his father so much himself. It had been nearly four months since his last episode, and D'mitri was grateful. He hoped it would be a very long time before it happened again, but he knew it wouldn't be. It was rare that Burian went so long being lucid.

Ava's laughter broke through D'mitri's worrying. He listened as Burian's deep laughter accompanied her softer one. "I do not jest. D'mitri was bent over, looking into the underbrush, when the thing charged, slamming into him so hard that the boy's feet left the ground."

Ava cracked up, and even though he loved the sound of her laughter, D'mitri was a little embarrassed because he realized what story his father was telling Ava. D'mitri spoke up. "Pai, you are not telling her this tale."

"Too late," Ava chuckled. "I wish I could've seen it. I would pay to have seen your face when the pig's head slammed into your butt."

Burian slapped the table with an open hand. "That was

the best part. The poor cub didn't know what hit him. He tumbled ass over elbows a good fifteen feet before he rolled to a stop."

Ava covered her mouth and looked at D'mitri with sparkling eyes.

Burian laughed harder. "He just sat there, stunned. He looked to me, but I was laughing too hard. He leapt from the ground, his temper pushing him, and charged the creature, but the thing wheeled on him and ran straight for his brother."

Ava shook her head, her eyes wide with curiosity and laughter. "What did Nicolai do?"

"He screamed like a banshee and scared the little thing so bad it squealed and swung around to run the other way. Nicolai jumped on its back and rode the thing a good twenty yards before it shook him loose and disappeared into the underbrush."

"It got away?" Ava asked, a hint of disappointment in her tone.

"Not a chance. My boys are ruthless. They ran after the poor creature, and before I could follow, I heard it squeal again. After a few moments, Nicolai came back into sight with blood on his face."

Ava gasped.

"Seconds later, D'mitri emerged from the brush with the blade in his hand. He looked up at me, and as he extended the weapon in a steady hand, he said with utter calm, 'For you, my father.' I knew that moment both my sons would be great men."

With a soft smile, Ava asked, "How old were they?"

Burian's pale eyes settled on D'mitri, and he said with such pride. "Six years, exactly."

Ava's wide eyes turned to D'mitri. The awe he saw in those amber and electric-green depths made him smile.

"Do not look at me as if a rarity. All Jagara young are taken into the jungle and taught to hunt for themselves."

"At that age? Really?"

D'mitri nodded, and Burian spoke proudly. "Not so young usually, but I knew my boys to be special, just like their mother."

Burian's eyes took on a slightly hazy quality. And for a moment, D'mitri wasn't sure if it was from his illness or just his mind touching on some distant memory.

D'mitri waited until Burian smiled at Ava with tears in his eyes. "My Dalah was a heartbreakingly beautiful Jagara female. She had the most generous heart I have ever known, and she loved with everything in her." Burian took Ava's hand. "Your mother was the same way. She had so much love to give everyone, especially you." He brushed her cheek with the gentlest of touches. "I see so much of her in you. Not just your features but the fire in your eyes. You will keep my D'mitri on his toes. I have no doubt."

Ava's eyes shifted to meet D'mitri's, and the two of them stared at one another for a long moment.

Drawing her attention back to him, Burian brought Ava's hand to his lips and said, "I know you only just met, but I can see how much your short time together has affected him. I have not seen him so happy since his Awakening. I know it is you and the promise of the life you will have together."

Ava didn't know how to respond to that. D'mitri could see it in her eyes.

Burian's expression grew serious, and he said to Ava, "I expect lots of young to fill this home."

Ava opened her mouth to speak, but nothing came out. She just stared at him, completely at a loss. Now she really didn't know what to say. D'mitri knew exactly how she felt. He stared at her when she looked to him, as if for help.

All he could think of was how much he would enjoy trying to make his father's command happen.

18

Ava enjoyed breakfast with Burian. The food and the conversation. Well, all but the filling-the-house-with-children part. She wanted kids. She always had, and D'mitri made her want them even more. But filling a house? She wasn't so sure about that.

Ava followed D'mitri down the trail toward their swimming hole. With her thoughts preoccupied, they got there sooner than she expected.

When they burst through the trees, D'mitri leapt into the river without slowing. Ava slowed, however, stopping near the edge. She waited until D'mitri surfaced before she backed up to the tree line and then ran as hard as she could. Leaping with all her strength, Ava launched herself and landed almost as far as D'mitri had.

She surfaced and D'mitri immediately dragged her into his arms. He stared down at her, his expression serious, and the way he looked at her made her nervous. "What is it?"

D'mitri cupped her cheek. "I know we only just met,

and I do not want to scare you. But I want what meu pai asked of us. Whether it's two or twenty, I want to have little ones with you. Whatever you want, I will give it to you."

Ava didn't know what to say. Something inside her screamed, *Yes! Yes! I want all that too!* But logic told her they were moving entirely too fast. They'd just met a couple of days ago. Why were they both so eager to rush things? They had all the time in the world.

When D'mitri looked a little lost, his bright eyes searching her expression and the unshed tears burning in her eyes, Ava didn't know what to do. She wanted to respond to the beautiful things he'd just said to her, but she didn't know how.

Resting his forehead against hers, D'mitri rasped, "Tell me I have not scared you. That you want to have my children."

Ava slipped her hands back into his hair and sighed. "I want it more than you will ever know."

She could feel the worry in D'mitri's mind. He wasn't convinced.

Ava lifted her head, her eyes meeting his. "When I held your sweet little niece yesterday, all I could think about was how I wanted our child cradled in my arms just like that. And I don't remember ever wanting anything so much in my life."

D'mitri smiled and pressed a kiss to her lips. "Good, because you have no idea how much seeing you holding a little one in your arms affected me."

D'mitri's hand slipped between them and rested his palm on the flat expanse of her belly.

"I cannot wait to see you swell with the life of our child."

The intensity in his eyes was nearly too much for Ava to bear, but she forced a breath and slid her fingers over his. Ava stared into his pale eyes for a long moment before she said softly, "I can't wait either."

D'MITRI LAID his mate in the grass near the water's edge and sat back on his heels to take in the sight of her naked form stretched out before him. Slowly letting his eyes drift over Ava's glistening body, D'mitri admired every inch of her, watching the beads of water slide over her tanned skin. He couldn't stop himself from leaning down and capturing some of the droplets with his mouth.

Ava stiffened as his lips touched the inside of her knee. But when D'mitri looked up at her and met her excited eyes, she gave him a nervous smile. He stretched out between her legs as he gently spread them wider. He kissed his way up the inside of her thigh, smiling to himself when Ava squirmed and made impatient little noises.

D'mitri took his time, enjoying the journey to her heated core, and when his lips brushed her sensitive flesh, Ava gasped, her hands instinctively going to his hair. For a few heartbeats, he didn't know if she would push him away or pull him closer. But when D'mitri looked up her naked torso and over the puckered peaks of her pert chest, he was nearly undone by the look of pure, unhindered passion in her wild eyes.

Unable to bear the intensity of her heated gaze, D'mitri

turned his focus back to her drenched core and inhaled her heavenly scent before he set out to feast upon her.

Ava made inhuman sounds as he licked and sucked on her sensitive flesh, and it only served to drive his need for her even higher. Just when he thought he could take it no more, when he was overwhelmed with the sight, scent, and taste of her, Ava cried out. She clutched at his head and his shoulders as her body shuddered and her sweet release spilled onto his waiting tongue.

When her arms fell limp at her sides, D'mitri looked up at Ava's flushed face. The breathless, contented little smile she gave him made him want to devour her all over again. But that would have to wait. He needed to be inside her.

She must have read his mind, because Ava got a sudden burst of energy. She forced D'mitri onto his back and climbed on top of him. She leaned in, and just before her lips touched his, she whispered, "We're not done yet."

REACHING BETWEEN THEM, Ava took hold of D'mitri's hard shaft. She gave him a slow, firm stroke as she stared down into his pale eyes. When a low groan of pleasure escaped his open mouth, Ava repeated the motion.

When she finally touched her lips to his, D'mitri gripped the back of her head and held her to him for a deep, intense kiss as she slid her tight fist over him again and again.

She loved the feel of his hard, warm flesh gliding against her palm. His deep groans of pleasure shot jolts of sizzling heat straight to her center.

The way he gripped her hair, the feel of his mouth opened against hers as he struggled to breathe through the pleasure.

His deep, ragged groans and the way his muscles tensed told her he was close. D'mitri suddenly pulled away from her mouth, his breath shooting in and out of his lungs.

Ava lifted her head, and the sight of him had her core clenching all over again. His head was back, his eyes squeezed shut. The look of absolute ecstasy on his gorgeous face. A man on the verge of coming completely undone. Knowing that she was the reason behind his pleasure, that she took him to the edge, and she could easily tip him over. Truly a thing of beauty.

But Ava wasn't done. She didn't want him to finish like this. She wanted him inside her when he came. The second her hand stilled, D'mitri's eyes snapped open, and he growled from between clenched teeth. "Do not stop."

Ava shifted her weight, aligning their bodies so his swollen tip kissed her overheated core. "How's this?" she rasped before she sank onto him with a long, slow descent.

D'mitri's eyes went hazy, and the words that left him were indiscernible. Ava wanted to remain in control, but D'mitri was a man on the edge. He gripped her hips and forced her to keep moving. He was so close to losing control that it only took two full strokes before they both flew into a mind-numbing orgasm.

Ava collapse on D'mitri, every ounce of strength leaving her body. Neither of them moved for a long time. They simply floated in a haze as their minds and bodies recovered.

When Ava could think straight again, she shifted her

body into a more comfortable position and lay with her head resting on her mate's sweat-slicked chest. Her entire body felt more relaxed than it ever had, and despite the heat still radiating between them, D'mitri held her close. One hand was buried in her hair and the other traced lazy circles up and down her spine.

Ava had never felt so comfortable with anyone in her life. Never felt so safe. So cherished. Is that what having a mate was like? Or was it something deeper?

That train of thought steered her back to the conversation with Grandi, and then the one with Burian. They knew the story she grew up on. But it wasn't just a story to them, was it. It was a part of their past. They'd both known her parents. And judging by how he'd reacted, D'mitri did too. Or at least knew the story well.

"D'mitri?"

"Hmm?" he hummed against her hair.

"How old are you?"

His hands still. "Thirty. Why? Does my age matter?"

Ava snickered and pressed a kiss to his chest. "No. I was just thinking. I saw your reaction when Grandi called me the Cherished One. How stunned you were. You knew exactly what he was talking about."

"What does that have to do with my age?"

Ava shifted so she could prop her chin on his chest. "If you are thirty, that means you were seven when my parents died. Did you know them? Do you remember them?"

D'mitri's curious expression softened. "I have a vague memory of your mother. Sitting on Grandi's back porch with Gianna and my mother, while Nicolai and I played in the yard."

Through their mate bond, Ava could see the hazy,

disjointed memories. The glimpse of a woman who did look eerily like herself. Same heart-shaped face and dark skin. The smile.

Ava's heart ached with jealousy. She had no memories of her mother or father. Only a handful of pictures that Lilah kept. And all she knew about them were from the stories her aunt told her. She still couldn't believe Lilah had kept the truth about their deaths from her.

When her eyes began to sting with unshed tears, she cleared her throat and asked D'mitri, "Do you remember when it happened? When my father died?"

His pale green eyes met hers again. "No. But I know the story. My father told me and Nicolai many times about Zorion and Nara, their tragic end, and the baby girl that meant so much to them. To everyone."

Ava's brows drew together. "What do you mean by everyone?"

D'mitri brushed her hair back from her cheek and tucked it behind her ear. "Every Jagara life is precious. Especially with less than fifty of our kind remaining."

That little fact stunned her. "I'm assuming it hasn't always been like that."

"No." D'mitri shifted his attention to the canopy above them. "There was a time when our numbers were great. Each tribe had many more Jagara than our entire population has today."

Ava's brows shot up. "What happened?"

"Sickness. Poachers." His face fell. "The Naymati."

The sudden change in his tone made Ava's heart skip a beat. "My aunt mentioned the Naymati. Who, or what, are they?"

"Ancient creatures who dwell in the caves beneath the

jungle. They only come out at night, and they survive off the blood and flesh of their prey. Local human lore calls them *bruxso*."

Ava's eyed widened. She'd heard of the *bruxso* before. They were essentially the vampires of Portuguese folklore. Lilah had told her many stories about them. "*Bruxso* are real?"

"More or less. They are not immortal like the legend says. But the Naymati are dangerous. Not only are they vicious, but they possess an unnatural power of persuasion."

The image of the creepy man from her dreams popped into her head. Was he a Naymati?

Ava sat up, suddenly uneasy with their surroundings. "Ali said she was abducted by one last year. Should we even be out here?"

D'mitri pushed himself onto his elbow. "No need to worry, *Amanté*. We are perfectly safe. The Naymati will not leave their caves during the day. They cannot tolerate the sun."

Ava let out a relieved breath. "Good to know."

D'mitri stretched and stood, offering Ava a hand. "Come on. I will take you back to my home. We can get cleaned up and get something to eat."

Ava took his hand and let him help her to her feet. She, for sure, needed a shower and some food in her belly. She felt starved.

They took their time, talking as they strolled along the paths back to D'mitri's. He told her about how lonely he'd been since Ali had come into his brother's life. How much he longed for his own mate to come. And the indescribable relief and joy he felt to finally have her by his side.

Ava could understand those feelings. "It's strange. I always had this feeling that something profound was missing in my life. I always assumed it was just because I never knew my parents, but now, I feel like that void in the center of my chest doesn't feel quite so vast."

She felt D'mitri's eyes on her, but she kept her focus on the trail ahead of them. But he gave her hand a squeeze. "I lost my mother when I was young, and I only have a handful of memories of her that are my own. The people around me keep the rest of her memory alive. And while I can sympathize with you over the second-hand recollections of a lost parent, I can only imagine how it must feel to have none of your own."

Ava didn't know how to respond to that. So, they walked in silence for a while before she grew curious. "What do you do for a living? I'm not keeping you from your work, am I?"

D'mitri smirked. "I am self-employed. I *work* whenever I feel the calling."

Ava arched a brow at him. She didn't miss the way he put emphasis on the word "work." "What exactly do you do?"

"Carpentry has always been a passion of mine. I love being able to take a piece of wood and make it into something more."

Woodworking? Huh. That explained why he smelled of sawdust. "What do you build?"

"All sorts of things. But mainly furniture now."

"Really? I'd love to see some of your work."

"I can take you down to my workshop later. But first, I feed you."

When they finally reached his home, dinner was

almost ready, so they went up to take a quick shower together.

Over dinner, Burian told Ava more stories of D'mitri's childhood. And after, D'mitri did as promised and led her down the hill to his workshop.

It wasn't exactly what she expected. She didn't know why she pictured some primitive shed. The outside was weathered, but the building was solid. What she found inside when D'mitri pushed open the door was incredible.

For one, the place was unusually clean. And it smelled amazing. She understood why D'mitri always smelled so good. He must have spent a lot of time in there. Because even after a fresh shower, she could still smell the faint hint of warm sawdust on his skin like it was a part of him.

A massive table sat at the center of the vast room. Along the left wall, stacks of lumber lay drying on racks. Some of them enormous slabs of gorgeous wood. Against the far wall was a line of breathtaking hand-carved furniture. A workbench stretched the length of the right wall, and above it, every conceivable tool he might need for creating such masterpieces.

Ava approached the back wall to get a closer look at some of his work. Up close, it was even more incredible. The intricate designs carved into the back of a set of high-backed chairs was stunning. She ran her fingertips over the sealed work of art. "This is beautiful, D'mitri."

He stepped up beside her. "Thank you."

Ava moved to the next piece. A long, narrow table: the top smooth as glass and tapered legs carved with symbols similar to the ones tattooed on Ali's and Nicolai's forearms.

Her favorite piece was a chest with a depiction of the

jungle carved into the lid. She studied it carefully and then turned to D'mitri. "You are more than a carpenter. You are an artist. These are amazing."

She thought she caught a hint of a blush touch his stubbled cheeks before he turned toward the worktable. "It is something I have loved since I was a boy. I once had this place filled with so many things I barely had room to move around. My father convinced me to sell some of them to make room. I didn't want to get rid of any of it. I loved everything I ever built in here, but I knew I couldn't create much more if I didn't do something."

Ava nodded. "It must have been hard for you."

He stared down at the piece of half-carved wood in front of him for a long moment. "I sold one set of chairs to a family across town. Seeing how happy the wife was to get those chairs, the true appreciation in her eyes when she saw them, I knew I couldn't be selfish and keep everything I made."

Ava smiled. "That's sweet."

He cleared his throat. "Soon word got out about my work, and I managed to clean this whole place out in less than a month."

"Wow."

"People from all over came to me about custom furniture, and it sort of took off from there."

Ava smiled as he ran his hand over a raw piece of wood on his worktable. "Must be satisfying to have something you love to do be appreciated by other people."

D'mitri shrugged. "Yes, but I also just enjoy the process of creating things with my own hands."

For some reason, seeing the man so passionate about his hobby-turned-profession made Ava feel things in unexpected places. The man was very good with his hands. She could personally vouch for that. And she would give anything for him to touch her right that moment.

Ava hadn't realized she'd been projecting her thoughts to him, but when D'mitri's head slowly turned toward her, Ava's breath caught in her throat. His eyes had taken on that familiar iridescent sheen again. The man was aroused. Again. And she couldn't complain.

When D'mitri turned to fully face her, butterflies took flight in her stomach. She didn't know what she expected, but she let out a startled squeak when he lifted her up onto the wide table in the center of the room.

D'mitri's mouth crashed into hers. He kissed her long and deep, until she had to come up for air.

He worked loose the button of her jeans and ordered her, "Lift up."

She planted her palms on the flat surface and lifted herself enough for him to peel her pants off.

The second her legs were free, he told her to lie back.

Ava dropped onto her elbows and let him press her thighs wide to make room for his thick shoulders. There were no gentle kisses up the inside of her thighs or teasing build-up. D'mitri dove straight in like a man starved and she was the only sustenance he needed.

Ava's body came alive with a jolt the second his mouth connected with her sensitive center. In an attempt to anchor herself, Ava sank her hand into D'mitri's silky hair and held on tight. But that only spurred him on.

He made the most animalistic sound, his fingers digging into her hips as he doubled his efforts. He devoured her, his tongue and lips setting her body ablaze.

Ava threw her head back and let the pleasure wash

over her. Never in her life had she come apart so fast. She lay stunned, legs trembling as she tried to catch her breath.

———

D'MITRI COULD HAVE SPENT all night with his mate spread out before him, but he knew the hard wood table beneath her couldn't be comfortable. Scooping Ava up, he carried her up to the house and straight to his room, where he deposited her on the bed.

He had a feeling he would never get enough of her. And judging by the look in her hungry eyes, as he stripped off his clothes, she felt the same about him.

For the next half-hour, they pleasured one another. But every time he came close to coming, D'mitri would back off and focus on Ava.

As she came down from yet another release, D'mitri looked up at her from his place between her spread thighs. He read something in her hazy thoughts that triggered his need to claim her, to mark her as his. He licked her sweet juices from his lips, knowing this time would be different. He only hoped she would enjoy it as much as he knew he would.

Rising to his knees, D'mitri looked down at her from beneath his heavy lids and commanded gruffly, "Turn over."

Still breathing hard from the last release, Ava gave him a questioning look.

"On your hands and knees," he growled.

Ava hesitated a moment before she did as he said. Her starburst eyes were bright with nervousness and excitement as she looked at him over her slender shoulder.

Ava shivered as D'mitri dragged his hands up the backs of her thighs and over the curve of her nicely rounded bottom. He loved her soft, feminine curves, and when his eyes met hers again, he said hoarsely, "I will take you like this." His rough palms moved up her back before sliding down her sides. "I am going to mark you, and I might lose myself for a bit," he warned.

Ava's bright eyes were nearly glowing when she asked shakily, "What do you mean by 'marking'?"

When he visualized himself sinking his teeth into the soft flesh at her neck as he buried himself in her tight sheath, Ava gasped and started to pull away from him. But D'mitri gripped her hips and held her in place. Through gritted teeth, he said hoarsely, "Do not worry. It will be pleasurable." When she still tried to pull away from him, he whispered into her mind. *Trust me.*

Ava looked at him with wide eyes, her breaths coming in short, shaky bursts, but she finally nodded. "What are you waiting for?"

D'MITRI'S fingers dug into the flesh at Ava's hips, and with a rumbling growl, he slammed into her. Ava cried out, on the verge of being frightened by the sudden change in him, but the wild part of her wanted this. The first hard thrust sent such an intense feeling rippling through her core that her arms nearly gave out beneath her. But D'mitri didn't allow her to regain her balance. He gripped her hips harder, and on the second deliciously rough invasion, Ava sank down as far as she could, pressing her cheek against the soft bedding beneath her.

D'mitri continued to move inside her with an almost desperate pace. Ava had a fleeting thought that she should be uncomfortable with her ass in the air, but when D'mitri slammed into her again, her thoughts left her completely. She just closed her eyes and absorbed every feeling her mate inflicted on her overly sensitive body.

Ava had never been one to like it rough, but with this man, she loved every intense moment, crying out breathlessly with his every thrust. She was verging on release, hanging on to the ledge, her trembling hands gripping at the blanket. Overwhelmed with the way D'mitri took her and the animalistic sounds coming from him, she didn't know how much more of this she could take.

Shocking her, D'mitri suddenly yanked her upright. She wasn't sure what he was doing until her back met his hard chest, and he gripped her chin in his work-roughened hand and tilted her face away from him.

"You are mine," he growled. And without warning, he sank his teeth into the soft flesh where her shoulder and neck met. It hurt, but the pain was short-lived. An unexpected jolt of pleasure shot through her entire body like a lightning bolt.

Overwhelmed with sensation, Ava didn't know what to focus on. The heat of D'mitri's mouth on her. His teeth embedded in her shoulder. The feel of him frantically moving inside her. The animalistic sounds rumbling from deep in his chest. All of that would have been enough to send her over the edge. But what did her in was their mental connection.

Not only could she feel her own pleasure, but also every sensation wreaking havoc on D'mitri's senses as well. With one final desperate thrust, he took them both barreling headfirst into oblivion.

———

STILL BURIED DEEP INSIDE HER, D'mitri sat back on his heels, taking Ava with him. Still cupping her chin with one hand, he caressed her abdomen with the other. With his breaths still rasping, he held Ava's trembling body against him, reveling in the ripples of pleasure still pulsing through her core.

D'mitri drew a deep breath, steadying himself before he released his hold on Ava's neck. She gasped when his teeth left her flesh, and her core tightened around his overly sensitive shaft.

D'mitri groaned, holding her against him and Ava brought her hands up to cover his. *That was so intense. And a little scary, honestly. But it was incredible.*

Knowing how sensitive she must be, he took his time, lapping gently at the tender punctures on her neck before he slipped from the warmth of her perfect body and eased her down onto the bed.

D'mitri settled on his side, still holding his mate close.

She was quiet for a long time before she asked, "Are you alright?"

D'mitri kissed the top of her dark head, smiling at the idea that she was worried about him. "I should ask you the same."

She ran a hand over his as it lay resting on her bare hip. And when D'mitri pushed himself up onto an elbow and forced Ava's head around so that he could see her eyes, she whispered, "What?"

"I did not hurt you?"

Ava smiled. "No."

Relief flooded him, and when Ava turned onto her back, D'mitri rested his head against her sternum and drew in a deep breath. As he exhaled, Ava slipped her hand into his hair. Turning to look up at her face, he eased even more when he saw that she was staring at the ceiling with a blissful expression.

D'mitri closed his eyes and relaxed into his female, allowing himself to doze.

va woke with a jolt. Disoriented, she searched her surroundings. It took a moment to remember where she was. Then she saw D'mitri sprawled next to her, sound asleep. Not even her gasping for air or her trembling body stirred him in the least. And she was glad. She didn't want him to see her so out of it.

Ava felt horrible. Aching all over. Cold sweats. Exhausted, yet every nerve ending in her body firing like a low-level current ran through her. Shaking like a leaf, she crawled out of bed and snagged D'mitri's shirt off the floor. She couldn't sit still. She had to get outside and breathe some fresh air before she screamed from sheer overwhelm.

With stiff, jerky movements, Ava slipped into her jeans and quietly made her way onto the balcony. She drew a few deep breaths, taking comfort in D'mitri's scent on the shirt she wore, but no matter how comforted she felt, she still felt claustrophobic.

Ava made her way down to the neglected garden and

wandered around, peering at the sad sight. She wanted to get on her hands and knees and pull the weeds, prune the plants, and restore the garden to its original glory. But that would have to wait. For now, she had to go. She needed to move.

Without a second thought, Ava broke into a jog and angled toward the trail that led into the jungle. She had no plan, no idea where she was going. She just needed to escape the overwhelming restlessness she felt.

With every stride she took, the faster she went, until she barreled down the narrow path. Little by little, the tension melted away.

So focused on the run, she didn't realize how far she'd gone until she reached the river where she and D'mitri last swam. Without a second thought, she stripped off her clothes and dove into the water.

It felt good to be out at night. The warm water enveloped her like a soothing hug. But her joy didn't last. She couldn't fully appreciate the moment alone. Without D'mitri there, it just felt empty.

Reaching out to him, Ava tested their connection. She caressed his mind and found him still in deep sleep. Not wanting to disturb him, she eased away from his mind, letting go of the connection.

She tried to enjoy the swim, but despite the symphony of nocturnal creatures in the surrounding jungle, she felt utterly alone. And just like that, every ounce of tension and overstimulation she'd felt before came creeping back in.

That was when Ava realized her mistake. She didn't want to be alone. She wanted D'mitri. She should have woken him up instead of slipping away in the middle of the night.

Dragging herself out of the river, she got dressed again and headed back up the slope toward the trail that led back to D'mitri's home. She made it a mere twenty yards onto the narrow path when she sensed it. Someone watching her. The second Ava saw him, her heart sank.

———

D'MITRI, wake up! I need you!

He sat up in the bed, his heart hammering in his chest. Ava wasn't in bed next to him, where she'd been when he'd fallen asleep. She was gone. And by the sound of things, she was afraid.

Please hear me! The desperate but faint plea echoed in his mind and had D'mitri leaping from the bed.

His first thought was that her Awakening had come, but when an unmistakable image of a Naymati flashed through his mind, he growled aloud. "Where are you?"

D'mitri felt Ava slipping away from their connection, but he got a vague image of their swimming hole. Without another thought, D'mitri ran for the balcony and leapt over the railing without touching it. He shifted in midair and landed in his jaguar form.

Eating up the distance between the house and the jungle with his long strides, he tore down the path with a speed he'd never accomplished before. His woman, the one he'd waited his entire life for, was in danger. The enemy was with her, but D'mitri refused to let the vile creature take her from him. She was coming home tonight, and she would never leave his sight again.

———

"HELLO, BEAUTIFUL."

The tall, pale man took a slow step in her direction. Those eerie, dark eyes bore into hers, holding her captive. Her first instinct was to run, but she felt frozen in place by his intent stare.

"I see you are distressed."

She didn't want to answer, but Ava found herself nodding anyway.

"You need not suffer."

The man's low, soothing voice drew her in. Like a helium balloon, bobbing on the end of a string, she felt herself floating closer.

The man reached out a hand and whispered, "Yes. Come with me. I will ease you."

Just as she felt her feet begin to move, she heard a rough yet firm voice. "Ava."

The dark eyes of the man in front of her shifted toward something behind her.

D'mitri, she whispered, but as she turned, she knew it wasn't her mate standing in the shadows.

"Move away from him." The rumbling voice distorted as his shadowed figure morphed into a giant jaguar. The animal stalked toward Ava, the wide red-brown head low and his deep-gray eyes focused straight ahead. Ava's first instinct was to take a step back, but that would only move her closer to the other man.

Without warning, the jaguar launched itself forward, and Ava hit the ground to avoid the impact. She rolled onto her stomach, and as she saw the jaguar land, she knew that it hadn't been aiming for her. Instead, he slammed hard against the other male's chest.

As the two of them rolled to a stop. Gone was the

gentle, coaxing man. In his place was a creature as ferocious as the jaguar.

Seeing his long, sharp teeth, Ava slowly pushed herself onto all fours and inched her way into the underbrush just off the trail. She watched wide-eyed as the two fought. Snarling, snapping teeth, swiping claws, and the primitive blade in the pale man's hand. All of that made the fight even more frightening, but she couldn't look away.

Even with some distance from the fight, Ava could still feel the ground tremble beneath her as the two slammed into one another repeatedly. She knew that it wouldn't end pretty for one of them. Suddenly, the jaguar let out a horrendous sound and leapt away. Covering her mouth, Ava watched as the big cat stumbled and then righted itself.

She worried that pale-skinned male had gotten the upper hand, but then she noticed blood trailing from his temple. The bright red streaked his white hair, and four distinct lines in the thin fabric along his ribs.

The panting, angry male tossed a look toward Ava before he spun around and left so fast that she barely saw him go.

The growling jaguar turned to Ava. He took one step in her direction. Then another. And as he stalked toward her, his jaguar form melted away. And striding toward her was a man that took her a moment to recognize.

Shocked, she sat up and breathed, "Darien?"

20

Ava should have been uncomfortable about the fact that the man, who had been as a brother to her, was striding naked in her direction. It should have been awkward, but all she saw was the blood dripping from his face and running down his thick chest.

Ava scrambled to her feet and slammed into her cousin with a force that drove the air from his lungs. But Darien folded her in his arms and held her tight.

Sobbing, Ava pressed her face into his chest, unfazed by the blood. Years had passed since she'd last seen him. Yet here he was in the middle of nowhere when she needed him the most.

Darien pressed his face into her hair and breathed, "Are you okay?"

She nodded against him but refused to let him go.

"Ava," he said, prying her arms from around his middle. When she lifted her head to look up at him, Darien searched her face, wiping at the blood on her cheek. "What are you doing out here?"

Before she could answer, a jaguar burst from the underbrush and slammed into Darien, taking him to the ground. Darien didn't fight. He lay perfectly still, keeping eye contact with the big male on top of him.

She didn't know how she knew, but when she realized that the angry beast atop her cousin was D'mitri, Ava lunged forward. "D'mitri, no!"

He whipped his big black head around and snarled at her, effectively stopping Ava in her tracks.

Maintaining eye contact, she pleaded. "Please don't hurt him. He's not fighting you."

He was touching you!

She nodded. "He saved me."

D'mitri snarled again. *I will not have a strange man, Jagara or not, touching my mate. Especially not a naked one.*

Ava shook her head. "He's not a stranger. He is my cousin. Darien."

That gave D'mitri pause. He glanced down at the male pinned beneath his massive jaguar form. They stared at one another for a long, tense moment before D'mitri reluctantly backed away.

Shifting back into his human form, D'mitri demanded, "What happened?"

Darien explained what he'd come across and how he'd attacked the Naymati male.

D'mitri turned to Ava. "What the hell were you doing out here?"

She could feel his anger, but it surprised her to have him shouting at her instead of relieved she was safe.

"Tell me what you were thinking," D'mitri barked.

Unexpected tears stung her eyes. She felt like a little

kid being scolded by her elder. Stammering, Ava managed to answer. "I…I don't know. I just had to get out."

D'mitri stalked right up to her and gripped her arms. "You cannot be out after dark. I told you this. It is too dangerous for you."

Ava opened her mouth to argue that she hadn't been thinking about any of that. The only thing on her mind was easing that relentless restless feeling burning in every inch of her body. But the way D'mitri snarled down at her, she couldn't form the words to explain herself. Especially with his hands gripping her so hard.

"You're hurting me," Ava breathed, trying to pull away from him.

D'mitri released her and she saw a flicker of unknown emotion in his blazing eyes. He paced away, throwing a glance at Darien, who had pulled himself into a seated position. Her cousin watched them carefully, his focus on D'mitri.

D'mitri snarled at him, showing teeth that seemed nearly as long as they'd been in his jaguar form.

Darien rose slowly and took a step in Ava's direction. "She is fine, friend."

D'mitri peeled his lips back farther and growled, "I am not your friend, and you are not mine!"

Darien held up his hands. "I am not your enemy. Ava is my blood, and I protected her from the Naymati."

"You let him get away!" D'mitri spat.

"Calm," Darien soothed. "She is safe."

"For now!"

Ava cut in. "D'mitri—"

He wheeled around and, towering over her, he snapped, "Do not talk to me, woman! You will go home, where you belong, and wait for me while I finish this properly."

And just like that, Ava went from shocked by D'mitri's uncharacteristic behavior to pissed as all hell. Before she could even register her own anger, she slapped D'mitri hard across his face.

Never in her life had she hit someone like that. Not anyone she cared about, anyway. And despite the stunned expression on D'mitri's face when he righted himself, Ava didn't care. No one talked to her like that. Especially not him.

"Fuck you," she panted. She'd never felt such rage in her life. "Do not ever talk to me like that again."

His eyes glowed with such intensity, Ava didn't know how he would react. But he just stood there, staring down at her, his breaths coming in ragged draws. And that did nothing to improve her mood.

"I don't need this from you right now. Or ever, actually. I'm pretty freaked out by what could've happened tonight, and you're yelling at me. What is wrong with you?"

"After everything I told you, you left the house at night! That was stupid!"

With tears shimmering in her eyes, Ava said to him, "If you can't offer me a little comfort right now, then just get the hell away from me."

Something flashed in his too-bright eyes before he turned to Darien. "Make sure she gets home safely, or nothing will stop me from ripping out your throat next time I see you."

And then D'mitri turned and disappeared into the jungle.

"THANK YOU," Darien said hoarsely.

Kaela gave a shy smile and asked Ava, "May I help with anything else?"

"No. I think we have all we need. Thank you, Kaela." When Darien pulled on the thin pants she'd given him, Ava pointed to the kitchen table. "Sit."

Darien sat in the sturdy chair closest to him, but he didn't relax. His eyes constantly shifted as if searching for some hidden threat.

Ava laid her hand on his shoulder, drawing his attention back to her as she said softly, "It's okay, Darien. It's safe here."

His eyes met hers and he sighed. "I know. I've just been alone for a long time. Being around others is difficult for me."

Ava wanted to ask him why. Where he'd been all these years. If he ever planned to come home. But she let the questions fall. And instead, she gave him a sad smile. "I won't keep you here long. Just want to doctor your wounds. That cut on your cheek looks a little deep."

Darien scoffed. "It's a scratch. I've had much worse than this out there with no first aid kit."

Ava could see that. He had all sorts of scars on his arms and torso. A thick one bisecting his right eyebrow. Another up near the hairline, close to his left temple. Looked like the last eight years had been a little rough.

Why he'd chosen to stay away, she couldn't be certain. And sure, she'd like him to come home. But she knew he wouldn't until he was ready. She didn't know if he ever would be, but at least she finally got to see him. Even if it was under terrifying circumstances.

She gave his shoulder a squeeze. "It's good to see you."

Darien covered her hand with his much bigger one. "It is good to see you too. I've missed you."

"I missed you too." She studied him for a long moment and shook her head. "You look so different."

Darien smiled. "As do you, cousin."

Ava laughed softly. "I guess that's what happens when you go eight years without seeing somebody."

He looked a little stunned by that bit of information. "Has it really been that long?"

"Feels longer," Ava admitted.

She saw the flicker of sadness in her cousin's eyes. Or maybe regret.

"It's okay, Darien. We miss you, but it's okay."

He shook his head, his jaw clenching and unclenching as if fighting back emotions.

When his eyes met hers again, Ava saw a faint shimmer of tears beginning to form. Her heart broke for him. Unable to hold herself back, Ava stepped close and wrapped her arms around him. After a moment of hesitation, Darien's strong arms pulled her tight against him, and he hugged her like she was his lifeline.

A lump formed in her throat, but she swallowed it down and held onto him until he pulled away. Neither of them said anything more about the subject. Ava just offered him a small smile and then turned back to the emergency kit Kaela had left on the counter.

She got to work cleaning his wounds. Then cut little butterfly strips for the one on his cheek and slathered some antibiotic ointment on the abrasions on his chest and shoulder. "There. All done."

"Thank you."

Ava could see Darien's restlessness growing, so she nodded toward the back door. "Go get some air. I'll join you when I get this stuff cleaned up."

Darien didn't hesitate. He slipped out the back door and Ava could only hope he would stick around a little longer.

Once she finished cleaning up the mess and put the kit away, Ava walked outside, relieved to find her cousin still there. Ava settled on the steps and watched him pace near the edge of the garden.

His movements reminded her of one of those lions you see pacing in the glass enclosures at the zoo. Not that Ava had ever been to a zoo before. But she'd seen them on TV plenty of times.

Without looking in her direction, Darien told her, "Go back inside. Your man will blow a gasket if he comes back and you're out here."

Ava rolled her eyes. "He can kiss my ass. Besides, nothing is going to happen right here in the yard. No one is around. Especially not one of those guys."

Darien half-turned, looking at her over his shoulder. "And how do you know?"

"I would smell them." She tilted her head back and drew a deep breath in. "And I don't. Just animals. You. And the faint hint of D'mitri's lingering scent."

Darien lifted his chin and breathed in. "You're right. I can't scent any danger."

Ava just sat and watched as he resumed his pacing.

After a long silence, Darien muttered, "I wonder if he

found the Naymati." He turned to her again. "Do you see or hear anything?"

Ava shook her head. "I don't want to. The last thing I want is to talk to him after what happened earlier. Honestly, I just want to go get in a hot bath and then go to bed. I'm exhausted."

"Well, go on up. I'll stick around and keep an eye out until he gets back."

"When he does get back, he can sit out here with you. I don't even want to look at him after the way he acted."

Darien sat next to her. "He is a Jagara male. When it comes to our mates, our emotions can be quite intense. He reacted the way he did out of fear of what could have happened to you."

Ava scoffed. "That's bullshit. There is no excuse for the way he talked to me."

"Don't stay angry with him, Ava. He loves you."

Ava laughed. "He barely knows me. We only met a couple days ago."

Darien's brows shot up. "Wait. What?"

Ava sighed. "Yeah. This is all pretty new."

"You haven't had your first emergence?"

Ava didn't like the sound of that. Though no one had talked about it yet, she instinctively knew what he meant. Her jaguar. She hadn't even really thought about it. Or when the time would come. Unable to speak, Ava shook her head.

Everything she'd been feeling before she'd gone out into the jungle on her own came flooding back. The restlessness. The overheated feeling. The shakiness. Is that what was happening? Was her time coming soon? Tonight?

Ava released a shuddering sigh. "I think I'm gonna get a bath and go back to bed."

Darien studied her for a long moment before he nodded. "If you need anything, I will be out here."

Ava gave his arm a squeeze and stood. Before she went inside, she felt the need to say something to him. "I know why you've stayed away all these years, but just know, no one blames you. Your mother misses you, Darien. You should go see her before you disappear again."

Ava saw a faint shimmer in his pale blue eyes. Darien cleared his throat, obviously trying to fight back his emotions. "I don't know if I can."

Ava hugged him. "Well, if you decide to go, she is staying at the Juani family home."

21

After her bath, Ava lay in D'mitri's bed, wondering when he'd be back. Had he found the Naymati? Were they fighting? Was D'mitri safe? The possibility of any harm coming to him made her sick to her stomach. She couldn't stand the idea of him lying hurt in the depths of the jungle, or worse, lying lifeless at the hands of their enemy. An enemy that had taken her parents from her.

She didn't want to think like that. Honestly, she didn't want to think about D'mitri at all. She was still angry with him for the way he'd reacted to the situation. Sure, she shouldn't have gone out alone at night, but that didn't justify the way he'd spoken to her.

Was Darien right, though? Had D'mitri only been stressed over the situation and just didn't know how to handle it? Did he love her? Did she feel that way about him in return? Could she love that beautiful, wild man already? No. It wasn't possible yet. They'd only known each other a few days.

Ava grabbed D'mitri's pillow and hugged it close. After everything that had happened, she didn't want to crave him. But the masculine scent still clinging to the soft fabric woke a hunger deep inside her that she knew only he could satiate.

The wind picked up outside, the breeze fluttering the hanging fabric surrounding the bed. Ava drew a deep breath in, hoping the fresh, fragrant air would relax her like before. But it didn't.

Instead, a peculiar tingling heat washed over her, skittering across her every nerve ending. She sat up, thinking she might pace around the room to burn off some of her excess energy, but she stumbled the moment she stood. She caught herself on the hanging fabric and swayed before stepping clear of the bed.

She tried to focus on other things, but her mind grew hazier with every shaky step she took. She sat on the small sofa for a moment. When her vision righted itself, she dropped her head into her hands and sighed. The strange feeling was easing.

Ava rested her head against the arm of the sofa. She needed sleep, but just as her mind eased a little, her entire body shuddered. Something was wrong, and she feared she knew what it was.

She shook uncontrollably, and she was covered in a layer of sweat. Ava forced herself to breathe. She wanted D'mitri because he was the only thing that could calm her, but she didn't want to call out to him.

Determined to try to deal with the situation herself, just like she always had, Ava slid off the sofa and headed for the bathroom to dry herself off. She only got a few steps when her legs wobbled, and a pain shot through her skull and down her spine. She stopped where she was and leaned against the wall.

The second wave hit her, and she curled in on herself. Her breathing came quicker, and her head spun. Another wave washed over her again. Shaky and incredibly nauseous, she stumbled into the bathroom and all but fell to her knees in front of the toilet.

She barely got her head over the opening before the retching started. The heaving seemed to go on forever, but when it finally subsided, Ava let herself slide to the floor. She didn't get much of a respite before another wave began to build.

A knock on the half-closed door startled her, but when she saw Kaela peeking around the jamb, relief washed over her. Ava didn't want anyone to see her in such a vulnerable state, but she also didn't want to be alone.

D'MITRI TORE through the jungle, following the scent of the Naymati. The musky, earthy scent was something his father had warned him about, something Nicolai and Ali had described to him. The scent hung in the air like the morning mist, enraging D'mitri even more when he thought of how close the creature had come to taking Ava from him.

He ran through the thick underbrush, down a path that wasn't really a path. He zigzagged through the jungle, knowing the enemy was gone but hoping to catch the Naymati's scent trail to where he rested during the day.

No such luck though. He reached the river and knew that the Naymati had already crossed it. D'mitri dove in and swam hard for the other side. He dragged himself out and onto the opposite bank. He searched for a fresh scent. But nothing. He had lost the trail.

Angry, he paced up and down the bank, trying to catch the scent once again. Nearly a hundred yards up-river, he caught a faint scent and concentrated, pacing back and forth. But just as he caught the trail, a feeling of dread washed over him.

Ava. Something was wrong.

The moment he reached out to her, D'mitri knew what it was. Her Awakening. The time had come for her jaguar to emerge. He could feel it. Though he was miles away from her, it ripped through him as if it were his own, and it nearly took him to his knees.

Damn it. He was so close to catching up with the Naymati. He could nearly taste the blood of his enemy. He wanted nothing more than to find the brazen male and rip him to shreds. But Ava needed him.

Whatever decision he made, it felt like a loss. Because either way, he failed his mate. If he continued his pursuit, she would be left alone to suffer through her first emergence on her own. If he abandoned the chase of his enemy, he could be there for her when she needed him most. But the Naymati had already scented her. D'mitri had no doubt the vile creature would come for her again.

He didn't have much time to choose, but when Ava reluctantly called out to him through their mate bond, the choice was made for him. He knew she still felt angry with him. But her fear and discomfort overrode that anger. She needed him.

Decision made, D'mitri wheeled in the direction of his

home and ran with all his strength and speed. He only hoped he could reach her in time.

Minutes later, a sharp pain lanced through his gut, making him stumble.

D'mitri, Ava called out to him again.

The almost frantic desperation in her voice made his heart skip a beat. But he steadied himself, leapt a narrow section of the river, and let his mind touch hers with reassurance. *I am coming, Ava. Just breathe.*

Her relief was palpable. Unfortunately, her respite didn't last long. Fear and pain came in waves. D'mitri forced himself to breathe through every crest and fall, all the while reassuring her that he would be with her soon.

No more than a mile away from his home, the mate bond flickered. Ava was fading, and that scared D'mitri even more than when he'd thought the Naymati had taken her. He felt the connection slip away completely just as he leapt onto the balcony and rushed into his room.

His mate's scent filled the space, but the potency tripled when he followed the trail into the bathroom. To his surprise, Ava wasn't alone.

Kaela sat on the floor with Ava's head in her lap. Her slender shoulders slumped with relief the second she saw him in the doorway. "Thank the heavens. I am so glad you made it in time. She is close."

Ava lay curled on her side, her arms tight around her middle, and her body shaking uncontrollably. Close was an understatement. Her jaguar could emerge at any moment.

D'mitri dropped to his knees beside them, and the second he pulled Ava into his lap, the tension in her body eased a fraction. But he wasn't fooled by the lull in her discomfort. He'd been there seven years ago. More was coming. Soon.

D'mitri carried her to the bed and sat down with her. He brushed her hair from her face. Her breaths came in short, panting draws, and the shakes increased again. He hated knowing the pain and discomfort she felt. And how much more she would suffer before the night was over. If he could endure it for her, he would.

Kaela touched his shoulder. "She will be okay, D'mitri."

He looked up into her dark eyes. "Thank you for staying with her. I'm glad she wasn't alone."

Kaela looked down at Ava. "For someone who only recently learned of our nature, she is handling it well. She is brave and strong."

D'mitri stroked Ava's cheek, and as her panting grew heavier, he wondered how much longer she had to suffer. Even as he had the thought, Ava's eyes slowly opened, and she looked up at him.

Soon. It would be soon. Her irises had changed. He'd thought they were beautiful before. But with the iridescent sheen of her jaguar, they left D'mitri speechless. Never had he seen eyes so resplendent.

He knew when the time approached. She didn't have to speak. He saw it in her eyes, and in the way her body grew restless. Her breaths grew more labored, and the crumbling wall she'd erected between their minds finally fell completely.

The wave of pain washed over him like it was his own. It stole his breath and took him back to the night of his own Awakening.

Ava's eyes squeezed shut. She arched in his arms, and

though he could sense her fear and feel her pain through their mate bond, she didn't make a sound. She endured wave after wave without so much as a whimper.

Sliding his other hand over her shoulder, down her arm and back up again, he tried his best to soothe her. *I am here, Amanté. Just keep breathing. It will pass soon.*

Ava drew slow, even breaths, staying surprisingly calm. Until the very end, when a low, growling moan escaped her throat, breaking the silence of the room. Her body pitched to the side, and with a hard shudder, her jaguar emerged.

Of all the times he'd imagined his mate, he never expected her jaguar to be so perfect. She was all tight, lean muscles under the beautiful black coat. Her beautifully frightening face and the four new dagger-like teeth that had emerged. She was quite a sight.

22

Ava opened her eyes to see the faint light of morning through the open double doors of the balcony. The shadow of a male figure stood near the railing, and for a second, she found it a little hard to breathe. The events of the night came barreling through her mind like a freight train. She expected D'mitri to be pissed for quite some time, but when she'd called to him, he had been there for her.

Sitting up slowly, Ava drew the sheet around her, tucking it under her arms when she rose from the bedding. She stepped onto the cool stone of the balcony and saw the muscles in D'mitri's back tense even more. Though she made no sound, he knew that she was there.

"Good morning," she whispered, her throat feeling scratchy.

Without looking at her, he answered in a strange tone. "Good morning, Ava."

She watched his hands grip and release the railing several times, as if he were agitated. She had a feeling he was still angry about the night before, but she'd thought since he'd come back, that he'd stayed with her and helped her through the change, that he was over it. Clearly, he wasn't.

When Ava moved to stand next to him, D'mitri didn't look at her. He just sighed heavily and pushed his dark hair from his face. She was about to ask him if he was all right when he said roughly, "I am sorry for how I behaved."

Ava didn't know what to say. She couldn't tell him it was okay, because it wasn't. He'd surprised her, scared her a little, and hurt her feelings more than anything or anyone ever had. Even as much as her aunt had hurt her, it was nothing compared to the despair she felt over the way D'mitri had treated her, and that had royally pissed her off. She didn't like being vulnerable to anyone, but she'd opened herself to him completely. He might as well have slapped her and spit in her face.

"I was overwhelmed."

"I know the feeling," Ava whispered.

D'mitri tilted his head back and looked up at the sky. Ava's gaze followed. The frothy clouds were aglow like smoldering embers. The oranges and reds feathered over the bottoms of the clouds, accenting the crisp blue of the morning sky. It was beautiful, but it was nothing compared to the way the new light touched D'mitri's tan skin.

A rush of air left his lungs, and his head fell forward. "The fear of losing you…" He looked over at her. She could see the pain and the regret there in his pale green eyes. "Can you forgive me for what I said to you?"

She didn't know why, but she forgave him. The hurt that radiated from him was nearly unbearable. She could hear the rambling in his chaotic thoughts. The pain, the anger, and the genuine regret were too much for her. She knew he was suffering, feeling tremendous guilt over the way he had reacted. It was true. He'd been so afraid of losing her that he didn't know how to react. And in the warm, morning light, they stood next to one another, uncomfortable and unsure of where their relationship headed.

D'mitri held fast to the railing, his knuckles white. Ava could see his uncertainty, but she ducked under his arm to stand between him and the railing. She looked up into his eyes and said with more emotion than she intended, "I forgive you."

D'mitri dropped his forehead to hers. His hand found its way into her wild hair, and with a shuddering breath, he rasped, "Thank you."

Ava looked deep into D'mitri's watery eyes, and she could see that Darien had been right. D'mitri loved her. She didn't understand why it had happened so fast, but she felt the same intensity for him. Touching her fingertips to the edge of his hard jaw, Ava placed a gentle kiss on his warm lips.

"D'mitri," she whispered against his mouth. When he grunted in reply, she slipped her hands into his hair and whispered next to his ear, "Love me."

He lifted his head. His intense eyes met hers, and he cradled her face in his hands. "I have loved you since that first dream of you."

With a faint smile, Ava tugged at the sheet she'd tucked around her. And when it hit the floor, she whispered, "Show me."

D'mitri lifted her to him and carried her back to bed. He took his time, loving her slowly. Thoroughly. He made sure she understood the depth of his love for her, and that she knew it would only continue to grow.

When they lay spent, D'mitri stared up at the ceiling for a long time before he said. "I think it is time to go."

Ava let her head roll toward him. "Where are we going?"

"You must leave the jungle. It is not safe for you here."

She frowned, watching him carefully.

"I will not have you in danger anymore. This ends today."

Ava felt tears come to her eyes. She couldn't believe he would say such a thing after what they'd just shared. She rolled away from him and started pulling on her clothes. She couldn't deal with this roller-coaster of emotions.

Ava froze when D'mitri came up behind her and wrapped his arms around her. He nudged her hair aside with his nose placed a gentle kiss to her nape before he rested his chin on her shoulder. "Share your home with me, meu amor. Let us live there, where it is safer for you, where you are far away from the threat of the Naymati."

Ava closed her eyes and realized that she had completely misunderstood. He hadn't meant that they were over. He'd only meant that he didn't want her in danger anymore. With a heavy sigh, she leaned back into him, relieved that she'd misunderstood.

"What is wrong?"

Ava placed her hands over his. "Nothing. I would be glad to share my home with you."

While Ava finished getting dressed, D'mitri pulled on a fresh pair of pants. She could feel his eyes on her. And when she turned to face him, she could see something else was on his mind too.

Nervous, Ava asked him, "What's going on in that head of yours?"

"You will not like it."

Ava frowned. "What?"

D'mitri slipped his arms around her and drew her close. "I think you should talk with your aunt before we go."

She dropped her head to his chest and sighed.

"You know you cannot leave this undone."

"I don't know if I'm ready for that conversation though."

D'mitri slid a soothing hand up and down her back. "Sometimes we must do things we do not feel ready for. It is time to speak with Lilah."

Ava sighed again. "I know, but what if I can't forgive her?"

D'mitri placed a gentle kiss to her forehead and smiled. "You already have, love."

She supposed she had, but was she ready to talk to Lilah?

"We can think about all that later." D'mitri gave her a gentle squeeze. "For now, let me feed you. I can feel your hunger."

They made their way downstairs to join the others. Ava hadn't realized just how hungry she was until she caught the scent of bacon frying and freshly baked biscuits.

Burian sat at the table, a book in his hand. And Kaela stood at the stove. She smiled at them over her shoulder. "Good morning. How are you feeling, Ava?"

"Better than I expected."

"If you're hungry, this will be ready soon."

"I'm starved," Ava admitted.

Kaela nodded toward the table. "Your cousin left you a note."

Feeling ashamed that she hadn't even thought of Darien since she woke, Ava rushed to the table and grabbed the letter. It read:

My sweet cousin,

I'm sorry I couldn't stay, but civilization just isn't for me anymore. I know Mama will be upset that I didn't come see her. But give her a big hug for me and tell her that I love her.

I hope you and D'mitri are happy together, and maybe one day I will see you again. Until then, take care of that mate of yours.

I love you, Ava.

-D

Ava looked up at D'mitri with tears in her eyes. "That's it?" She swallowed hard. "I mean, it's more than I expected. But it's still not enough."

23

After having breakfast, they told Burian and Kaela their plan to go back to Louisiana. D'mitri was worried about leaving Kaela to take care of his father on her own, but she insisted that they would be fine. She told him that if she needed anything, she could always go to Nicolai or Marius.

Burian completely agreed, telling D'mitri that it was time for him to go and live his life with his mate and stop worrying over his crazy father.

They didn't waste any time. They went back up to D'mitri's room and Ava helped him pack his things. It was well after lunch by the time they finished gathering his necessities. They said their goodbyes to Burian and Kaela, and then stopped by to say goodbye to Nicolai and Ali as well.

DeMario was in the yard when they came up in front of his house. Seeing their clasped hands as they approached, a wide smile broke across his face. "Hello, you two."

D'mitri raised a hand in greeting, and Ava gave a shy smile.

"I will be finished here shortly, and Lilah should be returning from her walk soon. If you are hungry, we have some leftover sandwiches from lunch."

"Thank you. That would be nice. I'm starving."

DeMario smiled and nodded in understanding. "Help yourselves to some food. There are also fresh tomatoes laid out."

They thanked him and quickly made their way into the kitchen, making a few turkey sandwiches. They stood there smiling at one another as they ate.

Ava took an extra slice of tomato from between D'mitri's fingers and laughed when a drop of the juice ran down her chin.

D'mitri leaned down, capturing the droplet before it fell, and then followed the path back up to her mouth. Ava's heart did a funny little flip when he sucked her bottom lip into his mouth and his teeth scraped over the soft flesh as he pulled away.

A groan escaped her throat, and D'mitri's let out a hoarse, amused chuckle.

When he straightened to his full height again, his gorgeous smile faded the second his focus shifted to something behind Ava.

Without turning, she asked, *Is it Lilah?*

Yes. Would you like me to leave you two alone?

She shook her head. *Please stay. You calm me.*

With a faint smile, D'mitri placed a lingering kiss to her forehead before he went to sit down.

"You two seem to have bonded quickly."

D'mitri responded, his tone neutral. "She is easy to grow attached to."

"I know what you mean."

Ava heard a hint of emotion in her aunt's voice, and she wanted to see the expression that went with it, but she was a little nervous. Giving herself time to quell her anxiety, Ava picked at a piece of turkey lying on the platter and popped the small bite into her mouth before turning.

When her eyes met Lilah's, Ava knew the conversation was coming whether she was ready for it or not. Lilah wouldn't let it go until they worked things out. Not talking and being unable to fix things between them had probably upset Lilah. That was one of their rules: never let the sun set on your anger.

Without even preamble, Lilah said, with tears in her eyes, "I've always worried I'd made the wrong decision in keeping this part of your heritage from you. Raising you outside of the Jagara world kept you safe from the fate so many our females have suffered over the generations. But in keeping you away, I robbed you of the joy of connection to our people. To the tribe lands and the jungle. I'm sorry you didn't get to experience a Jagara childhood. And I'm sorry for keeping the truth about your parents a secret. Can you ever forgive me?"

After what had happened with the Naymati, or could have happened, Ava understood her aunt's choices. Sure, she missed out on a lot. But she'd also had freedoms, opportunities, and experiences in Louisiana that she wouldn't have had in the depths of the South American rainforest.

Ava took a deep breath and leaned back against the

counter. "Tia, I know you love me, and I understand you only wanted to protect me, but I still wish you would've told me the truth. All of it."

Lilah exhaled a ragged breath, her chin quivering. "So do I, love."

"It would have been nice to be prepared for all this."

"I didn't realize how close you were to your emergence. I tried to tell you everything the other night, but—"

Lilah came closer. Her hand cautiously hovering between them. After a moment's hesitation, Lilah brushed her fingertips over Ava's jaw, before she cupped her cheek. "Look at you. Glowing."

Ava hugged Lilah. "Promise me one thing. Be honest with me from now on."

"I will."

"And Tia?"

"Yes?"

"I do forgive you." Lilah squeezed her, and Ava closed her eyes. "But you were right. It is dangerous for me here."

Lilah pulled away and looked at Ava's expression. "What happened? Are you okay?" she breathed, carefully looking her over.

"I'm fine. Don't worry. Just a close encounter with a Naymati."

Lilah gasped, covering her mouth with both hands.

"Tia, I'm fine. He never even touched me."

With a voice that trembled, her aunt asked, "What happened? How did you get away from him?"

Ava looked at D'mitri, unsure how to tell her aunt what had happened, that her only son had come to her rescue and then disappeared without even coming to see his own mother.

Tell her, Ava.

Closing her eyes briefly, Ava looked back at her aunt and said, "Darien saved me." When Lilah's eyes grew wide, she continued, "Just as I was approaching the Naymati, Darien came out of nowhere and chased him away."

Lilah breathed, "My boy?"

Ava nodded, watching the tears fill her aunt's eyes.

She sank into the nearest chair. "How is he? Is he well?"

Ava nodded. She could see that Lilah knew she wouldn't see him. She knew Darien wouldn't come. Ava cleared her throat, but she was unable to speak again. She just reached into her pocket and pulled out the letter Darien had left for her.

Lilah read the letter, and with tears rolling from her bright eyes, she smiled up at Ava. Ava knew that this short letter was enough for Lilah, who hadn't heard a single word of or from her son in so long. Just knowing he was alive and well was a huge worry lifted from her. Ava could see her aunt's spirit lift.

"He looked so good, Tia. You would not believe how big he is. He's huge." She looked to D'mitri and then back to Lilah. "He's bigger than D'mitri and taller by several inches."

Lilah's eyes flared. "Good Lord!"

"I know. I couldn't believe it either. The last time we saw him, he was a skinny teenager. But not anymore."

Sadness crossed her features, and she whispered, "My boy is gone."

"No, Tia. He's still there. Only grown. He's a man, but your boy is still in there."

She searched Ava's face for a moment and then nodded, almost reluctantly. "You're right." With a small smile, she added, "Now give me the hug he asked you to give me."

24

Three Months Later…

Ava's kitchen filled with the delicious aroma of sautéing vegetables. She didn't mind cooking, but ever since D'mitri had come to stay with her, she hadn't made a single meal. He'd said he wasn't a cook, but he always came up with the most mouthwatering recipes.

Not only did he cook for her, but in the beginning, he'd fed her and bathed her too. It was weird at first, but when he'd explained that it was tradition among the Jagara to care for their mates during all stages of their Awakening, Ava had accepted it. For a while.

It was nice to come home from work and be pampered. But she was beginning to feel guilty about letting him do so much for her. It was time to speak up. "D'mitri. Can we talk about something?"

He turned to look at her, quickly assessing her. "Everything okay?"

She nodded. "Yes. I just want to say how much I appreciate everything you do for me."

D'mitri's face lit up. "It is my pleasure, Amanté. I am happy to take care of you."

"I know. And I don't want to hurt your feelings, but I think it's time I start pulling my weight around here again."

He tapped the wooden spoon on the edge of the pan and sat it down. When he turned to fully face her, Ava worried she'd still managed to hurt his feelings. After a tense few moments, he sighed and approached her. Brushing the hair that had fallen from her braid, he tucked the strands behind her ear. "I understand, but I need to pull my own weight as well."

Ava smiled up at him. "You do more than your share."

"You work," he argued. "Let me take care of everything else."

Ava shook her head. "At least let me feed and bathe myself."

D'mitri sighed, looking put out. "Fine."

"And we take turns cooking."

D'mitri arched a brow.

"We are partners. We need to share responsibilities." He opened his mouth to speak, but Ava pressed a finger against his lips. "Partners."

D'mitri took her hand and placed a lingering kiss to the palm. "We are mates. Not partners. But yes, I see your point."

"Good. Now that that's settled"—she nodded toward the stove—"you get back to that, and I'm going to get a quick shower."

Ava felt refreshed and revived when she rejoined D'mitri in the kitchen fifteen minutes later. Now that she had someone to come home to in the evenings, she didn't feel quite so weary when she got home from work.

D'mitri always greeted her with a smile and genuine interest in how her day went.

Ava sidled up next to him at the stove. "Smells good."

D'mitri tugged her against his side with his free hand and kissed the top of her head. "It is almost ready."

"Good. I'm starved."

A muffled ringing came from her bag by the door. Someone was calling. Ava extracted herself from D'mitri to go see who it was. It was the middle of the week, so it couldn't be Lilah calling from Keintara for her weekly chat.

Ava frowned when she saw the name lit up on her phone screen.

When she answered, Maggie's chipper voice came across the line. "Hey. How are you?"

"Good. Just about to sit down and eat with D'mitri. What's up?"

D'mitri turned, curiosity drawing his attention to her.

"Okay, I won't keep you long then. I just wanted to update you. I know it's sort of last minute, but something came up and we're moving our wedding up to this next weekend. I don't know if you can make it, but Greg and I would love for you both to come. I can pay for your flight if need be."

"Yeah. I can talk to my boss and get a couple days off. Should be no problem."

"You sure?"

D'mitri nodded and Ava smiled. "Yeah. Absolutely. We'll be there."

"Awesome."

"Is everything okay?"

Maggie chuckled. "Yeah. It's just that my fiancé knocked me up and I don't want to look like a whale when we get married."

D'mitri's brows shot up and Ava's eyes flared. "Oh, wow. Congrats! That's awesome!"

Maggie snorted. "Not so much when you have an August wedding and you are due in September."

Ava laughed.

"Also, I wanted to do it before the morning sickness hits. I want to enjoy my honeymoon."

"Very true."

After a short silence, Maggie cleared her throat. "Anyway, I'll let you go, and we'll see you two next weekend."

When they ended the call, Ava turned to face D'mitri. "Well, that was unexpected."

LATER THAT NIGHT Ava and D'mitri lay facing each other, his hand drifting down her side, over her hip, and back up again. They'd just had the most amazing sex, and even though he was a little unsteady on his feet, D'mitri padded naked into the kitchen to get them something to rehydrate.

The last time Ava had felt so drained was that night with Joseph, but that was for a completely different reason. And not nearly as enjoyable. Hard to believe only a few months had passed. Honestly, it felt like a lifetime ago.

"Who is Joseph?" D'mitri asked from the doorway, his unhappy tone startling her.

Ava let her head roll to the side to see him standing there with a glass of juice. "A friend."

"A friend that you slept with," D'mitri said, making it a statement instead of a question.

"Technically, I guess. But I didn't have sex with him."

D'mitri just stood there, practically glaring at her as if he didn't believe her.

Ava sat up. "I mean, that was the intention at the time, but it didn't play out that way."

He closed the distance between them and slammed the cup down, half its contents sloshing out onto the side table. "You are my woman!"

Ava shot to her feet and crossed her arms over her chest. "Yes, I am. What's your point?"

"How would you feel if I was thinking of another woman after we had just made love?"

She had to admit, he had a point. She hated the idea of him thinking about another woman. Even worse, touching and kissing another woman.

"You kissed him?"

Something in D'mitri's angry tone triggered her own anger. "First of all, that isn't what I was even thinking about. But now that you mention it, why does it even matter? It happened before I ever met you. I'm sure you've kissed other women before me."

"No. I have not."

That gave Ava pause. "Wait. Never?"

D'mitri shook his head. "Why would I when I knew I would have my mate one day?"

In that moment, no matter how aggravated she felt with him, she wished she never even looked at another man before him. "I wish I could say the same. But I do have a past, and you need to accept that. If you can't, this isn't going to work between us."

D'mitri's face fell. "I only just found you, and I already push you away with my jealousy."

With a heavy sigh, Ava sank back down onto the bed. "Look. I watched a friend go through an intense, toxic relationship. It started out with mental crap but escalated to physical abuse. And I refuse to put myself through that kind of shit."

"And you think I could hurt you like that?" The disbelief in his tone made her look up at him again.

"I don't know," she admitted. "I barely know you."

D'mitri sank down in front of her and took her face in his hands. "I would never hurt you, Ava. I might be careless with my words or lose my temper from time to time, but I will never intentionally bring harm to you."

Closing her eyes, Ava forced herself to breathe. She thought she knew that, but after seeing how angry he was about her simply thinking about another man, she didn't know what to believe.

"Ava," he whispered. "Look at me."

When she lifted her eyes again, he continued.

"You give my life meaning. Without you, nothing else matters."

"Then you need to get better control of your temper. My past, no matter how distant or recent, is just that. My past. I am with you. That should be what matters."

D'mitri rested his forehead against hers, his big warm hand resting on her nape. "I apologize for my reaction. I will do better."

Ava let out a long sigh.

After a bit of silence, D'mitri pulled back and looked at her. "Tell me about that night. I will keep myself composed and listen to you."

Ava shook her head. "I don't want to fight with you anymore."

"I want to know. Please, tell me."

She stared up at him for a long moment before she spoke. "Are you sure?"

When he nodded, Ava got comfortable on the bed and sat back against the headboard. He climbed up beside her and waited for her to begin.

"Well, it all started with the dreams, I guess. Then when I met Ali and Nicolai, I was startled. Thinking I was dreaming about another woman's man was one thing, but catching myself daydreaming about him with her sitting right there made me feel like a shitty person."

D'mitri reached over and took her hand. That small gesture gave her the strength to admit to the next bit of information.

"No matter how hard I tried, I couldn't stop watching him and thinking about what it would feel like to have his hands and his mouth on me. And I hated that feeling." Ava reached over with her other hand and traced along D'mitri's knuckles. "So, I had to do something to distract myself from those thoughts and his voice in my head."

"So, you drank to forget."

Ava nodded. "I drank a lot. And by the time Joseph started talking to me, I was already feeling the effects. We had a few more drinks together, and when I couldn't take any more of Ali and Nicolai's affectionate displays, I knew I had to do something."

D'mitri cupped her cheek, forcing her to look at him. "I am sorry you were so confused. If I had known, I would have explained things to you much sooner."

"But you didn't know. And it isn't your fault."

"No. It was your aunt's fault for keeping you in the dark all these years."

She ignored his comment. She didn't want to get into that again. She'd moved on from that and forgiven Lilah for the choices she'd made. Right now, she just wanted to get the rest of the conversation over with.

Taking a deep breath, she continued. "So, after I'd had enough, I took Joseph up to my room. I intended to use him as a distraction, and no matter how much I tried to push through the building guilt, I just couldn't do it. Just thinking about being with him felt wrong. I panicked, and the whole situation made me feel sick. It could have just been the alcohol, but I threw up everything in my stomach."

D'mitri closed his eyes as if he hated that she'd gone through all that.

"After, Joseph cleaned me up and carried me to the bed. Though I don't remember a lot beyond that point, I do know that he stayed with me all night and made sure I was okay. Long story short, we talked about it the next morning, he understood why I had done what I'd done. We ended the conversation by agreeing to be friends even after all that."

D'mitri's gaze grew distant. And after a long silence, he asked, "Will he be there this weekend?"

"Probably. He's one of Maggie and Greg's closest friends."

Ava could see that D'mitri wasn't all that happy about it, but he didn't say more.

25

A va and D'mitri arrived at Maggie's early in the afternoon. After being greeted by the bride-to-be, they were shown to their room to get settled and cleaned up after their trip.

D'mitri showered and then put their things away while Ava took a long, hot bath. She was determined to relax a little before they joined the others downstairs.

They made their way down to the library, where everyone mingled and chatted cheerfully about the coming wedding. There were maybe twenty people total, and Ava recognized most of their faces from the engagement party.

She stood chatting with Maggie and Ali near the piano, while the guys hovered nearby, having a conversation of their own.

Probably an hour later, something in the air shifted. Ava glanced over at D'mitri, wondering if he felt it too. Only to discover that his eyes were riveted on something across the room. Though his mind was closed to hers, she had a feeling what—or who—he'd just seen.

Sure enough, when her eyes followed, she spotted a small group of people talking near the bar. Joseph was one of them. And his curious gaze was trained in their direction.

Ava reached out and took D'mitri's hand, drawing his attention to her. *You okay?*

His eyes flickered back to the group. *I do not like that he is looking at you like that.*

Honestly, he's probably more curious about you. Last time I saw him, I was a bit of a wreck. And now, I have you here with me.

D'mitri didn't answer, but she could hear how uneasy he felt with Joseph's presence. She just wished she could make him more comfortable. Reassure him that there was nothing to worry about with Joseph. Let him see that Joseph was a good guy. And despite one night of what-the-hell-was-I-thinking, Joseph was a friend. Nothing more.

D'mitri looked down at her, his bright green eyes boring into hers. *I hate that he has seen my mate in such an intimate way. That he knows what every inch of your perfect body looks like naked.*

Mostly naked, actually. But she didn't need to point that bit out.

A low, frustrated growl echoed through their mate bond. *That does not help.*

Ava's face heated. She hadn't meant for him to hear the thought. *Sorry.*

D'mitri finally took a calming breath.

Will it make you feel better if you meet him and see that there is nothing between us other than friendship?

No. I do not wish to be near him.

At some point, he's going to talk to us. You can't avoid him all weekend.

I can try.

D'mitri's pouty tone made her laugh. Several people tossed a curious glance their way.

Ava gave his hand a little tug. "Come on. I want you to meet a few people."

He didn't put up much resistance. Instead, he stayed quiet and let her escort him over to the small cluster of friends. Felicia broke away from the group to give Ava a hug. "Ava, it's good to see you again. You look amazing."

Ava offered a timid smile. "Thanks. You too."

Felicia made a sound of protest. "Please. You're practically glowing." She turned her attention to D'mitri and smiled. "It must be this handsome beast of a man."

Ava laughed at her wording, thinking just how right she was. She then turned to "the beast" and introduced him, "Felicia, this is D'mitri."

She offered her hand. "Nice to meet you, D'mitri."

"And you as well, Felicia."

Knowing just how much D'mitri's charm affected a female, Ava ignored the little glimmer that appeared in Felicia's eyes. She refused to react. D'mitri was hers. All hers. Instead, she looked at the others and noticed their curiosity.

She took a step toward them, and Wayne smiled. "Hey girl, how've you been?"

"Good." She smiled.

He turned to D'mitri and offered a hand, "I'm Wayne. You must be D'mitri."

D'mitri reluctantly shook his hand and nodded.

Gareth and Kurt gave a quick nod when Ava introduced them, but Mandy only gave him a polite smile, and Debbie a shy wave. When Ava introduced Joseph, he stepped forward and reached out to D'mitri. "Nice to meet you."

When D'mitri didn't immediately take Joseph's offered hand, Ava felt a hint of panic begin to rise. He only left him hanging for a heartbeat, but it felt like an eternity for Ava. Then he finally took Joseph's offered hand and nodded.

Gareth cut into the awkwardness. "How was South America?"

Ava smiled. Obviously, Maggie had already told everyone her business, which didn't bother her, but she knew D'mitri didn't like it too much. Even if she wasn't hearing his thoughts, she saw him shift uncomfortably. Absently rubbing the inside of D'mitri's forearm, she smiled at Gareth. "Beautiful. I would've stayed if I didn't have to go back to work."

D'mitri squeezed her hand gently.

Mandy spoke up, looking at D'mitri. "I heard from Mags that you haven't been away from South America much."

He nodded. "This is only my second time."

"How do you like Louisiana?"

D'mitri looked down at Ava before he answered. "Though it is far from what I am accustomed to, I like it very much."

"I love your accent," Debbie said softly. "It's beautiful."

"Uh..." D'mitri shifted his weight as if uncomfortable, but politely replied. "Thank you."

THE REST of the evening was a success. D'mitri managed to relax a little and chat with some of the guys while Ava went upstairs with the girls for a while.

The next morning, the two of them took a bath together before they met the bridal party and several other guests in the dining room for breakfast.

The day was long. They rushed around helping Maggie get the last-minute details taken care of and, whenever possible, Ava would find D'mitri wherever he was and steal a kiss or two before tearing herself away to get back to whatever task she'd been appointed.

At a quarter 'til six, Ava made one final sweep before she returned to Maggie's room to inform her that every-thing was in place and ready for the wedding to begin.

Maggie was practically bouncing in place, and Ali had to tell her several times to be still, so she didn't mess up her makeup. The bridesmaids were dressed in deep-burgundy satin dresses that hugged their beautiful curves and brushed against the tops of their feet, allowing just enough of the gorgeous shoes to peek from beneath the hem. They each had their hair twisted into a tight knot at the base of their skulls.

Maggie, though, was even more stunning. She wore the most beautiful gown Ava had ever seen. The top dipped in the middle to show a tasteful amount of cleav-age. The cap sleeves sat slightly off the shoulder. Her already small middle pulled in tighter with a waist cincher covered in small, stitched flowers, each was a tiny white pearl at their center. The skirt of the gown draped over

Maggie's shapely hips and hung in flawless beauty down to the floor as the train stretched out behind her.

Maggie stared at herself in the mirror with a blank expression. Ali asked her in a soft tone, "You okay?"

Maggie nodded without taking her eyes from the mirror. "I'm just thinking about how different this is from what I had planned."

Ali assured her friend. "This is beautiful, Maggie."

Maggie whispered something that only Ali heard. In response, Ali laughed. "Girl, you don't have anything to worry about. Greg is madly in love with you. You should have heard him talking to Nico this morning. He is unbelievably happy. He can't wait to be your husband."

Ava spoke up. "It's true. I heard him bragging about you to the other guys at the engagement party."

Maggie looked at her. "Really?"

Ava nodded and Ali added, "He's looking forward to his life with you and all the kids you two are going to have. You know he is."

Maggie hugged Ali and said something in her ear before pulling away and started to fan her face. Maggie took the tissue Ava offered and smiled through the tears that threatened to spill. "Thank you. For everything. I couldn't have pulled this day off without you two."

Tears stung Ava's eyes as well, but she fought them back.

Maggie cleared her throat. "Alright. Let's get this thing started." She smoothed her hands over her hips and asked, "How do I look?"

Ali chuckled. "You look perfect. Nothing is out of place."

Ava smiled at Maggie. "You really do look beautiful. I

can't wait to see Greg's face when he sees you in that dress."

Maggie beamed. "I can't wait to see him. The man looks good in a suit."

Ava made her way down to the living room and found Judge Crane, telling him Maggie was ready before she found D'mitri at the back of the room waiting for her. She gave him a quick kiss. "You ready?"

When he nodded, they slipped out the double doors. The bridal party was waiting in the hallway. While the others stood quietly chatting, Debbie snickered from behind her bouquet as she watched the flower girl and ring bearer enjoying the candy they'd "found" in her purse.

The soft music started, cuing Ava and D'mitri to open the doors and let the first pair into the room. After they'd moved halfway down the aisle, the next two stepped up. Once all three couples had entered, Ava and D'mitri closed the doors and waited for Maggie to step into place.

When the music changed and the traditional wedding march began, they opened the doors and watched Maggie glide into the room, accompanied by small gasps and whispers as she moved. Ava and D'mitri waited, watching her walk toward Greg, who was in complete awe of his bride.

Ava took D'mitri's hand, and they made their way to their seats. Throughout the entire ceremony, Ava could feel D'mitri's eyes on her frequently, but she focused on the happenings at the front of the room.

When Greg and Maggie were pronounced husband and wife, everyone was on their feet clapping and cheering.

The beaming couple left the room, heading straight for the stairs. Then everyone else slowly made their way into the library for the reception.

By the time the newlyweds returned, everyone had already had a drink or two or, in some cases, more than that.

Judge Crane introduced Maggie and Greg as Mr. and Mrs. Hartwell. Everyone cheered and clapped, and Ava even heard someone belt out a stadium whistle. Looking around, she spotted Debbie standing on a chair with two fingers in her mouth. The whistle cut off short when Gareth snatched her off the chair and dipped her, her back arching over his arm as he planted a kiss on her lips.

A gentle hand on Ava's back drew her attention away from the odd couple, she turned to look up at D'mitri. Before she could say a word, his mouth found hers. He kissed her slow and deep before lifting his head.

Ava forced a breath and smiled up at him. "What was that for?"

D'mitri shrugged a single shoulder. *Just felt like kissing my mate. Got a problem with that?*

"Not one bit."

After the newlyweds shared their first dance, D'mitri tugged Ava onto the dance floor.

He surprised her with his moves, and when the song ended, he stood there looking down at her with the oddest expression.

Unable to read his thoughts, Ava asked, "What is it?"

He whispered, "May I speak with you in private?"

She nodded and let him lead her onto the patio, where the setting sun seemed to make everything glow a beautiful orange red. "Tell me, D'mitri," she said when he stared down into her eyes with a peculiar intensity. One that she hadn't seen in him before.

He took her face in his hands. "This day has forced me

to realize that we have not even discussed marriage for us."

Ava's mind was suddenly reeling at the probability of where this conversation was going, but she could only stand there and stare up at him.

"I have waited a long time for you, and now that you are here, I have been content with just that." D'mitri slid his thumb over her bottom lip before he continued. "My purpose is to be your mate in every way, including as your husband. Why was I so blind as to think you would be happy with only being with me?"

Ava tried to speak, but no words came. She just closed her mouth and shook her head.

"You want a ring on your finger and my name on your wrist. You want the acknowledgement before all our people, and I want you to have it. I want you to be my wife, Ava. Say you will forgive my oversight and accept this humble proposal."

She stared up at him in disbelief.

"Say you will be my wife and make me the happiest man alive."

In complete shock, Ava turned to look out over the garden. She knew it must be beautiful in the summer, but right now, the last remnants of the snowfall from the previous day clung to the bare bushes and trees.

"Ava?" he whispered. When she still didn't answer, D'mitri dropped to his knees before her. Taking both her hands in his, he said, "Look at me."

When her reluctant gaze met his glowing green eyes, she nearly stopped breathing. He looked up at her with such ferocity she thought she might just melt.

"Ahava, Cherished One of the Parmali Tribe and of all

the Jagara people, I ask from my rightful place at your feet, the place where I will always belong, if you would give me the undeserving honor of being your husband."

Ava stared at him in awe of his words. The emotion in his voice and shining in his pale eyes. The sheer love she felt radiating from him was unbelievable. She knew she couldn't deny him. She took a shaky breath in, and he watched her carefully as she shook her head and then sank to her knees in front of him. "You don't belong on your knees, D'mitri."

"Answer me, Ava. Will you be my wife?"

Tears flooded her eyes, and with a beaming smile, she nodded. "Of course I will."

D'MITRI WAS OVERJOYED that Ava agreed to marry him. He didn't care when. All that mattered was that she said yes.

Ava looked over his shoulder and laughed. "I think we have an audience."

D'mitri turned. Several of the guests practically had their faces pressed against the windows. Maggie and Greg stood near the patio doors with Ali and Nicolai, all watching them with wide smiles on their faces.

"Great timing, D'mitri," Ava whispered and then kissed him once more before she climbed to her feet and moved back toward the house.

Halfway to the doors, Ali met them and hugged them both. "Finally!" she squeaked.

"I did not plan to do this here," D'mitri said quietly so that the other guests could not hear. "I did not want to take away from Maggie and Greg's big day."

"Nonsense," Maggie said, hugging him. "My day is almost over anyway. Besides, I was hoping you would pop the question soon. I feel honored that you chose to do it here."

Greg clasped hands with D'mitri briefly and patted his back. "Nothing like a wedding to make a man think about how much his woman means to him."

"Yes." D'mitri smiled, looking at Ava once more before he faced his brother.

With tears in his eyes, Nicolai blinked and cleared his throat, but he didn't speak. He and D'mitri touched foreheads briefly, and then Nicolai gave him a silent nod before they all went back inside where it was warmer.

After a few congratulations, D'mitri tugged Ava out onto the dance floor and ignored everyone else for a long while.

Eventually, they made their way to the bar and stood talking with Kurt and Mandy while they had a few drinks. Apparently, Gareth and Debbie had disappeared. Mandy said she hadn't seen either of them since the reception started.

"They slipped out together about thirty minutes ago," someone said from behind him. D'mitri turned to see Joseph reach for the drink the bartender had just set on the bar.

Mandy's eyes grew wide. "Are you serious?"

He nodded.

When Ava mentioned how they'd been kissing, Mandy gasped. "Really?"

"I saw it as well," D'mitri added.

"I knew he had a thing for her!" Mandy said and poked Kurt, who didn't appear surprised.

"Who has a thing for whom?" Maggie asked, reaching past them to grab another Coke.

"Gareth and Debbie," Mandy answered. "Apparently, they are taking advantage of one of your rooms right now."

Maggie threw her head back and laughed. "I didn't think he'd do it."

Greg frowned. "What?"

"Gareth took my advice and dragged Debbie upstairs," she said happily.

Greg blinked a few times before he said in disbelief, "Debbie and Gareth?" When Maggie nodded, he laughed. "Wow!"

They joked about how everyone in the old crew was with someone else in their little circle, apart from Katelyn and Joseph.

Katelyn looked at him. "You want to give it a shot?"

Joseph stopped the glass on the way to his mouth and gave her a funny look. "Are you serious? That wouldn't be weird for you?"

She shrugged, "No weirder than for you."

He continued to look at her for a few more beats before he shook his head and lifted his glass to his mouth. As he took a drink, Katelyn leaned closer and whispered something next to his ear. Joseph nearly choked, blowing bourbon right out of his nose.

Everybody watched in disbelief, and when Joseph finally stopped coughing, they all laughed.

"What did you say to him?" D'mitri heard Ava ask as Joseph took the hand towel the bartender handed him.

Katelyn smirked as Joseph wiped his face and the front of his shirt. "You don't want to know."

D'mitri was a little curious, but he was glad Ava didn't press.

The others teased Joseph relentlessly, making up what they thought Katelyn had said to him. D'mitri found himself amused by some of the commentary, and even though Joseph took it all in stride, D'mitri saw the moment he grew tired of the razzing. When Joseph turned toward the bar to get another drink, D'mitri almost felt bad for the guy. Almost.

Eventually, the subject moved on to something else. Katelyn tried to play it all off as though the whole thing had been a joke, but D'mitri saw the way her eyes kept finding Joseph no matter where he was in the room.

Eventually, when Katelyn disappeared, Joseph approached Ava and D'mitri again. "Do you mind if I steal Ava for a dance?"

D'mitri wanted to say no. Tell him to stay the hell away from his woman. But seeing the hopeful expression on Ava's face, he held his tongue and offered the guy a tight smile and a nod.

"Thank you," Joseph said before offering Ava his elbow.

Ava slipped her hand into the crook of the guy's arm and smiled at D'mitri. *Yes, D'mitri. Thank you.*

He had best behave.

He heard Ava's sigh as she followed Joseph out onto the dance floor.

———

D'MITRI SURPRISED the hell out of Ava. Though they'd talked about Joseph, she never would have expected

D'mitri to agree to let her dance with the guy. She almost told him no herself, but she had a feeling there was much-needed conversation to be had between them.

"So…" Joseph smiled down at her. "You're going to be Mrs.—"

She laughed softly, feeling some of her tension ease. "Montez. Yes."

Joseph shook his head. "Wow. Ava Montez. It sounds so Spanish."

"It's Portuguese actually. Well, Jagara." She glanced at D'mitri, whose fierce eyes were on the two of them. "Funny, we were both from the same area originally."

Joseph's brows went up. "Really?"

"Yeah. My parents grew up near where D'mitri lives now."

"Small world we live in."

"Tell me about it. His parents and mine were friends. Even Ali's parents were close to mine. Our mothers were best friends from what I hear."

Joseph looked a little distant for a moment. Ava waved a hand in front of his face. When he blinked, she asked if he was okay. "Yeah. I just realized that I never really had a chance with you."

She frowned. "Why do you say that?"

"I can see that the two of you are meant for one another. Just the way you look at him and the connection you seem to have. The way you seem to talk to each other without even speaking. It's amazing." He drew a deep breath in and let it out slowly. "Maybe I will find something like that one day."

Ava couldn't help but notice his eyes strayed toward the sofa near the back wall. The last place she'd seen

Katelyn standing with some of the others. Curious about his earlier reaction to whatever Katelyn had whispered to him, she had to know. "So, tell me. Do you have a thing for Katelyn?"

Joseph hesitated, his expression cautious. "Why do you ask?"

Ava snorted. "That's not a no."

He rolled his eyes.

"I probably shouldn't tell you this, but she's had a crush on you since freshman year of college. She used to talk about you all the time."

The comical way his brows shot up made Ava laugh.

"Don't look so surprised. You're a goodlooking guy."

Joseph's adorably freckled cheeks reddened ever so slightly.

She couldn't help but ask. "Is this a new development for you?"

"Honestly, I've always thought she was cute. But I watched her turn down every guy that ever asked her out, so I didn't bother."

Ava threw her head back and laughed. "You two are so bad. She never said anything to you because she thought you weren't interested."

Joseph stopped swaying completely. "How could I not be? I mean, look at her."

Ava laughed again. "Then what are you waiting for? Tell her how you feel."

"You think I should?"

Ava nodded. "Definitely."

D'MITRI FORCED himself to turn away from the dance floor. Seeing Joseph holding Ava close went against every protective instinct he had. He knew she was fine, that he could trust her, but his mind kept playing out scenarios on what had happened the night Joseph had taken her to her room.

Motioning for the bartender to pour him another drink, D'mitri forced himself to keep his back to the dance floor. He didn't want to listen in on their conversation, so he didn't tap in to her mind. He did, however, keep his mind wide open for Ava. If she needed him for anything, she would let him know through their mate bond.

He could feel her. She was enjoying herself with Joseph, and D'mitri forced himself to remember that this male was only Ava's friend. He just wanted the dance to be over already.

When the song ended, D'mitri finished the drink in his hand and swallowed as he turned to watch Ava stride back to him. But she was still on the far side of the room, and Joseph was looking down at her with such tenderness in his eyes.

A growl rumbled deep within D'mitri's chest. He started toward them. But before he could take three steps, Joseph lowered his head to Ava's, and D'mitri saw red when she tilted her head back as if accepting a kiss.

Pure rage boiled up, and he moved quicker than he should have in front of all those people. He couldn't stop himself. He had to get to his woman and break Joseph's neck for having the balls to kiss her.

26

W hen the song ended, Joseph leaned down and kissed Ava on the cheek. "Thank you. For the advice and the dance."

Ava heard the echoing growl in her mind just as Joseph stepped around her. She knew D'mitri was moving quickly in their direction, and it was already too late. Before she had a chance to turn and head him off, D'mitri struck Joseph in the chest with both hands, knocking him back a few steps. Joseph was shocked. As was the man he fell back against.

D'mitri spoke quickly in his native tongue, so quickly Ava hardly understood what he was saying, but she caught enough of his angry words to know that Joseph was in trouble. When she heard what sounded like "I will rip out your throat," she moved quickly, placing herself protectively in front of Joseph. "D'mitri, stop. What the hell?"

Nicolai appeared out of nowhere and stepped between her and his snarling twin. "Stop it! You are making a scene!" he snapped. When D'mitri didn't respond, Nicolai pushed against his chest, and ordered him, "Outside! Now!"

Ava was frightened not only for Joseph, but also for everyone witnessing the crazy scene, so she was glad when Nicolai forced his brother to take a step back. In shock, she looked at Joseph and whispered, "I'm so sorry."

He shook his head. "I'm fine."

Ava followed the twins as the small crowd quickly parted to get out of D'mitri's path. As soon as they were outside, D'mitri broke away from his brother and began to pace like a caged animal. He moved back and forth across the wide patio, his fury driving his every step.

Ava stood just outside the doors, listening as Nicolai tried to calm his brother. She hated this. She loved D'mitri, but this side of him terrified her. She understood him being unhappy about another man kissing her on the cheek. Especially one she had a history with. But it was how he responded that worried her.

This was the second time he'd reacted with way more aggression than she was comfortable with. She wasn't sure she could stay with someone so aggressive and possessive no matter how much she loved him. The more she thought about it, the more she watched him pace, the angrier *she* became. He was being ridiculous. He had no cause to act this way.

Ava moved past Nicolai, ignoring his restraining hand and stepping in front of D'mitri. "Stop it, now!"

He just stared down at her, his eyes blazing.

"You are being an idiot right now! Look at you!"

He growled.

"Oh, shut up! You are really pissing me off. You know that?" When he just continued to stare at her, Ava shook her head. "I can't believe you would behave like this after the discussion we had. Do you have no control? Do you understand what you could have done? What you *have* done? We talked about this, D'mitri. I can't be in a relationship like this. I won't."

"Do not threaten me, Amanté." His words were so hoarse she barely understood them.

"It's not a threat. I told you, and you didn't listen to me."

"Ava," Nicolai warned. "Do not push him."

She faced D'mitri's brother and snapped, "Don't push him? Are you kidding me? He just pushed me! Now back off! This is none of your business." Ava turned back to D'mitri and said to him, "You pushed me too far, D'mitri. I told you what would happen."

Nicolai spoke up again, "Ava, I don't think—" but he stopped when she glared at him.

Behind her the door opened, and she knew by D'mitri's reaction that it was Joseph. Snarling again, he moved as if to go around her, but Nicolai stopped him. Looking over his shoulder, he warned Joseph. "I would go back inside if I were you."

"I just wanted to try and help. I don't understand what happened."

"You are a fucking man-whore who thought he could take my woman. That is what happened!" D'mitri roared, straining against Nicolai's hold.

Nicolai looked at D'mitri, shocked at his language.

Ava snapped, "I said stop!"

D'mitri stopped his forward motion but refused to take his eyes from Joseph. Ava saw his irises take on the iridescence of his inner jaguar. His focus remained, as if on his prey. His breaths came in short, panting draws, and Ava could see his entire body trembling.

"He didn't do anything, D'mitri. He was just…" She took a deep breath. Her anger quickly faded. She didn't understand why, but she suddenly felt like crying. "I'm not doing this. I told you that I…" She turned her back to him and blinked away tears of frustration.

As she started toward the house, D'mitri asked angrily, "Where are you going?"

Ava faced him again and the calmest voice she could manage, she informed him, "I'm done."

When he only stared at her, she turned back to the house. Joseph asked if she was okay, but she just held up a hand and moved past him as she went back inside. Several people asked if everything was all right, but she ignored them and made her way through the crowd. She went up the stairs to the room she and D'mitri were sharing. He would have to find another place to sleep because he wasn't coming near her the rest of the night.

———

D'MITRI WAS angrier than he'd ever been before, and he didn't understand why he couldn't control himself. Seeing how much he'd upset Ava hadn't been quite enough to shake him, but when she said, "I'm done" and walked away from him, he knew he'd screwed up.

When she'd disappeared inside, Nicolai turned back to him with a perplexed look on his face.

D'mitri didn't know what to say. He was so confused, especially with the sudden calm that settled over him. D'mitri turned his gaze to Joseph and frowned. He should still feel rage toward the man, but there wasn't even the smallest bit of hostility left. With Ava gone, he couldn't care less about Joseph.

"Brother?" Nicolai asked, obviously sensing his confusion.

D'mitri glanced at the house and all the people peering out from the party, which seemed to have all but come to a halt because of the scene he'd made. He was ashamed and angry with himself because he knew he'd embarrassed Ava.

He wanted to go to her and apologize, but he knew the damage was already done. And she'd been dead serious when she'd said it was over. Closing his eyes, D'mitri wished there was a way to fix things. He wished he knew what the hell was wrong with him. He'd thought it was all Joseph, but he realized it was something about Ava that had him so angry before. How was that possible? He had waited years for her, and he loved her more than life itself, but something about her had set him off.

"D'mitri?" Nicolai said, taking a step toward him.

He took a step back and whispered, "Leave me alone." When his brother started to protest, D'mitri shook his head. "Let me go. I need to be alone."

He turned to Joseph and offered him a quick apology before disappearing into the darkness.

ONCE SHE WAS in her room and had locked the door, Ava sank down on the edge of the bed and let out a shuddering breath. Tears flooded her vision, and with the adrenaline beginning to wear off, the shaking set in. She couldn't believe what had just happened. Not even two hours ago, D'mitri had asked her to marry him, and now it was all over. What was she going to do? She didn't know how she could go back to her old life. Not after what she and D'mitri had shared. Still, she knew she couldn't live with a man who behaved so impulsively.

A knock on the door startled her from her thoughts. She didn't care who it was, she didn't want to be around anyone. "Go away."

"Ava. Please open the door."

The sound of Katelyn's soft voice made her squeeze her eyes shut. "I just want to be alone."

After a short silence Katelyn said, "I don't know what happened, but I'm sure everything will be okay."

"It won't," Ava whispered.

"What?" Katelyn asked.

"Nothing. Please, just go."

"Honey, I can't do that. You seemed too upset. Come on. Just let me in, even if it's just for one of my famous make-anything-better hugs."

"Maybe later, okay? I just need some time."

She heard a heavy sigh and her friend's retreating footsteps.

Ava moved to the window and looked out over the yard at the trees beyond. Most of them were bare, but there were groups of evergreens here and there still standing proud in the cold of winter. Something in her wanted to be out there. Breathing in the fresh air. But he was still out there.

Besides, no matter how clear the air, it wouldn't be the same as breathing in the scents of the jungle. And there was no hot, heavy dampness to cover her. And no symphony of the animals to lull her.

Ava didn't know how much time had passed when a soft knock brought her back to the present. When she didn't answer, a gentle, raspy voice broke the silence. "Ava, may I come in?"

It was Ali. And she sounded concerned. Join the club.

With a heavy sigh, Ava spoke up. "Like I told Katelyn, I just want to be alone."

"After what happened, I can understand that. But I need to speak with you."

Annoyed, Ava moved to the door and yanked it open. "'Need' is a strong word. Are you sure you aren't just being nosy?"

Ali's golden brows drew together, and she shook her head. "You don't have to be rude. I'm only trying to help."

Feeling like a total bitch, Ava sighed. "Sorry. I'm just a little edgy."

"You and D'mitri are both edgy. And I have an idea about what's causing it."

Ava crossed her arms over her chest. "I'm listening."

Ali glanced toward the stairs before she met Ava's eyes again. "I'd rather not discuss this in the hallway."

Understanding her caution, Ava stepped aside and let Ali in. If what she had to say had something to do with their Jagara nature, none of the other guests needed to hear any of the coming conversation.

Ali waited for her to close the door before she spoke. "I don't know exactly what's going on with D'mitri, but I will say that whatever that was downstairs, it was not the D'mitri I know."

Ava scoffed. "Then maybe you don't know him like you think you do."

"I know him well enough to know that he isn't acting like himself. And you've been with him long enough to see that too."

Ava looked away from her. She did know that. D'mitri was usually such a sweet, understanding man. He pampered her as much as she'd let him. The furious, irrational beast that she'd encountered tonight was not the D'mitri she had come to know and love.

But there had been signs that something wasn't quite right. His reaction the night of her encounter with the Naymati. The little outburst of anger the night he'd misunderstood her thoughts about Joseph.

Ali spoke again, interrupting Ava's thoughts. "There are things that happen between mates that can be intense sometimes. And I think what happened tonight is one of them."

Ava frowned. "And what exactly happened?"

Ali eyed her a moment. "To put it bluntly, I think your jaguars are restless."

"Restless?" Ava said flatly.

Ali nodded. "You have both been on edge since you got here. I noticed. Nico mentioned it too."

"Great," Ava muttered under her breath.

"We noticed because we've experienced the same. I know I feel antsy when I can't run or swim at least once every couple days. After a week, I'm a wreck. How long has it been for you two?"

Ava hesitated before she answered. "Since we got to Louisiana."

Ali's brows shot up. "That was almost three months

ago. No wonder you two are so moody. Not letting your jaguars out to run can make you irritable and impulsive. But if you go long enough, your jaguar will force its way out eventually."

Well, that was terrifying.

"I'm surprised it hasn't happened before now." Ali looked thoughtful. "Could explain why D'mitri looked so close to shifting."

He truly had. The change in his eyes. His voice. The growling. Ava had seen his jaguar just beneath the surface. Barely contained. And she'd feared D'mitri would lose control completely and his jaguar would break free in front of everyone.

"If you are going to stay in Louisiana, you two need to find a place to go run."

There was nowhere Ava would feel safe doing that. Especially that time of year. Hunting was a big thing where she lived, and she'd rather not get shot at.

Ali searched her eyes. "Look. I know you two decided safety was the most important thing. But maybe it's time to consider going back to Keintara."

Ava's stomach dropped. Sure, she'd love to go back, but the dangers that lurked there gave her major anxiety. She didn't want to ever see a Naymati again. Once was scary enough.

"I know there are risks. The jungle can be a dangerous place. Be it Naymati, poachers, or any other number of things. We all must decide for ourselves if it's worth the risk. Nicolai and I chose not to leave. But I understand where D'mitri is coming from. He has waited a long time for you, and now that he has you, he doesn't want to chance losing you."

Ava sat on the edge of the bed. "But he did lose me."

"Don't say that." Ali sat beside her. "I know the intensity between you two can be a bit much at times, but you have to understand—"

"I can't," Ava interrupted. "I can't be with someone who gives me emotional whiplash. I won't stay in a relationship where I'm treated the way he treated me tonight. The way he treated my friend. I won't."

"All relationships have problems. Especially in the beginning. You just need to learn how to work them out."

Shaking her head, Ava said, "I can't. I'm done with the drama. I refuse to live like that."

Ali sighed. "You've got to understand. It's different with Jagara. And worse for those of us who were raised human. But once you find your balance, it is all worth it."

"Even if it is worth it, how do we come back from what happened tonight? And how do I show my face here again? I've never been so embarrassed in my life."

"I know it seems impossible right now, but everything will work out. You two were born for each other. It would go against nature, against fate, if you weren't together."

Taking a deep breath, Ava said, "I don't think I could face him after all that's happened."

Ali smiled. "Sure, you can. You love him, don't you?"

"I don't like him very much right now, but yes. I love him."

"Then everything will work out. You'll see." Ali put an arm around Ava's shoulders. "I tell you what. Why don't I talk to Nico and see about you and D'mitri coming back with us?"

Ava knew D'mitri would never agree to that, so she nodded. "Sure."

WHEN D'MITRI FINALLY MADE his way back to the house, the partygoers had dispersed. Only Katelyn, Ali, and Nicolai lingered in the library. When he pushed open the door, they all looked up. Nicolai started to stand, but Ali placed a hand on his arm to stop him. They exchanged a few quiet words before Nicolai nodded and Ali rose from the couch. She looked up at D'mitri, "You want something to eat?"

He shook his head.

"You want to come with me while I get something? I'm starving."

He just wanted to go to bed, but Ali clearly wanted to talk to him alone, and he was too exhausted to argue. He sighed. "Fine."

Ali hooked her arm around his and tugged him toward the kitchen. Maybe he could talk to her about Ava and get her advice on how to move forward after the ridiculous incident earlier in the night.

She was a woman of their kind. She would understand the situation better than, say, Katelyn. He had no desire to speak with her anyway. He had a feeling that she didn't like him very much. And D'mitri certainly didn't want to talk with his brother. Nicolai would probably yell at him and call him an idiot the first chance he got.

D'mitri leaned back against the counter and watched Ali pull food from the fridge. Finally, as she began to pile things on a plate, she glanced at him. "How are you doing?"

"I do not know." He watched her spoon food onto her

plate, and after a long silence, he reluctantly asked. "How is Ava? Does she hate me?"

Ali laughed softly and shook her head. "She was angry with you, but she could never hate you. She loves you."

D'mitri didn't miss her use of the past tense. "Was angry?"

She put the plate in the microwave and hit the start button before she turned to face him. "Look, I'm not going to pretend to have all the answers, because I don't. But I do know that you both love each other very much. I also know that no matter what she said, the two of you belong together. You are mates, and it will happen. You will be together in the end, but something needs to change. We've got to figure out what is going on with you and figure out a way to fix it. The only question is what are you willing to do to make things right between you?"

Without a second thought, he answered. "I will do anything I must to make her happy."

A smile barely showed at the corner of her mouth, but Ali's eyes gave her away. She was pleased with his answer, but she still asked. "Would you be willing to go back to the homelands with her if that's what she wanted?"

He didn't want Ava in the jungle or anywhere near the Naymati colony.

Ali must have seen the answer in his eyes, because she shook her head. "Before you answer, I want to tell you something."

"Okay."

She turned to get her food from the microwave. "You sure you don't want some of this?"

When he shook his head, she poured herself a drink. She then explained her suspicions about how she thought that their edginess was because they had been away from the jungle for too long.

"What of the jealousy and the need to rip out Joseph's throat?"

Ali stared at him for a long moment and then shrugged. "I don't know. Maybe you are just a naturally jealous man, but I don't think that's it. Mainly because there were men everywhere who had their eyes on her all night, but that didn't seem to bother you. Maybe you sensed something in Joseph."

"No. It was Ava, because as soon as she was gone, the hostility vanished. I do not understand any of this. She is my mate. How could I feel like that? I was not myself. I had no control. How could I act that way?"

Ali appeared deep in thought for a few moments. She didn't offer any answers. Instead, she crossed her arms over her chest and asked. "So, are you two coming back with us?"

He didn't know. He wasn't sure where Ava stood on the subject. And he didn't have much hope after the way she'd reacted to his earlier behavior. He was afraid to ask, but he needed to know where his mate stood on the matter. "Have you talked to Ava about this?"

Ali nodded.

When she didn't volunteer more information, D'mitri pressed. "And she agreed to go?"

"No. That's why I think you two should talk."

Talk to Ava? After what happened? Even in the haze of his uncontrollable rage, he'd seen how done she was with him. Attempting to talk to her anytime soon was just asking for disaster.

27

Ava woke to the sound of her phone's alarm going off next to her ear. She pawed at it until it stopped shrieking. Then she rolled over, taking the covers with her and pulling them over her head. She knew she needed to get up. But she didn't want to move. She just wanted to lay there and enjoy her solitude a little bit longer.

Five minutes later, her alarm shrieked again. So, with a heavy sigh, Ava forced herself out of bed. While she brushed her teeth, she walked around the room and made sure she hadn't forgotten anything. She even packed D'mitri's things for him and set his bag next to hers beside the door. She only wished that the two of them could already be past the coming conversation.

Once she tucked her toothbrush into her bag, she decided to go down and grab a bite to eat.

She nearly jumped out of her skin when she opened the door and D'mitri fell into the doorway. Apparently, he'd fallen asleep sitting with his back against the door. She wanted to laugh at the surprised expression on his face, but he quickly recovered and got to his feet, turning to face her.

He stood there looking at her expectantly, but when she said nothing, he asked, "Did you sleep well?"

"When someone finally stopped banging on the door and left me alone."

"I was not banging..." he started. Then he took a calming breath before saying, "I am sorry I kept you up. I only wanted to speak with you."

Ava sighed again and tried to move around him, D'mitri reached out to stop her with a gentle hand on her forearm.

The second she lifted her eyes to meet his, she wished she hadn't. She wanted to pull away from him, but the sadness and regret in D'mitri's sea-green eyes held her in place. "I want to apologize for last night. I do not know what came over me, but I feel terrible."

Her gut clenched. She could hear the sincerity in his rough voice, but she wasn't sure if she was ready to discuss what happened. "D'mitri, I'm tired. Just let me do what I need to do, and maybe we can talk later."

He searched her face carefully before nodding. "When you are ready."

His hand fell from her arm, and when he turned to move farther into the room, Ava took a breath and headed downstairs. After the night she'd had, she could really use some coffee.

THE TRIP back to Louisiana was miserable. Ava didn't speak to him or touch him the entire four hours and fifty-three minutes it took to get back to her home. D'mitri hated that the conversation hovered over them, leaving things between them unresolved. But despite everything, D'mitri was glad to be headed back home.

He had missed the jungle these past months, and he couldn't wait to step foot in the homelands again. He knew the enormous relief he would feel the moment he stepped off the plane. And just knowing he would be free to unleash his jaguar would lift a huge weight from his shoulders.

He still worried about the Naymati, of course. He didn't want Ava in danger, but he knew her jaguar needed out as much as his did.

Nearly twenty minutes into the flight, Ali settled into the seat next to Nicolai. D'mitri decided to give the two of them some space, so he moved toward the back, where Ava reclined in her seat. Not only could he see her restless-ness, but as D'mitri sat next to her, he noticed how much stronger her natural scent was.

Frowning, he asked, "Are you well?"

Ava didn't look at him. She just shook her head, and her voice quavered when she spoke. "Please leave me alone."

D'mitri watched the tension in her features ratchet up that much higher, and he knew something was wrong. "Ava, you seem very bothered by something. Is there anything I can do to ease you?"

She sat up quickly and snapped. "You can leave me alone, you stubborn ass!"

Seeing that her eyes had taken on the sheen they got

when she was in her jaguar form, D'mitri frowned. He knew things weren't resolved between them, but he didn't understand her harsh reaction either. When D'mitri reached out to touch her, to try to calm her, Ava slapped his hand away and snarled, "Don't fucking touch me!"

Confused by her sudden defensiveness, D'mitri wondered why her jaguar was showing so close to the surface. He sat back, giving her a little room to breathe. Ava immediately got to her feet and paced the limited space the small jet afforded. Something was wrong. Her reaction wasn't just because of her irritation with him.

The need to comfort her overwhelmed him, but when D'mitri took a step toward her, Ava swiped at him with her claws and bared her lengthened teeth again.

Before he could even react, Nicolai stepped between them and placed a hand on D'mitri's chest. "Stop pushing her, brother."

Ali squeezed past them both and spoke softly to Ava, who didn't take her eyes from D'mitri. She just kept staring at him with an intensity that he had never seen in her before.

"Leave her," Nicolai said. "Come sit with me."

D'mitri took a step back but kept his eyes on Ava as she continued to glare at him.

"D'mitri, look at me." When he finally shifted his attention to his brother, Nicolai said, "Come on. Give her some space. She just needs you to back off for now."

Blinking, D'mitri shook his head. "I did nothing."

"I know. She just feels a little crowded, but she will be fine. Let Alessandra talk to her. She needs a few minutes of girl talk, okay."

D'mitri looked over his brother's shoulder only to see

that the women had disappeared into the back room of the plane and closed the door. His eyes met Nicolai's again, and he asked, "What did I do?"

Nicolai smiled. "Nothing that every other male hasn't tried since the beginning of time."

AVA PACED BACK and forth across what small distance the tiny room allowed before Ali said, "Come and sit with me."

Ava shook her head. "I can't."

As she made another pass, Ali sighed. "Look I know what you're going through right now. I know what you're feeling, but pacing in such a small space will not help. Trust me. It's only agitating you more." When Ava threw her an aggravated look, Ali nodded to the bed. "Please sit."

Ava didn't want to sit. She wanted out of the plane and away from everyone. Especially D'mitri.

"I'm pretty sure I know what's going on with you, and I can help."

With a heavy sigh, Ava sat on the end of the bed next to her. "So tell me."

Without even a hint of easing her into it, Ali said, "You are entering your breeding cycle."

Ava stared at her for a long moment, unsure she'd heard her right. "My what?"

"Breeding cycle." Ali repeated.

Ava blinked. "Tell me that it's not what it sounds like."

"Several times a year, Jagara females come into their cycles. They are much the same as a human woman's cycle, but we only get three or four a year. That makes it more intense. Not only because we have fewer but also because of our jaguar side. You are being testy with D'mitri because your jaguar senses that she isn't ready for mating."

Ava frowned.

"I think maybe that's also what was wrong with D'mitri. His jaguar probably sensed the change in you and became territorial. I don't understand why he wasn't that way with every man there, but I think maybe he was aggressive with Joseph because he perceived him as a direct threat. As competition."

Ava shook her head. "That's ridiculous. He knows better. We talked about that."

"That may be true, but a male doesn't see or think logically when his woman is in her cycle."

"So, it's like being in heat." When Ali nodded, Ava sighed and added sarcastically, "Awesome."

"I know it sucks, but it will get better. Once you figure it all out and learn the signs, you can plan accordingly in the future."

The thought of all this happening again made Ava want to scream. Or claw D'mitri's eyes out, even though it wasn't his fault.

"And something I didn't think about until now, it may go deeper than I thought."

Great.

"With the mate bond, your emotions can affect each other. Your scent grows. He gets territorial. You get irritated. He feels your frustration, and he gets more worked up."

Ava nodded. "And everything continues to escalate.

Makes sense, but it's so infuriating. I hate not being in control of my own body."

Ali placed a gentle hand on Ava's shoulder. "You will get through this. You'll see. By the time we land, you will feel better. And after a good run, you will want nothing more than to roll around in the grass somewhere with D'mitri."

Ava shook her head. "I just want him to stay away from me. This is so embarrassing."

"I understand how you feel right now, but it won't stay that way much longer. Trust me."

28

Ava felt like she was going insane. It didn't matter than Ali had told her how normal it was, Ava still felt embarrassed. The words "breeding cycle" made her cringe. As did knowing that she was, for lack of better explanation, in heat.

Ava wanted to deny it, but she felt the effects. The achy, overheated feeling. The need to rip D'mitri's clothes off and take what her body craved from him. Yet still feeling the urge to claw out his eyes if he came near her. What a confusing, frustrating load of crap. How could she feel such drastically contrasting things for one man?

Lying back on the bed, she closed her eyes and tried to focus on anything but him, but images kept flashing in her mind—images of the two of them intertwined, sweat beading on their skin, D'mitri holding her down, marking her...

Ava. D'mitri's deep voice echoed in her mind.

She sat up when she felt him move to the door again. Every sensation in her body amplified by his closer proximity, and she wanted to scream. She couldn't take much more. But what could she do? She had nowhere to go. No escape.

Let me in, Ava.

Closing her eyes, she sent back to him, *Leave me alone.*

"That is not what you want," he whispered from the other side of the door. "Let me in, Amanté."

Shaking her head, she rasped against the door, "Go away." She hadn't even realized that she'd moved from the bed, but now she stood with her hand against the door and her cheek pressed to the cool surface. "I don't want you near me."

But you do, my sweet female. You want me with you... in you. I feel your need like it is my own.

With tears of frustration in her eyes, Ava hissed. *Stop it!*

Why? I can ease your discomfort. All you need to do is open the door.

Please, D'mitri. This is so humiliating. All I want is.... She took a shuddering breath. *Just leave me alone.*

D'mitri whispered from the other side of the door. "I am sorry. I know this must be hard for you, but you do not have to be embarrassed."

"D'mitri, please let me get a grip on the situation."

He didn't say another word to her. He left her to her thoughts.

Several hours later, they reached their destination. Ava stayed barricaded in the bedroom until Ali knocked on the door. "The boys are already outside. I can walk out with you if you like."

Ava appreciated the gesture. She almost told Ali to go without her, but why delay the inevitable?

Flipping the latch, Ava eased the door open, and Ali offered her a gentle smile.

As soon as she approached the open door of the plane, Ava felt the pull. The scents hanging in the jungle air called her. She itched to run. Her jaguar clawed for the surface. She tried to fight the feeling, but the need was too strong. The moment her feet touched the ground, she couldn't deny it any longer. Without a single word to the others, Ava kicked off her shoes and jogged toward the tree line.

No one said a thing to her. None of them tried to stop her. And that felt freeing.

She plunged into the thick foliage, feeling the strain melt away little by little. Her mind let go of all the tension that had built up over the last few months. All the animosity she felt toward D'mitri after what had happened at Maggie's. And everything else that she couldn't even recall in that moment.

She paused long enough to shed her clothes. Freeing herself from the confines of her own body, she let her jaguar emerge with a joy so shocking that she wanted to cry.

D'MITRI WATCHED as Ava disappeared into the jungle. He wanted to go after her, but he wasn't sure she wanted him to follow her. He thought being off the plane and away from her scent would ease his need, but when D'mitri smelled the jungle, his wild side reached for the surface—

wanting out, needing out. Forcing his voice to remain calm, D'mitri reached out to Ava. *May I join you?*

He sensed her slowing her pace before she answered. *Take your time. I'm enjoying myself.*

His heart leapt in his chest. She hadn't told him no. Before D'mitri could stop himself, he responded. *You will enjoy yourself more when I reach you.*

To his surprise, a soft, flirty laughter echoed in his mind. *Then come and get me, wild man.*

His body surged. He could feel his jaguar clawing for the surface and he couldn't hold back any longer. He needed his mate. And he needed her now.

Ali cleared her throat, drawing his attention. "We'll take your things to your house."

D'mitri looked to his brother for encouragement.

Nicolai smiled. "Go get your mate, brother. Everything will be fine, I promise you."

D'mitri thanked them both and jogged into the jungle, his focus now fully on Ava. Her scent guided him on the right path. She hadn't taken a trail. She'd created her own, tearing through the dense foliage and hopping buttress roots until she found a well-traveled footpath.

A mile or so later, D'mitri came upon her discarded clothes. He gathered them up and brought the fabric to his nose. The jolt of arousal that shot through him nearly took him to his knees. Her scent was even stronger than it had been in the confines of the plane, and he knew without a doubt that Ali and Nicolai were right. Ava truly was in her breeding cycle.

If his uncharacteristic behavior over the last couple days hadn't been obvious enough, his body's reaction to her ever-increasing scent certainly convinced him.

D'mitri stripped out of his own clothes and let his jaguar emerge. He padded along the trail, following her lingering scent and the images in her mind.

He knew when she slowed to allow him to catch up. His body grew more impatient for hers by the second, and he knew he needed to try to make things right with his mate before he found her.

He nudged at their mate bond again. *Ava, I want you to know how sorry I am for my behavior before.*

Without even a beat of hesitation, she answered. *Don't worry so much, D'mitri. I forgive you. Just come and get me. We can talk later.*

Do not tell me that, he growled. *I may not be so tame when I reach you.*

A husky purring echoed in his mind, and she rasped, *I can only hope.*

He nearly stumbled when she pushed into his mind the image of the two of them intertwined, rolling in the tall, soft grass near the water's edge.

Ava headed for their favorite swimming hole. And being so in tune with her thoughts, he knew she was excited by his pursuit.

D'mitri knew when she reached her destination, and it didn't take him much longer to get there. He slowed just before he broke through the trees. When he stepped into the open, Ava stood near the ledge in her jaguar form, peering down at the water below.

She looked over her shoulder, and when their eyes met, D'mitri knew she wouldn't make his claiming her easy. He would have to work for it. It was only natural that this knowledge made him want her even more.

Sinking into a crouch, Ava pretended not to look at him

while he slowly prowled closer to her. His body screamed with the need to be inside her, and his jaguar was desperate for hers.

He cautiously moved closer, and she stayed where she was. He could see her body tense as he drew close enough to feel her body heat. And just as his front paws settled on either side of her, his beautiful mate hissed and lunged from beneath him.

Her scent drove him insane with the need to take her, and for the next forty-five minutes, neither of them said a single word to the other. Many times, when D'mitri was close enough, she would hiss or growl, swiping at him before she moved away again.

Finally, when Ava crouched in the lush grass near the ledge, D'mitri cautiously lowered his much larger body over hers, licking at her spine, urging her to relax under the ministrations of his rough tongue. She seemed to ease, and just to be sure she didn't get away if she panicked again, D'mitri settled his open mouth over her nape.

Sure enough, Ava tried to move away, but he clamped down and growled softly, warning her not to move. She started to fight him, but when he held her still and surged into her overheated body, she stilled, crying out with a wild, feminine sound that made the beast inside him roar.

Ava's mind reached for his, and when D'mitri heard her intense pleasure and the answering tremble in her body, his control shattered. He surged into her again and again, losing himself in the feel of her beneath him. When he felt his seed spill into her, D'mitri pulled himself from her, quickly leaping away as she wheeled around, swatting at him with her claws fully extended.

They lay ten or so feet apart, Ava watching him with

her wild, intense eyes for a long time. No coherent thoughts came. Just raw animal instincts, so when she turned her back to him again, D'mitri knew she was ready for another round.

They repeated this many times until they lay panting side by side. Ava let her jaguar slip away and she returned to human form, exhausted.

D'mitri was unsure how he felt when he saw the marks he'd left on her neck and shoulders. He didn't know whether to feel bad about the blood oozing from the multiple wounds or if he was proud of the marks he'd left, knowing that anyone who saw them would know she was his.

AVA LET her head roll toward D'mitri. He lay next to her, still in his jaguar form, panting as hard as she did. The deep connection she felt with him was like nothing she'd ever imagined. She thought it would be weird to be with him that way, but it wasn't. The two of them together in their jaguar forms was just as natural as it had been in their human form. Only, oddly, more intense.

Are you well? D'mitri asked.

Ava nodded, forcing herself onto her side to face him.

His eyes went to the place he'd bitten her. *Will you let me clean you?*

"Yes," Ava replied hoarsely and watched from under heavy lids as D'mitri eased closer.

Her eyes drifted shut when his warm nose touched her neck. Ava closed her eyes, sighing as his wet, rough tongue slid over her skin. D'mitri took his time licking the blood from her, and when he whispered in her mind for her to turn over, he continued unhurriedly caressing her skin until it was clean of all blood.

By the time D'mitri settled next to her, Ava was so relaxed that she almost fell asleep. When he laid a heavy paw over the small of her back, D'mitri rested his head on her bare ass.

Ava smiled, thinking how strange it was to lie there with him like that. He snuggled closer and lazily drew his tongue over the curve of her backside. She couldn't help herself. She laughed out loud.

What is funny, Amanté?

She giggled. "That tickles."

And this? He moved lower, sliding his tongue along the crease where her leg met her bottom.

Gasping, Ava rolled over, pushing at the massive black cat.

D'mitri's pale green, iridescent eyes slid over her, and a growling purr rumbled up from deep inside him. *Where do you think you are going?*

Ava breathed. "What are you doing?"

D'mitri moved over her again. He crouched low, the soft hair on his belly brushing her naked skin. After an intense stare, D'mitri lowered himself as he shifted back to his human form.

Seeing his face like this, Ava suddenly felt a little embarrassed about what had happened between them.

"Do not," D'mitri whispered. "That was pure beauty." When Ava shook her head and closed her eyes, he caressed her cheek with the back of his hand. "Do not be ashamed of what we did. It was raw and untamed, but it was love."

Ava lifted her eyes to meet his again, and when D'mitri

smiled, she could see the truth there. He was right. Unhindered love shone down from his bright eyes, and Ava knew that no matter the issues they had, things were going to be okay again. She only wished that they could remain in the jungle forever.

"We can," D'mitri whispered while he stroked her cheek. "We will. A Naymati threat will not run us from where we belong, from our home. Not again."

Ava searched his gorgeous face. "Our home?"

D'mitri nodded. "If you will still have me as your friend, as your lover, and your mate, I would be overjoyed if you chose to stay with me in my home. And make it yours as well."

Ava stared up at him for a long moment, searching his expressive face before she shook her head. "I will only agree to that if you promise me one thing first."

A flash of panic lit his eyes. "Anything, my love. What do you ask of me?"

"Promise that you will still be my husband too."

With a relieved breath, D'mitri took Ava's face in his hands and kissed her fiercely.

29

Ava settled into D'mitri's life, feeling good about the way things were going between them. The last weeks had been great, but all the lazy days were getting to her. Sometimes Ava caught herself wandering around the house or out in the yard, but there was only so much exploration you could do before you knew a place like the back of your hand.

Sometimes she would wander into D'mitri's shop and sit quietly, watching him slave over whatever piece of furniture he worked on. At the moment, he sanded a long, curved piece of wood. He was so focused on his task that he hadn't even noticed her standing in the doorway.

Ava could tell how much he loved what he did, and she was in awe of his incredible talent. She could sit for hours watching him. But lately, she often grew restless. She wished she had a talent or even just a hobby that she could dive into when she felt fidgety.

D'mitri sat up straight, stretching his arms over his head, drawing Ava's attention to his thick muscles. When he saw her standing just inside the open doors, he smiled. "Hello, meu amanté."

"Hey."

She'd tried to keep the weariness out of her tone, but D'mitri still noticed. "What troubles you?"

She couldn't tell him what was on her mind because she didn't want him to think it had anything to do with him or her surroundings. The jungle was great. She loved it there, and she loved D'mitri, but part of her missed her old life. She missed her job, her house, and her friends.

D'mitri rose from his workbench and made his way over to her. When he stepped close, Ava leaned back against the doorframe and looked up at him.

He brushed her cheek with his fingertips. "Tell me what bothers you."

"Just restless."

"Do you need to go for another run?"

Ava shook her head. "I need something to keep me busy. I need a hobby. Or a job."

"I can teach you how to carve."

Ava smiled up at him. "Thanks, but that's your thing. I need something of my own."

D'mitri's attention shifted to something over her shoulder. "Everything okay?"

Ava turned to see Burian standing just outside. He held out a cordless phone. "A call for you. Jameson Ferro."

Frowning, Ava took the phone, wondering what reason her old boss could possibly have for calling her.

D'mitri didn't look all that thrilled with the interruption. But he stepped outside to give her some privacy.

She brought the phone to her ear. "Jameson?"

"Hi, Ava. How are you?"

"I'm good. You?"

"Things are well overall. Busy as usual. My new assistant is settling in nicely."

"That's good."

He chuckled. "She isn't you, but she's a good fit, I think."

"I'm glad," Ava admitted. "I still feel bad for not giving you more notice."

"No worries. I understand life was changing for you, and we all need to adapt as things around us shift. And I'm good with change, Ava." He was quiet for a moment before he added softly, "I do miss you though."

"I'm sure you do," Ava laughed softly. "Did you ever make a decision on the Delcheki offer?"

"I've given it serious consideration."

Ava's brows shot up. "Really?"

"Yeah, I know. But I think you were right. I think it could be good for Ferro Corp."

Ava chuckled. "Did I say that?"

"Yes, you did. And I trust your judgment. That's part of the reason I'm calling. I'm meeting with Delcheki in a couple of days to check things out at the facility. And I know you don't work for me anymore, but I wanted to ask a huge favor."

"What kind of favor?"

"Will you go with me? Be a second set of eyes and ears?"

Ava was a bit taken aback.

"I understand that you don't like him. But neither do I. I just don't know if I can be unbiased because of his connection with my father. I would trust your judgment on this more than my own."

Ava rubbed her forehead. Jameson was right. She didn't like the guy at all, but Jameson was her friend, and she wanted to help if she could. "Where is the meeting?"

"I'm staying in Rio da Cidade. The facility where we are meeting is about an hour south of there."

Dropping her hand, Ava stared outside. "That's only a few hours from here."

Jameson laughed. "Nice."

Grey Delcheki was a real creep, but he was a smart businessman. If he was still determined to partner with Ferro Corp, this new venture into medical research must be important to him. And Ava was curious as to why.

Besides, it would give her something to make her feel useful again. "Okay. I'll go."

———

D'MITRI STOOD in the doorway, watching as Ava dug her bag from the back of the closet. He didn't want her to leave. And even though he sensed her reluctance, she'd told her old boss she would go. "I do not understand why you agreed to do this."

She moved into the bathroom and gathered her toiletries. "Because taking this contract would be huge for him and his company."

D'mitri crossed his arms over his chest. "What does that have to do with you? You do not work for him anymore."

"I know. But he's my friend and I want to help."

"You have your own life here with me now. Why is he asking this of you?"

Ava turned to face him, a tiny little frown creasing her

brow. "What is this, D'mitri? Why are you acting like a jealous teenager?"

D'mitri scowled at her. Jealous? He just didn't like the idea of his mate dropping everything for another man. Someone who was no longer a part of her life.

Ava released a tired sigh. "Look. I was his assistant for five years. He trusts my judgment when it comes to this sort of thing. I'm just going to feel out the situation for him, offer up my opinion, and then come back home. That's it."

"I do not want you to go." D'mitri didn't know what else to say or how to explain to her how he felt. Hell, he didn't even know for sure.

"It's only for a couple days." Ava leaned back against the sink and gathered her hair into a loose knot at her nape. "I would ask you to go too, but I know you have your commissioned piece that you need to finish."

That much was true, but D'mitri didn't care about a piece of furniture for someone else when his mate was leaving him to do a favor for another man. Maybe he was jealous. Or maybe he just didn't trust anyone else to protect her if something happened. Especially not a human. Even if the guy was a friend of hers.

"What else am I going to do while you're working? It's not like there's much for me to do around here, and like I started to tell you earlier, I'm going stir crazy."

"I can take breaks and we can go for more runs."

"That's not enough, D'mitri. I need to feel useful. You can understand that much, can't you? Wasn't that one of the things you struggled with in Louisiana?"

D'mitri growled, his frustration overwhelming him. "That was different."

Ava drew a deep breath and let it out slowly. "D'mitri, I love you. I really do. But I'm getting a little crazy just sitting around doing nothing all the time."

"You are with your mate. Does that mean nothing?"

"Of course. And I love being with you. But this has nothing to do with you."

D'mitri snapped. "It has everything to do with me!"

Ava let out a frustrated little growl. "I'm just helping him out. It's not like I'm getting my job back."

"But that is what you want. That's what you've been moping around about."

Ava looked at him like he'd lost his mind. "First of all, I haven't been moping. I'm going crazy. And yes, actually, I do wish I could have my job back. I'd love to have everything I used to have, but that's not happening, is it."

Her sharp words cut him deep. His heart breaking, D'mitri searched her face. "You want your old life?"

Ava nodded.

"You are not happy here with me?"

Ava frowned hard. "That's not what I'm saying. I miss my old life, my job, and my friends, but I love spending time with you and watching you work on your furniture. I just need more, D'mitri. I need something to do besides just sitting here with you and playing the good little wife type all the time as if there's nothing else in the world. I need some me time. Some time to feel useful. Can't you understand that?"

D'mitri's heart ached when her words registered. Forcing himself to speak, D'mitri said, "I understand I am not enough for you."

Ava cringed at his words and quickly corrected him. "That's not what I'm saying either."

Feeling his composure slip, he snarled, "That is exactly what you are saying."

Ava stepped up to him and jabbed a finger against his sternum. "Don't snarl at me."

D'mitri gripped her wrist. "Do not poke me."

She jerked her hand from him and snapped. "Then stop being a dick! What the hell is your problem?"

"My problem is that my mate prefers to be with another man rather than be with me."

"You know what? At the moment, yes!" Ava admitted, her tone harsh. "You're being an irrational asshole."

Not wanting her to go, not wanting her to be near the man she seemed to have such an uneasy feeling about, D'mitri took charge and stepped close to her. With assertiveness in his voice, he told her, "You are not going."

Ava was having none of it. She just lifted her chin and informed him. "Yes, I am."

"No, you are not!"

"Watch me." Ava growled back at him before she pushed by him and left him standing alone in the bathroom.

AVA FOUGHT BACK the urge to scream or punch something. She really wanted to punch D'mitri, but that wouldn't do any good. It would likely only hurt her hand.

That hardheaded man was going to be the death of her. She couldn't believe what an ass he was being about this. It was a trip that would probably only take half a day, and he was acting like she was never coming back.

Ava moved across the room and grabbed the phone.

"Jameson Ferro's office. May I help you?"

The chipper voice irritated Ava, but she said as politely as she could, "May I speak with Mr. Ferro, please?"

"He is on an important call at the moment. May I take a message?"

Ava drew a breath. "Actually, maybe you could help me with this. He has a meeting in a couple of days, and I was wondering which hotel he's staying in."

The woman hesitated. "I'm sorry, I can't give out that information. But if you'd like to have Mr. Ferro call you back, I can give him a message."

Ava blew out a breath. "Alright. Could you just tell him that Ava Brayda called?"

"Oh." The woman's tone changed. "Ms. Brayda, can you please hold?"

Ava frowned. "Sure."

Not thirty seconds later, she came back on the line. "I'm putting you through to Mr. Ferro now."

Before she could reply, there were a couple of beeps and a click before Jameson answered. "Ava. You needed something?"

"Yes. I was just wondering what hotel you are staying in once you get here."

"The Marriott. Why?"

"I wanted to get a room there."

"Alright. I will have my assistant call and reserve a room for you as well."

"Thanks, but I'll—"

"No, I'll take care of it," he insisted.

"You really don't have to do that. I plan to leave soon. I wanted to get there a day early and spend some time relaxing a little before the meeting."

With a hint of laughter in his voice, Jameson said, "A little alone time with your man to relax you for the meeting?"

"No," Ava answered flatly. "D'mitri isn't coming with me."

Behind her, the bedroom door shut with a little too much force, making her jump. There was a pause before Jameson asked, "Is everything okay with you two?"

"Yes," she lied.

"How's three days?"

"That's great, but…"

"No buts," Jameson said firmly. "I asked you to come. I'm paying."

Knowing he wouldn't take no for an answer, Ava sighed. "Fine. Thank you."

"Was there anything else you needed?" When she said no, Jameson's voice softened a little. "Are you sure you're okay?"

"Yes. I'm fine, but I have to go. I need to pack. I'll see you when you get here."

"See you soon."

Ava hung up the phone and exhaled a ragged breath. She wasn't okay. She just didn't want to think about it right now. She just wanted to get her stuff and get the hell out of there. She could think later.

D'MITRI RETURNED FROM HIS RUN, and after getting something to drink, he went up to his room to find Ava gone and a note on the bed that read:

I'll be gone for a few days. I hope that allows you plenty of time to pull your head out of your ass. —Ava

D'mitri dropped onto the edge of the bed and forced himself to breathe. Ava really had left him. He'd hoped some time alone would've helped her calm a little, but obviously it hadn't. She had taken advantage of his absence and packed her things.

Looking at the open closet, D'mitri could see that she'd wasted no time. She'd been in such a hurry to leave him that she hadn't bothered to close the door.

His first instinct was to go after her, but he didn't even know where she was. Besides, if she wanted to be away from him so badly, he'd give her some space. She'd be back in a few days. Hopefully.

va stood at the floor-to-ceiling windows with a glass of wine in her hand. She'd ordered a bottle in the hopes of taking the edge off. But after only three sips, she realized she didn't have the stomach for it.

She sat the glass on the table beside her and stared out over the treetops at the setting sun. All she could think about was D'mitri. They were supposed to be fated mates and have this cosmic, epic bond. But they just couldn't catch a damn break. Their relationship had been nothing but one big roller-coaster ride. She knew every relationship took work, but it felt like every time she thought it was going well, something happened to screw it all up.

She understood that D'mitri was protective, and he could be possessive at times, but occasionally he went overboard. This was one of those times.

She couldn't believe that he thought her need for more meant that she didn't want to be with him. Why couldn't he understand that she wasn't accustomed to sitting around doing nothing? Yes, the lovemaking, running in the jungle, and cooling off in their favorite swimming hole were all great. But she could only take so much relaxation.

Ava turned away from the window and sighed. As big as her room was, it still felt claustrophobic. She had to get outside and get some fresh air, or she was going to lose her mind.

After slipping her shoes on, Ava made her way downstairs and wandered the gardens. All the exotic flowers were beautiful, but they made her think of the neglected garden at D'mitri's home. Which, in turn, made her think of D'mitri. Again.

Frustrated, Ava followed the stone path, through the garden and around to the far wall at the back of the property. She needed to run. That's the only thing that would help at this point, and it couldn't happen in the confines of the hotel's fence.

She glanced up at the sky. Still plenty of daylight left for a quick run.

Ava hopped the rough wall and moved into the jungle. She let her senses reach out and she took in her surroundings. The sights, scents, and sounds were the perfect distraction. She found a narrow path and as she fell into an easy jog, the suffocating feeling began to fade.

She gradually increased her pace until she ran flat-out down the trail. She let the anxiety slowly seep out of her as she barreled through the jungle, running until she stumbled across a wide, beautiful pool. She had to stop and admire it for a bit. Not only to take in the breathtaking view, but because her legs felt like rubber, and she needed a break.

Ava dropped to the ground near the water's edge. It was unbelievable. The center was a deep emerald green, the shallower parts a rich aquamarine, and the rim of the calm pool a pale green. The same shade as D'mitri's bright eyes.

Though surrounded by the magnificence of the jungle, Ava couldn't fully enjoy it. Because no matter how upset she was with him, she wished D'mitri was there to share it all with her.

Ava didn't know how they would work things out, but one thing was certain, their relationship was doomed to fail if something didn't give. If they couldn't figure it all out and compromise, she'd just have to go back to the way things were before he'd come into her life. After every- thing they'd shared, she didn't want to live without him.

Tilting her head back, Ava looked up at the thin sliver of visible sky above her. So much for a quick run. She'd been so deep in her thoughts that she didn't notice how fast night approached. Could she make it back to the hotel before the darkness fully set in?

The thought of encountering a Naymati again made her shudder. She never wanted to see another of those terri- fying creatures again.

Forcing herself to her feet, Ava began walking back in the direction she'd come, hoping she'd be able to find her way back again. She hadn't gone very far before she became abruptly aware that she was not alone. She stopped moving and searched the foliage around her.

As if she'd manifested him, a man stepped onto the trail a few yards in front of her. The very sight of him made her heart race. Ava knew he wasn't the same male as before, but he was no doubt a Naymati.

Her eyes drifted over his tall, lean frame. She took in his odd, angular features, his pale skin, and equally pale hair. His eyes were as dark as the other male's. Still, there was something different about the way he looked at her.

"Hello." His low, deep voice was marked with the strange, yet beautiful accent of his people.

Ava backed away, angling toward his left, hoping to find a way around him and get back to the hotel, where it was safe. Moving off the trail, she continued to back away from him, making a wide circle around him, hoping to reconnect with the path behind him.

But then he moved toward her.

Ava's heart skipped a beat.

He paused, holding his hands up and said in a soothing tone, "I did not mean to frighten you." When she continued to move away from him, his eyes shifted to something behind her. "Please stop. I will not harm you."

For some reason she wanted to believe him, but her instincts screamed that she was in danger. And knowing he had the ability to make her listen to him, to do anything he said, Ava turned to run. She made it maybe three steps before the ground dropped from beneath her feet. She tried to right herself and grab for the ledge as she fell, but her finger slid over the loose earth, finding no purchase.

One moment she was falling. The next, a cool hand gripped her wrist, stopping her descent. Before she had a chance to fully register what happened, she found herself standing on solid ground again, her body pressed tight against the Naymati.

Her breath caught in her throat, and she tried to pull away from him. But he only held on tighter. "Calm. Do not run again. I will not harm you."

She stared up at him, her eyes wide.

"Promise you will not run."

Ava saw something in his eyes that she couldn't explain. A genuine concern for her safety. And though she didn't trust him, she reluctantly nodded.

He stared down into her eyes for a long moment before he slowly released her and took a couple steps back. Instinct demanded she get to safety, but part of her knew she needed a plan. She had to better observe her surroundings before she acted again.

It felt like the bottom dropped out of her stomach when she saw the deep ravine a few paces away. With the darkness creeping in around them, she could barely see the bottom. And only then with her Jagara eyes.

Feeling dizzy, she caught her balance on the tree beside her and forced herself to take slow, calming breaths. Things could have turned out much worse.

The tall male shifted uncomfortably, his hand reaching out as if he wanted to steady her, but he didn't touch her. "Are you hurt?"

Ava shook her head. At least, she didn't think so. Maybe a couple scrapes on her hands and forearms. But other than that, she felt fine. Just a little in shock at how close she'd come to dying. And the little tingling unease in the back of her mind. She needed to get out of there, and back to the safety of the hotel.

She eyed the Naymati for a long moment before she whispered. "Thank you for not letting me fall."

The Naymati bowed his head. "You are most welcome." When he lifted his dark eyes again, he added, "I am Tynan. What is your name?"

"Ava."

"You should not be here, Ava. It is not safe for you."

Though he had just saved her from what would have

no doubt been a horrifying fall to her death, Ava still didn't trust him.

"This," he said, nodding toward the ledge, "would likely have killed you, but it would be much more pleasant than what fates await you at the hands of my kind."

Ava's heart thudded hard, and she forced a breath. "If you're trying to put my mind at ease, that is the wrong thing to say to me."

"Sweet female," Tynan said, taking a step closer to her. "I am no threat to you. But others of my kind are. You must leave here."

Ava frowned. "And you're just going to let me go?"

He nodded. "But I ask that you allow me to accompany you back home."

Yeah. No. She didn't want him to know where she was staying. He might come back for her. "And if I say no?"

"No matter. I could not allow you to go alone, and I am sure your male would not like it if you did." Tynan laughed, startling her. "I am sure he would not like it if I walked with you either."

"Definitely not."

"Then let us go," Tynan said as he motioned for her to lead the way. "It will ease my mind if I know you are safe with your people again."

Ava didn't move. She wasn't about to tell him that her people were not around. That she was alone in Rio da Cidade. Instead, she asked him, "Why are you helping me?"

Tynan hesitated a moment before he answered. "Because you look very much like someone I once knew. The fate she suffered affected me in ways I would never tell another of my kind."

Ava frowned. "Why? What happened to her?"

"She and her male were made an example of. Because he hid her from the others, keeping her to himself, she was killed in front of the entirety of the Naymati people, and he was banished by his brother. To make matters worse, they did not allow him to keep his child. They told him if he ever returned, they would kill the boy as well."

Ava's heart ached for the man. But mostly for the boy. "How terrible."

"Yes." Sadness crept into Tynan's dark eyes. "I have never understood why my people treat females as only a means of furthering our numbers. I always felt a female should be treasured because of her rarity among our kind. But that has never been the case in my lifetime."

"That's why you want to help me?"

Tynan nodded. "I do not want you to share the same fate as that female."

Ava's stomach turned when a thought came out of left field. Could the female have been her mother? No one really knew what happened to her. Was it possible that this had been her fate? Had her mother been taken by the Naymati male and murdered by the others when they found out?

Ava had to know. "You said I reminded you of her. Obviously, she was Jagara." When Tynan nodded, Ava steeled herself and asked. "How long ago did she die?"

"Twenty cycles ago," Tynan said without hesitation.

Twenty? Maybe the female he spoke of wasn't her mother after all. Ava's mother had died almost twenty-four years ago, but to be certain, Ava asked, "Are you sure?"

"I remember it well. It was the eve of my ninth birth celebration."

Ava turned back to him and asked in disbelief, "You were that young? And you watched her die?"

"Yes. As I said, it was a lesson to everyone." Tynan shifted his weight, his gaze darting around them.

Ava glanced around, reaching out with all her senses, but she didn't feel anyone or anything else near them except for the animals. Frowning up at him, she asked, "What is it?"

"I will feel much better when I get you out of Naymati territory."

Yeah. She knew the feeling. She'd had no idea she was in their territory. She'd just assumed he'd wandered into Jagara territory.

TYNAN ENJOYED the silent company of the petite female as they moved through the jungle toward a location known only to her.

When he had first seen Ava, he'd thought her presence was a trap of some kind, but after scenting the area and smelling no other, he'd made himself known to her.

The feeling that his father had told him about—the feeling the Jagara caused in his kind—was much stronger than Tynan had expected. He hadn't recognized it for what it was until it was too late. Now that he had her close to him, her scent amplified the feeling. But he somehow pushed it aside, determined to get her back to her own people.

When they finally approached the central river, Tynan hesitated. He'd been told all his life not to cross this river. This was the first time he'd even been close to it, and he normally wouldn't have come this far, but something compelled him to stay with her.

When Ava noticed he'd stopped, she watched him for a moment, her entire body going visibly tense as she looked around. Once she'd determined there was no threat nearby, she turned back to him. "What's wrong?"

"That river marks the Naymati/Jagara border. If I cross it, I will be in Jagara territory, a place I told myself I would never enter."

A slight frown touched Ava's brow as her odd eyes moved over the water before she focused on him again. "You don't have to come any farther."

Tynan stared at her for a long moment, struggling between everything he'd ever been taught and the need to stay with her to make sure she arrived home safely.

"I'm sure I'll find my way back from here," Ava added.

Tynan forced a hard breath and shook his head. "I cannot leave you until I know you are safe."

"I'm safe in Jagara territory." Even as she said the words, he could see that she didn't fully believe it.

Tynan shook his head. "Just because I know better than to cross to Jagara territory does not mean others of my kind will obey the law. In fact, I am sure most do not when given the opportunity. Especially now that it is rumored that the current generation of Jagara is entering their breeding years."

Ava's eyes flared. "Yeah. If you're coming, let's get moving. I suddenly don't want to be out here anymore."

Once they crossed the river, Tynan grew nervous, but they picked up the pace a little. And when they finally approached the stone wall separating them from the tall human building, Tynan stopped near the tree line.

Ava turned to him. "Thank you for walking with me."

Tynan searched her beautiful, hauntingly familiar face. "Thank you for trusting me and for allowing me to accompany you. You do not know how relieved I am that you are safely home."

Ava thanked him again.

"Pleasant resting, Ava."

She gave him a tentative smile. "Goodnight, Tynan."

"Yes, it has been," Tynan whispered to himself as he watched her move across the small clearing and hop the fence.

Ava was one of the most beautiful creatures he had ever laid eyes on, and it saddened him that he would probably never see her again.

31

Ali smiled as Violet made content little sounds as she wiggled her chubby little toes and occasionally kicked to splash the warm water. Violet loved the river as much as her parents, but she oddly hated baths. Grandi had said happily many times that the little one was wild at heart, and it would take much to tame her when she grew older. But Ali didn't mind. She was just glad she didn't have to raise her daughter in the city.

Ali looked up when she heard someone walking leisurely along the trail, slowly approaching her. She grew still and, as if she too sensed Ali's unease, Violet grew quiet as well. Ali couldn't see anyone yet, but she breathed the air in, and when the familiar scent came to her, she smiled.

As he came into view, Ali greeted him. "D'mitri. It's good to see you."

"It is good to see you too. How are you?"

"As well as can be expected with Nicolai away," Ali

laughed. "I've discovered this to be the only thing to calm her when she's upset."

D'mitri crouched near the water's edge as Ali moved closer to him. He smiled down at the two of them. "A true Jagara."

Ali chuckled softly. "Watch this."

She lifted Violet, but the second the water no longer surrounded her, she let out a high-pitched shriek and kicked her chubby little legs.

The surprised look on D'mitri's face made Ali laugh. And when she lowered the angry little monster back into the water, Violet instantly grew quiet. Ali lifted her again, and Violet let out another shriek.

D'mitri let out a loud belly laugh when Ali lowered Violet's feet back into the water. "A true Jagara, indeed."

Ali snorted. "This time when I lift her, will you take her? Otherwise, we'll be here the rest of the day."

D'mitri held out his hands, happy as always to take his niece. When Ali lifted Violet from the water, sure enough, the piercing cry came again. But as D'mitri lifted the little one to his chest and began speaking softly to her in his native tongue, Violet grew quiet and snuggled close, just like she always did. She really did love her uncle.

And the feeling was mutual. Ali loved that her little one had such a strong bond with D'mitri. And as she watched D'mitri closed his eyes and laid his cheek against Violet's damp curls, she knew he felt the same. He visibly relaxed as he rubbed her little back and continued speaking to her.

Ali could see that her sweet brother-in-law needed the connection in that moment, just as much as Violet did.

Something troubled him. And Ali wondered if it had anything to do with Ava's absence.

Climbing from the water while D'mitri was occupied, Ali pulled her clothes on before turning back to him. While it was natural for their kind to be nude much of the time, she'd never fully embraced that freedom around the others.

Once dressed, Ali invited D'mitri inside for a bite to eat. He declined the food, but he did follow her into the kitchen and sat at the table with Violet while Ali grabbed a snack.

"So," Ali kept her tone casual as she settled into the chair across from him. "Where's Ava this morning?"

D'mitri looked at her, something drifting over his expression before quickly vanishing. "That is why I came to see you. I need your advice."

She arched a brow. "Okay."

Shifting his weight, D'mitri asked with a slightly anxious tone, "Has there ever been a time when you were not happy here—with Nicolai? Have you ever felt like he was not enough for you? Like you wanted more?"

Ali shook her head. "No."

D'mitri sighed. "You don't ever miss your old life?"

Understanding where this conversation was going, Ali asked, "Did Ava tell you she felt that way?"

D'mitri nodded.

Ali drew a deep breath and sat back in her chair. "She actually said you weren't enough for her? That she wasn't happy with you?"

He shrugged. "More or less."

Ava eyed him carefully. "Those were your words?"

D'mitri looked down at Violet, who now lay sleeping in his arms. "Maybe."

AVA HAD SPENT most of the day trying to relax, but all she could seem to think about was the Naymati male. Tynan had saved her life last night. He hadn't tried to take her or hurt her, which went against everything she'd been taught about his kind. He'd seemed concerned that she was out there alone in the jungle, and he'd walked her back to the hotel to assure her safety. Was he only trying to gain her trust, or was he truly different from the others?

The phone rang, startling Ava from her thoughts. Relieved for the distraction, she answered. "Hello?"

"Good evening, Ava."

"Jameson. Hey."

He chuckled. "You sound much more cheerful than the last time I spoke with you. I take it your time has been relaxing."

"More or less."

"Well, I'm calling to see if you would like to join me for dinner."

Ava checked the clock. It was nearly six. "Sure. What time?"

"Now, if you're up for it."

She glanced at her blue-striped pajama pants and frowned. "Um, I'm not exactly dressed for dinner."

"No matter. I was thinking of ordering in. I would love nothing more than to kick off my shoes and share a bottle of wine with you."

Ava laughed. "Yeah, I think I could use a few drinks."

"So as far as dinner," Jameson asked, "is there anything specific you want?"

"Not really. Just whatever is on the menu."

Jameson laughed. "Alright. My room or yours?"

"My room is fine."

"Excellent. I'll see you shortly."

Less than ten minutes later there was a knock at her door. Standing on her toes, Ava looked through the peephole, and when she confirmed it was Jameson, she opened the door for him.

He hesitated, his eyes sliding over her before he smiled. "Hey."

Ava nervously looked down at herself and then back to him. "What?"

Jameson shook his head. "It's just that in all the time I've known you, I've never seen you without your heels. I hadn't realized you were so…" A small smile of amusement pulled at the corner of his mouth before he finished, "…petite."

Ava rolled her eyes.

"Just an observation."

Jameson followed her into the main room and sat in the armchair while she settled on the couch again.

As Ava tucked her feet beneath her, Jameson smiled. "You look so different like this." When Ava frowned, he explained, "Your hair has grown so much."

"Yeah," she said nervously, pulling the chaotic mess back from her face. "And it's a little wild. The humidity brings out the natural curls, and I can't do anything with it."

"I like it. It suits you."

Ava laughed. "You have no idea."

AFTER DINNER, Ava and Jameson sat out on the balcony with a bottle of wine. He didn't mention it, but he noticed she hadn't eaten much. Truthfully, she'd barely touched her food. But he didn't point it out. He just sat in the decently comfortable patio chair and updated her on the goings on in his life. She looked like she needed the distraction.

They talked about work, his new assistant, and the woman he'd met at a client party two weeks ago.

"Is she potential Mrs. Ferro material?" Ava asked with a playful smile.

Jameson hesitated, unsure how to answer. He and Sara had only been out to dinner a handful of times. She'd let him kiss her on the third date, but that was as far as things had gone.

He couldn't ignore the fact that something about her felt different. Not only was Sara the most beautiful woman he'd ever seen, but he felt a deeper connection with her already than he'd ever felt for his ex-wife.

He didn't want to jinx it, but what was the harm in admitting, even if only to Ava, that the thought had crossed his mind. "Possibly."

"Good. Even if nothing else, at least you're getting laid."

A little thrown off by her comment, he laughed. "Yeah."

Ava poured herself another glass of wine and leaned back in the chair. Propping her bare feet on the bottom rung of the railing, she sighed. Jameson watched as she stared up at the darkening sky. "What are you thinking about?"

Ava looked over at him, a sad smile on her pretty face. "D'mitri."

"You want to talk about it?"

Ava held his gaze for a long moment before she set her glass on the little table between them and leaned forward in her chair. She was quiet for so long Jameson figured the answer was no.

He sat forward in his chair and searched his friend's profile. "I know it's none of my business, but I've never seen you like this, and it worries me. Are you not happy here? Are you not happy with D'mitri?"

Ava shook her head. "It's not like that. I love it here. I love being with D'mitri, but I'm having trouble adjusting."

Jameson frowned. "What are you having trouble adjusting to? Is it the difference in pace?"

Ava nodded. "That's part of it. The last weeks have been like a long vacation. It's been great, but I'm ready to get back to work. I can't sit at home and do nothing all the time. I'm too used to staying busy."

Jameson nodded. "I can understand that."

"He doesn't," Ava said softly.

"You are from different worlds, Ava. It's going to take some adjustments on both your parts."

Ava nodded. "I know. I wish he could understand that I need more than just to be happy with him. He didn't even want me coming to the meeting."

Jameson frowned. "Why?"

Ava shrugged, but he could sense that wasn't true. She knew. She just didn't want to talk about it.

She let out a shuddering breath and stood. When she

moved to stand near the railing, Jameson set his glass on the table and followed her. He stood beside her, and when she didn't look at him, he asked, "You okay?"

"I'm fine," she quavered before clearing her throat. "I just really hate fighting with him."

Jameson leaned forward, resting his forearms on the railing. Without warning, an uncontrollable sob broke from Ava's throat, and when Jameson looked at her again, she had tears streaming down her face.

"Hey, don't cry." Jameson shifted uncomfortably. "I'm not good with tears."

Ava laughed roughly. "Then you picked the wrong subject."

"I'm sorry."

Ava's chin quivered. "It's barely been a day, and I already miss him."

"Hey," Jameson said as he moved close to her. "Come here."

Ava let him pull her into his arms, and the moment she wrapped her arms around him, another sob broke free of her throat. Jameson hated seeing her like this, but he could do nothing but hold her until her sobs stopped.

D'MITRI HAD SAT for over an hour listening to Ali take sides with Ava. She'd explained to him that though she enjoyed being a wife and a mother, her writing was still a big part of her life. She used that to occupy her free time, so she didn't go crazy from being inactive.

Ali also explained how different Ava was from herself and how even though she didn't miss her old life, she could understand how someone as independent as Ava might.

D'mitri thought long and hard about that. Ali had to explain that Ava's need for more had nothing to do with him, that it was simply a matter of needing to keep her mind busy because she wasn't used to living such a simple life.

He could see how someone who was so accustomed to always being on the go could grow anxious when forced into such a slow-paced life.

Feeling bad for not recognizing Ava's needs, for denying them when she had told him so herself, D'mitri knew he had to apologize to her. He had to let her know how important she was to him, how much he needed her in his life, before his behavior finally pushed her beyond the point of forgiveness. He'd done enough since they'd met to make any normal woman want to leave, to just walk away. And Ava was right. He had been an irrational asshole, making the entire thing about himself when it had nothing to do with him.

D'mitri was worried Ava might not give him another chance, and even though Ali had advised him to just give Ava her space, to let her have a little time to do something that didn't involve her being up his ass, D'mitri had to go to her. He had to see her. He had to apologize for not seeing what she needed and providing it for her the way a good mate should. He needed her to know he would try harder to make her as happy as she deserved to be.

No matter what Ali had told him, and no matter how much she'd assured him things would be all right, D'mitri didn't like the silence between him and Ava. Having his mate not speak to him through their mate bond was unsettling.

So, against his better judgment and Ali's advice, D'mitri decided to make the trip to go see his woman. He needed to talk to her. He had to tell her how sorry he was for all the things he'd said, to tell her how much he loved her, and how much he wanted her to come home.

But when he arrived at the hotel, he thought maybe he'd made the wrong decision. She wasn't alone. And seeing her in the arms of another man stole his breath.

He knew Ava was angry with him, but seeing her cry over what had happened between them was devastating. His heart broke when he heard her say how much she missed him and then began to sob against her old boss's chest.

D'mitri wanted more than anything to be the one comforting her, but he knew what she needed more than she needed him in that moment. Ali had been right. Ava needed space.

D'mitri could see how important it was for her to do something that didn't revolve around him. She needed her job, and he knew he had to make that compromise for her.

AVA PULLED AWAY from Jameson and wiped the tears from her face. She sniffled. "I'm sorry I broke down like that."

Jameson gave her a sympathetic smile. "It's all right. Sometimes you just need a good cry."

Ava snorted.

He rubbed her arm. "I'm sure everything will work out."

She looked up at him. "And if it doesn't?"

"It will."

Ava drew a ragged breath and exhaled slowly.

"Hey. Why don't you go take a nice hot bath and then crawl up in the bed and get some sleep?"

Ava let out a rough laugh. "Yeah, that sounds like heaven right now."

"Come on." Jameson gathered up their glasses and the wine bottle.

Ava followed him back inside and watched him set everything on the coffee table before he turned to give her a hug. Ava pressed her cheek against his chest and whispered, "Thank you."

Jameson gave her a gentle squeeze. "Goodnight, Ava."

After seeing him to the door, Ava flipped the latch and leaned back against the door. She closed her eyes and exhaled a ragged breath. She couldn't believe she'd let her emotions get the better of her. And in front of Jameson, no less.

It had been good to see him, but she was glad she was alone again. She'd hoped he would be a distraction from the shit storm that was her life, but she should've known he would bring up the one thing she didn't want to talk about, the one thing she didn't even want to think about.

Pushing away from the door, Ava knew a long, hot bath was just what she needed, so she made her way into the bathroom. After finding the perfect temperature, she quickly undressed and climbed into the rising water.

Sliding down against the sloped back, Ava propped her feet beside the faucet and watched as the steaming water flowed into the deep tub with a roaring sound that reminded her so much of her and D'mitri's favorite swimming hole…only not nearly as loud.

They'd had so much fun, had so many enjoyable moments at their swimming hole. Thinking about all the times they'd gone there together made Ava miss him. She even missed all the teasing thoughts he'd sent to her. Who was she kidding? She missed his voice in her mind, no matter what he was saying.

Ava missed speaking to him as well, but as angry as he'd been when she left, she wasn't sure she wanted to test that connection again just yet. She couldn't face his anger again. Especially in that moment. She felt too raw.

She was hurt by his inability to see her needs. What if he couldn't understand? Did that mean there was no hope for them? She always had hope that anything was possible, but now she wasn't so sure. Could she walk away from him forever because she wanted a career? Or could she give up everything just to be with him? She loved him. She really did. Still, she wasn't sure she could do that.

The thought of never hearing D'mitri's voice in her mind again, of never having that connection again, broke her heart.

Ava refused to keep sitting there fretting over that stubborn man while her fingers and toes pruned in the rapidly cooling water. She'd cried enough for one night. For one lifetime, honestly. So, she pulled the plug and climbed out of the tub.

Once she'd dried off and dressed in her comfy pajamas, Ava moved into the bedroom as she towel-dried her hair. She turned on the TV, hoping to find something to watch, but as she turned to throw her towel onto the dirty clothes pile in the corner, she frowned. A small purple flower and a folded piece of paper lay on her pillow. How had she missed that? It hadn't been there earlier. And knowing that someone had been in her room while she was unaware was more than a little disturbing.

Cautious, she looked around the room, searching every nook and cranny. Once satisfied no one was there, Ava made her way back over to the bed and picked up the folded piece of paper. To her surprise, it was a note that read:

Ava,

You were right, and I am sorry I did not see what you need. Though I deserve whatever anger you hold, I hope you do not give up on me.

Forever yours,

D'mitri

She sat down hard on the edge of the bed, and with tears in her eyes she held the note to her chest. Not only had he come to her, but he'd left her the only words she needed to hear from him.

32

The trip home seemed longer than it was because, throughout the entire three and a half hours, all Ava could think about was D'mitri. What would he be like when she finally got home? Would he be happy to see her? Would he pull her into his arms and tell her how much he missed her? Or would he be distant and as unsure as she felt over how their reunion would go?

Many scenarios played out in her mind. Especially ones where he was still angry with her. But when she finally got home, none of those played out. The house was quiet. She saw no one as she made her way through the hall and went upstairs with her bag.

After putting her things away, Ava stood in the center of the room. The last few days had done her some good, but she was so glad to finally be home again. She'd missed D'mitri terribly, and standing there in their room, drawing in his familiar scent, she felt the tension ease a little.

Still reluctant to speak to him through their mate bond, Ava set out to find him. She did a quick search of the house, and when she found no one, she wondered where everybody was. She figured D'mitri was likely in one of three places. Either wandering the jungle, at their favorite swimming hole, or in his shop slaving away on some piece of furniture.

Ava made her way outside, and as she started down the path leading toward D'mitri's workshop, she spotted Burian. He stood in the middle of the long-neglected flower garden with a sad expression on his face. Ava stopped and watched him for a long moment, wondering if he was okay, but when he wiped at his eyes and turned, his expression lightened instantly. He gave her a bright smile and quickly approached.

"It is good to see you home." Burian gave her a gentle hug and put her at arm's length. "D'mitri has been miserable without you. Maybe now he will finally eat something and get some rest."

Ava frowned up at her father-in-law. "He's not been sleeping or eating?"

Burian shook his head. "Probably no more than you have."

The knowledge in his eyes made Ava wonder. Was she that transparent or was it simply expected for mates to be miserable while apart.

She really hadn't eaten much because her stomach just never seemed to settle. She'd end up feeling sick any time she tried. Besides, the only thing that appealed to her— food or otherwise—was being with D'mitri again.

She hadn't slept well since she'd left, and when she had slept, it hadn't been restful. She woke many times throughout the night, and each time she'd taken a while to settle down enough to go back to sleep. Being away from D'mitri had been miserable.

Burian gave her a gentle smile and nodded toward D'mitri's shop. "Go to him."

Without another word, Burian turned and headed the opposite direction.

Ava continued down the path and, as she approached the open double doors, she heard the familiar sounds of D'mitri hard at work.

She drew a steadying breath and stepped into the doorway. D'mitri's powerful body hunched over his worktable. His brows were drawn tight, a look of pure concentration on his gorgeous face as he chiseled away at the piece of dark wood in front of him.

Ava stood there watching him work, admiring the way his muscles flexed and released as he carved at his latest project. The way the light caught the beads of perspiration on his golden skin took her breath away. He was the most beautiful man she'd ever seen, and she loved him with every fiber of her being.

Ava could smell him from where she stood. Sawdust, clean sweat, and the raw mouthwateringly male scent that was all D'mitri.

His hands suddenly stilled. His head came up and his nostrils flared as if he'd caught scent of something as well. When he turned his head in her direction, Ava nearly stopped breathing. D'mitri was gorgeous, as always, but he looked exhausted. The dark circles under his eyes made his pale-green irises appear brighter than usual.

They stared at one another for a long moment before Ava cleared her throat. "Hi."

D'mitri set his tool on the workbench. Without looking

away from her, he straightened to his full height and turned to fully face her. "How was your time away?"

His careful tone gave her pause, but Ava swallowed hard and answered. "Informative."

D'mitri shifted his weight, the restless movement drawing her attention. Was he still angry? No. He was worried and waiting for her to make the first move.

Ava had never felt so awkward in her life. Not knowing what else to say or do, she nodded toward his workbench. "You've been busy."

"Yes."

His hoarse reply made her heart ache, but she pushed the feeling down and asked, "May I see it?"

When he nodded, Ava forced herself to move farther into his space. As she stepped close to him, she could see D'mitri tense. But when she saw what he'd been working on, her breath caught in her throat.

"It is not finished," D'mitri said nervously.

Shaking her head, Ava reached out and ran her finger tentatively over the intricate grooves in the wood. "This is beautiful already."

At the center of the piece lay two jaguars that faced one another, their foreheads pressed together in the classic Jagara display of affection. Ava had seen his carvings before, but this—even unfinished—was the best thing she'd seen him do yet.

"I tried to finish before you got home, but..." He trailed off when Ava looked up at him again. He drew a shaky breath. "It is for you. A small representation of my love for you."

The sincerity in those words made her heart ache, and

she managed to speak around the lump in her throat. "Thank you."

D'mitri shifted uncomfortably, clearly unsure what to say or do next.

With tears stinging behind her eyes, Ava whispered, "I missed you."

The relief that danced over his features washed over her as well. With shaky hands, D'mitri reached for her, taking her face between his rough palms. "I have missed you too."

To her surprise, he dropped his mouth to hers and pressed a gentle kiss to her parted lips.

AVA HAD ONLY BEEN GONE three days, but it seemed like an eternity had passed since D'mitri had last held her. Though she was the one who'd just returned, the feel of her soft, sweet mouth against his made him feel as if he was the one coming home.

Ava's arms came around him as she stepped in closer, and D'mitri released a ragged breath. "You do not know what being apart from you did to me."

Ava pressed even closer. "If it's even half of what I felt being away from you, I never want to do that again."

D'mitri cupped the back of her head and pressed his forehead to hers. "Then let us not do that again if we can avoid it."

Ava nodded.

D'mitri moved a hand down the curve of her spine, over the small of her back, and gripped her firm bottom.

The groan that left her throat spiked his temperature, and D'mitri claimed her mouth with a hot kiss.

The kiss seemed to go on forever, but when Ava pulled away, D'mitri growled. He wasn't ready to stop. He wanted more.

Apparently, Ava wasn't done either. She pushed him back toward the sturdy bench he'd made a few weeks ago. And when she told him to sit, he sank onto the hard surface. Ava looked him in the eyes and said breathlessly, "I want you inside me. Right here. Right now."

D'mitri ripped open his pants, and his suddenly painful arousal sprang free.

When Ava's starburst eyes widened, she yanked up her skirt and ripped off her lace panties. With the way she looked at him, D'mitri knew there wouldn't be time to savor her. Proving him right, Ava grabbed ahold of his throbbing shaft and sat hard on him, taking him all the way into her.

Their simultaneous cries echoed off the ceiling, and D'mitri knew everyone within a mile could hear them, but he didn't care. He was with his mate again, and she felt like heaven and hell all rolled into one.

Ava rode him hard and fast, never once breaking eye contact with him. When they both exploded with the most intense orgasm either of them had ever experienced, D'mitri pulled her hard against him and held her tight until their breaths returned to normal.

D'MITRI CARRIED Ava up to their room and made love to her slow and easy. Then they lay curled together in their bed with D'mitri's big body surrounding her. Ava smiled to herself when he nuzzled closer and release a contented sigh as he tucked his free hand between her legs.

They lay for a long time, listening to each other's breaths and heartbeats, and when Ava was about to drift into much-needed slumber, D'mitri whispered, "I want to do something for you."

Ava giggled. "I don't think I could handle you doing anything more. I am plenty satisfied. I promise."

He laughed and gave her a gentle squeeze. "I am glad I pleased you, but I was not the only one giving pleasure, meu amanté." Then he grew serious. "What I speak of are the ways I have failed you. I want to make you happy. Not only in matters of the heart and in bed. I want you to be happy in every possible way."

Ava turned in his arms. "What are you talking about?"

D'mitri brushed her hair from her face and placed a kiss to the tip of her nose. "My heart shattered seeing you so brokenhearted, and I never want that to happen again because I have been insensitive to my mate. I want nothing more than to make you happy."

Tears blurred her vision, but she blinked them away.

"I understand now how much you need something to keep your mind occupied. I tried thinking of a way to give you that and remain here where we are both so at home, and this is the only rational thing to do."

Ava frowned.

"If I expand my business further, would you be willing to help me? Would you be willing to be my partner? You can do whatever you want. I can teach you to carve, or you can run the business part of it if that is what you prefer."

Ava opened her mouth to speak, but when no words

came, she simply took his face in her hands and pulled his mouth down to hers, putting as much thanks into the kiss as she could possibly muster.

WHEN THEY FINALLY MADE IT out of bed the next morning, D'mitri and Ava joined Burian for breakfast. He didn't say much, but Ava noticed how he kept staring out the window. He was deep in his own world, seeming as sad as he had when she'd found him out back staring at the sadly neglected garden. Looking out at it even now, Ava could see how much potential it held.

She cleared her throat. "What's with the garden? Were you all not born with a green thumb?" D'mitri looked at her sharply, and she frowned. "What? It was a simple question."

Burian looked at his son and then to Ava. "My Dalah was the gardener in the family. Only she had the touch needed to maintain such…" He seemed to search for the right word, and then he said, with a slight smile, "… beauty."

Ava saw the sadness in his eyes, but there was also pride for his wife, the woman who had been gone for so long. Ava could almost feel it herself, and she'd never had the privilege of knowing the woman. She would just have to settle for D'mitri's memories of her and the stories Burian would no doubt tell.

Ava smiled. "I understand her love of gardening. I've always had the need to have my hands in the dirt. It's been driving me crazy not being able to do that here."

Ava saw a flicker of something in Burian's eyes, and

he exchanged a long look with D'mitri. Burian sat straight in his chair; his pale green eyes met hers again. "Since you will be living here indefinitely, would you be interested in rejuvenating the garden?"

Ava felt a funny little tickle of emotion in the back of her throat.

"I think my Dalah would be happy to share her little sanctuary with you."

Ava didn't dare look at D'mitri. Even though he'd tried, he failed to shield her from his sudden overwhelming emotion. She pushed away the thought and smiled at Burian. "I would love that."

33

A week into the garden rejuvenation, Ava stood at the center of a small circular clearing surrounded by a waist-high wall. Just inside the wall sat what looked to be six benches, three on either side of the walkway. The entire place was crawling with vines, and Ava wasn't sure where to start with that section of the garden.

Making up her mind, she pulled the overgrowth away until she revealed a simple stone bench. Once she cleared the surface, she sat down to take a break. Lately, for some reason, she'd been getting tired easier. She thought maybe it was her lack of appetite and how busy she'd been, but she suspected there might be another reason.

Shaking herself from the thought, Ava focused on the sight in front of her. She could already see the potential of the open space. A simple water fountain in the center would add to the serene atmosphere. Or left open, it could be the perfect spot for a small, intimate wedding.

Ava couldn't help herself. That one thought took her

down a rabbit hole of ideas. She pictured what it might look like with the surrounding garden in full bloom and the center space decorated for the occasion.

She and D'mitri hadn't talked about the particulars of their own wedding. They hadn't even set a date yet, but Ava liked the idea of taking their vows in his mother's flower garden.

After seeing pictures of what it once looked like, Ava hoped she'd be able to return it to its former glory. And maybe honor the woman who loved the space so much.

Ava felt D'mitri's presence in her mind before he spoke. *You are a kindhearted soul, my sweet mate. I am blessed to have you.*

Ava smiled. *How much of that did you hear?*

Enough to know that I do not deserve you, but I will spend the rest of my days trying to be worthy.

Ava snorted. *Don't be so dramatic.*

D'mitri's gentle laugh made her smile. It was nice to hear him sound so at ease after everything that had happened.

Ever since their last argument, he'd been so different. More like the man she'd first thought him to be. Every day, he made a point to do something for her that made her feel, for lack of better words, cherished.

D'mitri sent her a wave of love. *I will let you get back to work. I wanted to let you know I am almost done here, but I might be a bit late for dinner.*

Ava sighed. *That's okay. I'll wait for you. I'd like to finish this anyway.*

Then I will leave you to it. Enjoy yourself, Amanté. I will see you when I get home.

Ava moved to the next bench and began clearing it of

the vines. When she had finished with all six, she rose to stretch her arms over her head. She kind of liked the look of the ivy covering the short circular wall that wrapped around the area. She couldn't decide if she wanted to keep it or clean the vines from it as well.

Ava was deep in contemplation when she felt the short hairs at her nape stand on end. She instinctively reached with her senses the way D'mitri had taught her, and she could feel the presence of another. Slowly turning toward the disturbance, she saw him standing in the shadow of a nearby tree.

Ava hadn't realized night had fallen because her new eyes had simply adjusted to the difference in light. But seeing the Naymati standing perfectly still beneath the massive tree made her realize just how long she'd been out there.

Forcing a calm breath, Ava reached for D'mitri. *Where are you?*

I will be home shortly. Why? What is wrong?

She sent him the mental image of the Naymati.

The tall male chose that precise moment to step from beneath the low-hanging limbs. It was him. The one that Darien had run off. A slow, deliberate smile pulled at his lips like a villain in a comic. "It is good to see you again, sweet female."

Ava didn't say a word. She simply watched him.

"Come to me," the male whispered.

In an instant, she felt D'mitri's connection disappear like a switch had been flipped. And though she didn't want to, she felt the need to do as the terrifying male in front of her said.

"Let me take you from here and to a place where you

can belong." Ava took a step forward, and a triumphant smile curved the man's generous mouth. "You will be happier where you can have a true purpose."

"She has a purpose," a low voice said from Ava's right.

The Naymati broke eye contact with her, the connection snapping like an overstretched rubber band. His eyes went wide. "What are you doing here?"

"Stopping you from making a big mistake."

When Ava had shaken herself from the Naymati's compulsion and let her gaze follow his, she found Tynan standing just inside the circle, his full focus on the other male.

Tynan slowly moved closer to Ava, putting himself between her and the other Naymati. "Walk away before it is too late, brother."

"I will not. I will have her. She is mine. Find yourself another."

Tynan shook his head. "You should not have come here, Riku. Leave now or you will never live to see another moon."

The ominous warning didn't deter Riku. He let out a strange hissing growl. "You dare threaten me?"

"It is no threat. It is a promise. You came to their territory to take one of their women. They will not let you leave here alive. And I will not let you take her."

"So, stop me, *brother*." Riku hissed the last word.

"I do not wish to fight you. I am trying to save your life. Be wise. Resist the draw and leave before it is too late."

Ava peeked around Tynan, and Riku's gaze fell on her. Something in his eyes shifted, and he bared his teeth at Tynan. "You cannot have her."

When Riku lunged forward, Tynan met him halfway. Their bodies came together with such force that Ava felt the ground tremble beneath her feet. Mesmerized by their speed and their movements, Ava couldn't take her eyes off the fight. They were evenly matched, both strong and fast, and Ava watched nervously as they fought.

After seeing Tynan's gentle side, the viciousness he directed at Riku was both stunning and frightening. Seeing the two of them go up against each other so ferociously made her realize how much she should fear their kind.

Unable to look away from the fight, Ava watched wide-eyed as the males brutalized one another. When they broke apart, they were both breathing hard, their clothes torn and streaked with blood. Tynan ripped away his robing and tossed it aside. The sight of him bare from the waist up was a bit surprising. She could see the strength in him, but his long, lean frame wasn't something she expected to be beneath the thin material.

Tynan and Riku settled into a similar stance, both ready to pounce on the other if given a chance. Riku moved first, the impatience in his expression clear as he sprang toward Tynan. They both moved with blurring speed, and Ava had a hard time keeping track of the blows they each delivered.

Until it happened. Like a scene from a movie playing out before her, the two males slammed into one another. There was a pause where no one breathed. Ava knew someone was mortally wounded, but with blood on them both, it was hard to tell which one had received the fatal blow.

Riku and Tynan stared at one another for what felt like an eternity. Ava held her breath as she waited to see which of them had been injured. She watched in horror as Tynan suddenly dropped to his knees, clutching his midsection.

"No," Ava whimpered.

Riku spit on the fallen male and turned the force of his dark eyes on Ava. As he slowly moved toward her, Ava fought the tears stinging her eyes and she backed away from him. She made it maybe two steps outside the vine-covered walls when something in Riku's expression faltered.

Ava turned to run, but she hit the sturdy wall of Burian's chest. Her breath left her in a rush, and her father-in-law said, without looking down at her, "Go to the house, Ava."

She moved around him and started to do as he said, but her steps faltered when Burian spoke again.

With a tone she'd never heard from him before, he said, "Leave now or you will die this night."

Riku snarled. "I think not."

"Because of your arrogance and stupidity, you are about to take your last breath."

Riku threw his head back and laughed. "I am not frightened of you, old man."

Ava knew he was lying. She could see it in his eyes.

Burian knew it too, but he chuckled. "It is not me you should be worried about."

Before Riku could reply, a massive black jaguar slammed into him. The impact took them both tumbling across the circle, and they crashed into one of the stone benches, leaving behind a pile of rubble.

Ava hadn't even realized D'mitri was near until he'd leapt the wall and taken Riku down. Riku didn't stay down long though. He lurched to his feet and leapt the wall, disappearing into the overgrowth of the garden with D'mitri tight on his heels.

Go home, Ava! D'mitri snapped.

Please be careful. He is a fierce fighter.

D'mitri growled into her mind, *His fierceness pales in comparison to what he will suffer for coming after my mate.*

A pained sound came from across the wide circle, and when Ava turned to see Burian at Tynan's side, she quickly followed. Her breath left her when she saw how much blood covered him and how much had soaked into the ground around him.

His eyes were squeezed shut as Burian tried to stop the bleeding. His hands fell away from Burian's as he began to struggle to breathe.

"No," Ava choked out as she dropped to her knees beside him.

When she took his blood-soaked hand, Tynan opened his eyes and looked up at her. A weak smile touched his lips, and he forced out the words, "You are safe."

With tears in her eyes, she nodded. "I'm fine."

"Do not cry," Tynan breathed.

He coughed, and as blood bubbled from his pale lips, Ava felt the panic set in. She looked up at Burian and demanded, "Do something!" The apology in his eyes made her sob. "Please."

Burian shook his head. "I am sorry."

"He saved me!" Ava cried. "Help him. Please!"

Tynan's cold hand touched her face, startling her, and she looked down at him. "No...help. I am...finished."

Though she knew it was true, Ava's voice quavered, "No."

"Only…you…important…" he forced between gasping breaths.

Crying harder, Ava dropped her head to his shoulder. Tynan had risked his life to protect her from one of his own kind, and feeling the life leave him, Ava wished it didn't have to be that way.

When his hand rested on the back of her head, Ava's heart broke. Even though he knew his death approached, he was comforting her. As his breaths grew more and more shallow, Ava could only hope he was comforted by her and Burian being here with him.

When Tynan drew in an unsteady breath, Ava felt him shudder. This time, his breath left him on a slow, soft exhale, and Ava felt his hand fall away.

THE NAYMATI WAS FAST, but his speed was nothing compared to D'mitri's determination. He would not allow the bastard to escape this time. He would never have another chance to come for Ava again.

D'mitri took him down near the outer edge of the garden. The male shrieked when D'mitri's teeth sank into his leg, but no sooner had he hit the ground than he came around with a long knife and tried to slice into D'mitri's ribs.

D'mitri scarcely avoided the blade, but he knew he couldn't give the male a chance to use the knife again. With a quick swipe of his big black paw, D'mitri knocked the weapon from his hand.

The Naymati tried to roll away and get to his feet, but D'mitri pounced. Just when he thought he would have a clear shot at the male's throat, the Naymati came at him with another knife, this time catching him across the chest.

D'mitri leapt back, letting out a pissed-off roar. The Naymati managed to get to his feet, laughing as he licked the blood from the blade. "You cannot win, Jagara. I will have your woman."

D'mitri saw red. He attacked, tearing at whatever part of the male he could reach. And when his teeth sank into the soft pale flesh of the Naymati's throat, instinct kicked in. D'mitri wanted nothing more than to clamp down and squeeze until the fragile windpipe caved.

Unfortunately, that didn't happen. The Naymati continued to fight, clawing at D'mitri's face. Going for his eyes. So D'mitri jerked away, tearing the pale flesh of the male's throat.

The Naymati's hands came up, and he frantically tried to stop the pumping blood flow, but D'mitri knew there was no stopping it. Shifting back to his human form, he smiled down at the Naymati. "You will never have her."

He stared up at D'mitri with wide eyes as he tried to drag air into his lungs.

When only a nasty gurgling sound came, D'mitri smiled down at the creature. "I get to watch you die, not only for what you tried to do to my Ava, but for what you did to your own brother to have her." When the male's struggles weakened even more and his eyes began to haze, D'mitri leaned closer and snarled, "Now you will never hurt anyone again."

When the Naymati's eyes glazed over completely and his body fell limp, D'mitri checked to be sure there was no pulse, and then he hurried back toward Ava.

Throughout the entire encounter with the horrid male,

Ava had unknowingly been projecting everything happening with her. Knowing everything she was suffering had driven D'mitri even harder. It had been one of the reasons he'd snapped and why he'd been so cruel.

Hearing and feeling the sorrow his mate was feeling had been too much. Now he had to get to her and comfort her. But when D'mitri reached the garden's center, the sight before him nearly robbed his breath. Ava knelt beside the other Naymati with her head on his shoulder, and Burian sat across from her with a deep look of sympathy in his eyes.

Judging by the amount of blood loss and the Naymati's pained expression, D'mitri knew there was no helping him.

As the Naymati rested his hand on Ava's head, D'mitri wasn't sure how to react. Obviously, this male cared about her, and she returned his feelings. But the entire situation went against everything D'mitri had been taught about the Naymati people. Part of him screamed to get his mate away from his enemy, but seeing the way the male had protected her and the way he held her to him as he drew his last breaths made D'mitri second-guess his instincts.

The male opened his eyes and looked directly at D'mitri. As the Naymati drew his last breaths, something passed between the two of them. D'mitri bowed his head slightly in thanks, and the Naymati gave a faint smile before he inhaled one last shuddering breath. He closed his eyes for the last time, and his hand fell away from Ava as his breath left him in a long, soft sigh.

A heart-wrenching sob escaped Ava, and D'mitri moved to crouch beside her. The second he laid his palm on her back, she turned into his embrace and cried even harder.

34

D'mitri sat on the floor beside the bath and Ava lay staring at the ceiling. To anyone else, she might have looked in shock. But with her mind wide open to his, D'mitri could see her playing over and over everything that had transpired that night. She had so many what-ifs and I-don't-understands. So much guilt and regret.

"None of this is your fault, Ava."

She closed her eyes, her voice nothing more than a ragged whisper when she spoke. "It feels that way, though."

D'mitri reached out and brushed at the wet tendril of hair that clung to her cheek. "I know there is nothing I can say to ease your heartache, but I am here for you. Whatever you need."

Ava turned her head to look at him. "I know."

"Can I ask you something?"

Ava nodded.

"How did you come to know him?"

Though he could feel her reluctance to answer, Ava said, "My first night in Rio da Cidade was a bit much for me, so I went for a run."

She hesitated, as if she knew a fight was about to ensue, but when he didn't react, she continued. D'mitri listened patiently as she told him everything that had happened that night. He wanted to rage about her going out into the jungle alone after what had happened before, but he held his tongue. Not only was it in the past, but he knew if she hadn't gone, she wouldn't have met Tynan. And if she hadn't met him that night, he wouldn't have been there to keep the other Naymati from taking her.

D'mitri had much to be grateful for because of Tynan. He would have a future with Ava because of the male's sacrifice.

When Ava grew quiet again, D'mitri told her, "I understand if you want to go back to your home in Louisiana after all that has happened."

Ava sighed and closed her eyes. After a long silence, she shook her head. "I won't take you away from your home again."

D'mitri cupped her cheek. "If you do not want to be this close to our enemies, I will go anywhere you want as long as you are happy."

Ava smiled up at him, bringing her wet hand up to cup his stubbled cheek as well. "Thank you, but this is my home now. I won't let what's happened run me off. I'm happy here with you. I don't want to be anywhere else."

D'mitri turned his face into her small hand and kissed the center of her palm.

"Besides," she added softly, "if Ali and Nicolai can live here, so can we."

D'mitri leaned over the edge of the tub and gave her a gentle kiss. Resting his forehead against hers, he whispered. "Eu te amo."

Ava smiled. "I love you too."

35

N early a month had passed since Tynan's death, and Ava still had moments where all she could think about were the events of that fateful day, but for the most part, she was fine. Today was one of her good days.

She'd woke feeling a bit under the weather, but after getting out and taking in the fresh jungle air, she felt much better. Now she sat on the bank with her feet dangling in the water while D'mitri swam in lazy circles.

Her mind was a million miles away as she slid her thumb over the markings on her wrist. She loved the look of D'mitri's name in Old Jagara inked permanently in her skin. As she traced the symbols, Ava hummed a little tune. She'd been humming it quite often lately, and she smiled to herself, thinking again about that morning, when she'd realized the tune was a lullaby Lilah would hum to her when she was sick.

When D'mitri climbed out of the water, Ava watched him pull on his pants. He noticed her staring, and as he slipped his arms into his shirt, he didn't bother with the buttons as he made his way over to her. "What are you smiling about?"

"I talked to Aunt Lilah this morning. She told me that she's decided to sell the house in Louisiana and permanently move back to the homelands."

He snorted. "I am surprised it took her this long to decide."

Ava grinned. "I know. I'm shocked it wasn't on the market the second we moved back here."

D'mitri leaned down and dropped a kiss to her upturned mouth. He eyed her suspiciously. "Is that all you have to tell me?"

Ava's smile widened. She should have known that he'd picked up on something, even though she'd tried not to give anything away. "Actually, I have more news for you."

He crouched beside her, and she felt him pushing at their mate bond, searching for a clue. When he couldn't penetrate the barrier that she'd thrown up, he arched a single brow. "And? Are you going to tell me, or do I have to guess?"

Ava reached out to take his hand. She looked him in the eye and said, "I'm pregnant."

D'mitri opened his mouth to speak but paused and then shook his head. Just like he always did when he was feeling intense emotions, D'mitri abandoned English and said fiercely in his native tongue, "Do not joke with me about such things, woman. My heart could not take it."

Ava's hands found their way into his long, still-damp hair, and she looked into his eyes. "I would never joke about something like this."

D'mitri whispered, "You are really with young?"

308

Ava nodded. "I really am."

His eyes shimmered with unshed tears, and he smiled bigger than she'd ever seen him smile before. "I am to be a father."

Ava beamed up at him. "Yes."

D'mitri dragged her to him and laughed as he squeezed her tight. "I cannot wait to tell everyone."

EPILOGUE

Ava lay in the bed and smiled as D'mitri cradled their son in his arms. The awe and wonder on her mate's face, the tears of joy barely contained within the barrier of his lashes, was quite a sight to see. D'mitri was the picture of fatherly pride.

Staring down at his son, D'mitri smiled. "I have waited for you all my life, little one. Nothing can compare to the feelings you bring forth in me." He lifted his eyes and met Ava's gaze. "Except maybe your mother."

Ava chuckled softly. "Suck up."

D'mitri shook his head. "I never thought I could love you so much, but seeing what you went through to give me this blessing, I am overwhelmed."

Ava smiled up at him. "I love you, D'mitri."

He leaned down and pressed a kiss to her lips. When he pulled away, he asked her, "Would you like to meet your son?"

When she nodded, D'mitri settled on the bed beside her and placed the little one in her arms. Ava's breath nearly left her when she finally got a good look at her son's sweet little face. He looked so much like his father, and he even had the same little dimple in his chin. It was his green-gold eyes that held her attention most though. They were incredibly bright, like Violet's eyes had been, and it made Ava wonder if all Jagara young were born with eyes so unusually focused.

D'mitri reached over and smoothed a gentle hand over their son's head. "What is his name, Amanté?"

Ava shook her head. "I don't know. I thought of a handful of names for girls but never could think of a boy's name. Maybe he could be a Jr," she said with a smile.

D'mitri stared down at her for a long moment before he shook his head. Something shifted in his eyes, and Ava could see his nervousness. He cleared his throat before he asked tentatively, "Can we name him Tynan?"

Ava stared up at D'mitri, a lump forming in her throat. "If that's what you want."

D'mitri nodded. "If it were not for that male, I would not have you or my child. Even though he was Naymati, what he did deserves to be honored in more than just memory."

Ava smiled up at her mate with tears in her eyes. "Then our son's name is Tynan."

THANK YOU FOR READING!

I hope you enjoyed Ava and D'mitri's story.
Up next…
Book three of the Jagara Tribes series.

Until then, check out my other books:
Given
Assertion Trials
The Betrayal
Lost Zendori

FOR THE LATEST BOOK NEWS

Sign up for my newsletter:
www.melainarayne.com/newsletter

Or follow me on Facebook:
facebook.com/melainarayne